Death

Death of a Murderer

RUPERT THOMSON

ISIS
LARGE PRINT
Oxford

First published in Great Britain 2007
by
Bloomsbury Publishing Plc

Published in Large Print 2007 by ISIS Publishing Ltd.,
7 Centremead, Osney Mead, Oxford OX2 0ES
by arrangement with
Bloomsbury Publishing Plc

British Library Cataloguing in Publication Data
Thomson, Rupert
    Death of a murderer. – Large print ed.
    1. Police – England – Suffolk – Fiction
    2. Psychological fiction
    3. Large type books
    I. Title
    823.9'14 [F]

ISBN 978–0–7531–7858–4 (hb)
ISBN 978–0–7531–7859–1 (pb)

Printed and bound in Great Britain by
T. J. International Ltd., Padstow, Cornwall

Acknowledgements

I am indebted to the staff of the West Suffolk Hospital in Bury St Edmunds, and to various police officers at the Suffolk Constabulary and the Cheshire Constabulary, and to the staff of the Cambridge City Crematorium, without whose patience, cooperation and expertise this book could not have been written.

CHAPTER
ONE

When the news came through on the car radio, Billy sat quite motionless, unable to do anything but listen. He was parked on Norwich Road, outside a place called Glamour Gear. Lying on the seat beside him, sealed in an envelope of transparent plastic, were the ballet shoes he had promised to collect on his way home. The windscreen was starting to mist up, but he could still see out. An ordinary street in an ordinary English town. Friday afternoon. Lights on in all the shops, the pavement wet with rain . . .

He didn't have any particular thoughts about the woman's death. He didn't feel sorry, or relieved, or cheated. It was vaguer than that, and more powerful. The woman had been involved in the murder of at least five people, three of them young children, and she had been feared and hated ever since. Children had been savagely abused in front of her by her own boyfriend, and she had gone along with it; she had even, possibly, tortured one of them herself. The victims' bodies had been buried on a high, desolate moor to the east of Manchester. It had all happened years ago, in the sixties, but people had never forgiven her for what she had done. Never forgiven, and never forgotten. And now she had died, of natural causes, in a hospital twenty miles away. It was one of those heightened moments when you make a mental note of your surroundings, and yet the whole thing felt oddly muted, scaled down, like watching an explosion through a telescope. Certainly, it never occurred to him that her death might affect him directly; he had no idea, at that point, that he was about to become part of the story.

The phone rang three days later, on the Monday evening, while he was watching a TV programme about the mystery of the pyramids. He would be leaving for work before too long, so he let his wife, Sue, take the call.

"Yes, he is," he heard her say. "I'll just get him."

Eyes bright, almost silvery, she held the phone out to him and mouthed the words *It's for you*. These days there was an exaggerated quality about her that he found bewildering: she would get excited over nothing, and angry over nothing. They had been together for fourteen years, married for ten, and yet he seemed to see her less clearly now than he had at the beginning.

Moving across the room, he took the phone from her and turned towards the window. Though it had already been dark for several hours, he parted the curtains and put his face close to the glass. He could just make out the dim shape of his car, and the low brick wall beyond.

"Billy Tyler here."

"Billy? Are you all right?"

He had expected it to be one of his colleagues from the police station, but the voice on the other end belonged to Phil Shaw. Billy had acted as Phil's probationer when Phil joined the force in 1992, which meant he'd had to show Phil the ropes, to guide him through those tricky first few weeks. He had known even then that Phil had a good career ahead of him. They'd got on pretty well, though. He used to have Phil over to the house for takeaways — curries in the kitchen, with plenty of cold lager — or if the weather was fine he would light the barbecue. Now, ten years later, Phil was a detective sergeant.

"You've seen the news?" Phil said.

"Hard to miss," Billy said.

Over the weekend, he had bought most of the papers, and they had been full of articles about the woman. They had referred to her as "a sick killer", "a monster" and "the devil"; her name, they said, was synonymous with evil. Many of the front pages had reprinted the picture that had been taken when she was first arrested, the picture that had captured so much more than it was intended to, not just the woman herself but the nature of the crimes as well, the atmosphere in which they had been committed. There she was, perfectly preserved, despite the thirty-six years she had spent behind bars: the sixties beehive hairdo, the sullen, bruised-looking mouth and, most potent of all, that steady black stare, so full of defiance and hostility, so empty of regret. There, too, was her boyfriend, the psychopath from Glasgow, who had initiated her into a world of pornography, sadism and murder. And there were the victims. Those little faces — for they were never blown up large, like hers. That old-fashioned, ham-fisted black-and-white. They were

3

lost in time, it seemed, as well as to their families. On Saturday, the *Sun* had published a partial transcript of the sixteen-minute tape that had been played in court. It was a recording of the torture of one of the children, and it had shaken even the most cynical of reporters. Billy would have been nine when the trial started, and, naturally enough, the details of the crimes had been kept from him. All the same, he thought he remembered grown-ups talking in shocked whispers and glancing at him across their shoulders — his mother's best friend, Betty Lydgate, and Auntie Ethel, and Mrs Parks from next door — and a chill seemed to hang over that part of his childhood, as if, for a while, the sun had been obliterated by dark clouds. After reading the transcript, Billy went for a walk in the woods behind his house, a cold wind rushing through the trees, but he couldn't rid himself of the woman's voice. *Hush hush. Stop it or I will forget myself and hit you one. Will you stop it. Stop it. Shut up.*

Phil Shaw was saying something, though. Billy heard the words "supervise" and "operation", and now, for the first time, he understood why Phil might be calling.

"We need you tomorrow night," Phil said.

He was giving Billy the job of guarding the woman's body. It would be her last night in the mortuary, he said. The funeral was scheduled for Wednesday evening, though no one knew that yet; that information had not been released. He was sorry, but Billy would have to work a twelve-hour shift. They were short on numbers. Still, at least there'd be some overtime in it.

"Will you be there?" Billy asked.

"I've been here since 4a.m. on Friday when they realised she was going to die."

Billy could imagine the grim smile on Phil's face. Phil might sound calm, even matter-of-fact — one of his strengths was that he never lost his composure — but he would be feeling the strain. It was such a sensitive situation. There was so much that could go wrong.

They talked some more about what was being planned and what would be required, then Phil gave Billy directions to the hospital, which Billy jotted down on a notepad next to the phone.

"What is it?" Sue asked, the moment he hung up.

He decided not to tell her, not just yet.

"I've got to work a seven-to-seven tomorrow," he said, then he went and sat in front of the TV again.

His programme about the pyramids was over.

CHAPTER
TWO

"It's just a job," he told Sue as he left the house on Tuesday evening. "It's a job, that's all." But when he saw her mouth fold down at one corner he knew that he had failed to convince her, and he, too, felt that his words had fallen short, that there was something basic, something significant, that he hadn't managed to convey. He couldn't delay any longer, though, or he'd be late.

He turned the key in the ignition with the door open on the driver's side, hoping she might relent at the last minute and give him her approval — he hated leaving for work with an argument hanging in the air — but once he had fastened his seat-belt and shifted into gear he had to shut the door and ease the car out of the drive. What else could he do? Although she was standing only a few yards away, she still hadn't said anything. Her head was lowered, and the brass coach-light on the porch behind her prevented him from reading the expression on her face. Indicating left, he pulled out into the road, and in less than five minutes he was on the A14, heading west.

As he drove, he glanced at his mobile from time to time, but it stayed quiet. He followed a white van for several miles, the words GREYHOUNDS IN TRANSIT painted on the back. Where was the nearest dog-track? He couldn't think. The night was bleak and raw. Wind hurling the trees about. It seemed like an eternity since there had been any warm weather, but it was only November.

He yawned loudly, not bothering to cover his mouth. Usually, when he was working a night-shift, he slept from about nine in the morning until three or four in the afternoon, but that day, for some reason, he had woken at one, and even though he felt exhausted he couldn't seem to fall asleep again. On going downstairs, he had found Sue in the lounge, fitting a photograph of their daughter, Emma, into a frame, and it was then that he told her what he would be doing. Hopelessly mistimed, no doubt, bungled, in fact, but he would've had to mention it sooner or later. They'd never kept too many secrets from each other — and besides, it was unusual, wasn't it? It was like being part of history.

When Sue heard the woman's name, her reaction was immediate and vehement. "Don't go, Billy. Stay here, with me." He was so surprised that he couldn't think of anything to say — and she was already inventing excuses for him. "You could call in sick. There's that flu bug going round." But he hardly ever took time off because of illness — not like his old mate Jim Malone, whose nickname, tellingly, was "Virus" — and anyway, he didn't feel he could let the sergeant down, not at this late stage. Losing her temper, Sue told him that he only ever thought about himself. He was pig-headed. Blind. She didn't mind him sitting in a mortuary. He'd done that kind of thing before. What upset her was the contact with evil, the soaking up of some dark influence — the shadow that might cast over their lives. She had always been full of superstition, but where in the past it had been just one aspect of her character, a thread that zigzagged through her, an endearing quirk, now it had become the prism through which she viewed the world, and he began to wish he had dreamed up a decent lie for her, something out of the ordinary and yet believable — a prison riot, a strike, a demonstration. He had been caught off guard, though. He'd been too slow. Once again, she asked him whose body he would be dealing with, obviously hoping that she had misheard or misunderstood, and that he would come up with a different name this time, one that meant nothing to her. When he repeated what he had said, struggling to contain his irritation now — "I already *told* you, Sue" — she had tugged on his arm, reminding him, uncomfortably, of Emma, and there had been tears in her eyes, something that often happened if she was frightened. He didn't respond, though, and she whirled away across the room. She stood facing the window, with her hands knotted at her sides. He could see the patch of fuzzy hair at the back of her head, the legacy of a car crash she'd had the year before, and there was a moment when a crack opened in his heart, and he almost went over and took her in his arms. *All right, love. I won't go.*

It would have been so easy.

Later, when he was in the kitchen, making his sandwiches, she attacked him again. By that point she had worked herself up into a state of outrage. How could he possibly justify what he was doing? Why was he prepared to put his whole family at risk? What sort of person was he? He couldn't believe the extent to which she had blown the danger out of all proportion, and yet she spoke with such conviction that he was beginning to doubt himself.

"All I'll be doing is sitting in a room," he said.

"Yes, but it's *her*, isn't it?" She wouldn't say the woman's name; she didn't want it in the house. "What she did —" She shuddered. "It's not healthy to be close to something like that. It's just not healthy."

Some*thing*, he thought. Not some*one*.

"But she's dead," he said.

She shook her head slowly, a gesture she would use whenever he was clearly in the wrong.

"I can't afford to be superstitious, Sue, not in my line of —"

"I read something in the paper yesterday. Apparently, twenty funeral directors have refused to handle the body. *Twenty funeral directors.* Now why's that, do you think? Are they superstitious too?"

"That's different."

"And what about the crematoriums? How many of them said no?" She let out a dry laugh. "I'll be amazed if they manage to dispose of her at all."

Billy sighed and looked away. In the next room, Emma was sitting cross-legged on the carpet, watching *The Sound of Music*, the volume turned up far too loud.

"Can you make it quieter, Emma?" he called out, but she didn't hear him.

Well, perhaps it was for the best, he thought. At least she wouldn't realise they were arguing.

"It's not about superstition, Billy," Sue was saying. "It's about keeping your distance. It's about not letting the wrong things rub off on you. You should know all about that. You're a policeman."

"I won't see her," he said. "I won't even set eyes on her."

Sue's head snapped in his direction, as if he had finally come out with something truly horrific. Her lips tightened and then shrank, and she looked down at the kitchen floor. She seemed to be staring right through the tiles to what lay immediately beneath: the foundations of the house, the dark, damp earth — the end of everything.

"It's my job," he murmured.

In the lounge, Julie Andrews was singing that famous song about the hills being alive.

Not long afterwards he had to leave. Sue followed him outside, but she didn't wave him off, or even say goodbye. She just stood on the gravel in her ribbed sweater, looking cold.

10

CHAPTER
THREE

When he first met her, in the late eighties, her name was Susie — Susie Newman — and there was so much in that extra syllable, that hidden "z". There was a kind of fearlessness. There was laughter. There was sex. Back then, she was always Susie, never Sue. At that point in his life, Billy had been a police officer for almost a decade. Thanks to Neil, a schoolfriend who had joined the force at the same time, he was called "Scruff" — Neil had caught him in the equipment room, polishing the badge on his helmet — but as nicknames went it wasn't too bad, not when you considered that two of his contemporaries were known as "Vomit" and "The Perv". For the first few years he had lived in "the Brothel", the single men's hostel located behind Widnes police station, but then, at the beginning of 1985, he had moved into a small flat of his own on Frederick Street. He had already failed the sergeant's exam, but he'd taken it because you were supposed to, not because he wanted to, and he had long since decided that he was happy being a constable. In the early days he would go about on foot, calling in at various business and shops. Later, he would drive around in the area car. A lot of what he did was listen.

It was the side of his job he liked best, this chance to mix with all sorts of people, to establish some connection with their lives. He liked knowing everyone, and being known.

One bright June morning he stopped at a local garage for his usual cup of tea. They had a new girl working in the office, and he decided to go in and introduce himself. Putting his head round the door, he saw that she was typing. He waited until she sensed his presence and looked at him, and then he stepped into the room.

"I'm Billy Tyler," he said.

He asked her a few questions, nothing too personal. It turned out that her stepfather had found her the job. He ran a second-hand-car dealership in Stockport. Not just any old cars. Jaguars. Ferraris.

"It's only for the summer," she said. "After that, I'm thinking of travelling. India, maybe — or Thailand . . ."

Her eyes had gone misty, opaque, and he wanted to kiss her there and then. He wanted to kiss her eyes back into focus.

"Susie Newman."

Standing in that poky office, with its threadbare carpet and its dog-eared girlie calendar, he had repeated her name out loud. She watched him carefully, and puzzled lines appeared on her forehead, though there was also the promise of a smile at the edges of her mouth. But he'd been in a kind of dream. As soon as she told him her name, he'd had the feeling that it was familiar. Not that he had ever heard it before. No, it was more as if he had been propelled into his own

12

future, a future that included her, or even revolved around her. Her name seemed familiar because it was about to become familiar. It was a familiarity that hadn't happened yet.

He didn't mention any of this to Susie, though — not that morning, anyway. When he was twenty-eight, he had gone out with a girl called Venetia. He had been unable to conceal the extent of his infatuation, and it had spoiled everything. "I can't breathe with you around," Venetia had told him once. "You use up all the air." Over the years he'd learned that sometimes it's better to go slowly. When he finally told Susie about the feeling he'd had on hearing her name, it was two months later, and they were having a cup of tea in a place just round the corner from the garage, the Kingsway Hotel on Victoria Road. She let him finish talking, then she tucked her hair behind her ear and looked straight at him, her eyes so shiny that he could have been the first thing they had ever seen.

"I bet you say that to all the girls," she said.

He didn't laugh, nor did he attempt to deny it; he remained perfectly serious, and his gaze dropped to the tablecloth. Though he had spent weeks trying to work it out, what he had just told her still perplexed him.

"I've *never* said it before," he said. "I've never even *felt* it."

There was a moment when nothing happened, nothing at all, but they both knew what was coming, so those few seconds were slow-motion and yet urgent, the slowness and the sense of urgency simultaneous but contradictory, delicious too, like ice-cream wrapped in hot meringue. At last, she put a hand on the back of his head and drew him towards her until their lips were touching. After the kiss, they remained an inch or two apart, looking into each other's faces. He could feel the warm steam from his tea on the underside of his chin.

"Don't go travelling," he said. "Not yet."

CHAPTER
FOUR

If you see the sugar factory, you've gone too far, Phil had said, but Billy left the A14 at the Bury St Edmunds East exit, and the hospital showed up on signposts shortly after. He went through several roundabouts, then up a quiet suburban road. Trees on either side, large houses. Bury wasn't a town he knew particularly well. He had driven here one Saturday with Sue when Emma was a baby. They had spent an hour at a car-boot sale, and Sue had bought a bamboo wind-chime, which she had hung in their garden. On the first blustery day, though, their neighbours, the Gibsons, complained about the noise it made, and Sue had to take it down again.

He signalled left and turned into the drive, passing beneath the dark, flat branches of a cedar. The car-park was full. He waited, indicator flashing, while a woman backed out of a narrow space. Leaning close to the steering-wheel, he stared up at the hospital. It had been painted a curious mint-green colour, and modern bay windows jutted squarely from the façade. The place looked new, but cheap. It looked prefabricated.

Even from where he was, he could see the crowd gathered outside the main entrance. In his phone-call,

Phil had mentioned the press, and how they had been camped in the hospital grounds ever since the news broke. It wasn't anything they hadn't expected, he had said; in fact, they'd thought it would be far worse. During the past four days, the police had talked to reporters on a regular basis, keeping them informed, but no one had been allowed into the hospital itself. Not that some of them hadn't tried, apparently. One tabloid journalist had offered a nurse several thousand pounds in cash if she would smuggle him into the mortuary. They were after trophies, of course — a photograph of the corpse, a ring, a lock of hair. They wanted some kind of physical contact with the famous child-killer. They wanted to sense the power, the horror. They wanted a direct line to the unknown.

As Billy stepped out of his car, his foot caught in something and he looked down. The remains of a home-made placard lay on the ground, and though the soggy cardboard had dirt and tyre-tracks on it, the message was still legible. BURN IN HELL.

Locking his car, he straightened his uniform and then began to walk towards the hospital entrance. Faces swung in his direction as he approached. Microphones appeared. A TV camera was pointed at him, its tiny red light glowing. At that moment his mobile bleeped, telling him that he'd just received a text. It was from Sue. *Please come home billy.* The fact that she'd used his name meant her anger had died down, but there was still nothing he could do. He switched the mobile off and slid it into his pocket. Ignoring the questions he was being asked, he pushed through the crowd. He didn't open his mouth at all except to say "Excuse me". One scrawny man in a parka took hold of his arm, but quickly let go of it again when Billy turned and stared at him.

On entering reception, Billy saw Phil Shaw talking to a woman in a pale-grey suit. Phil was wearing a suit as well, navy-blue, with a white shirt and a purple tie. There were dark smears under his eyes, and his skin looked blotchy, porous.

"You have any trouble out there, Billy?" Phil said.

"No, not really."

"People seem to be behaving themselves — so far . . ."

Phil introduced him to the woman. Her name was Eileen Evans, and she worked for the hospital as an operations manager. If for some reason Phil was called away, she would be available to deal with any problems or enquiries. Billy felt Eileen's cool grey eyes move evenly across his face.

A pass had been organised for Billy's car, and he went outside and placed it in his windscreen. When he returned, Phil nodded at the constable on duty by the main entrance, then put a hand against the small of Billy's back and steered him down a long, bright corridor. They passed a snack bar, then a lift. The walls were white, with just a tinge of pink to them. Sometimes there was a row of plastic chairs. The air seemed taut, almost rigid, as if the entire hospital had taken a breath in the early hours of Friday morning and was still holding it.

A garden appeared on Billy's left. Built in an internal courtyard, Oriental in style, it had a pond with a miniature stone temple and a red wooden bridge. He wondered what Harry Parsons would make of it. Harry was a retired plumber who worked on the allotments behind Billy's house. If Billy ever found himself at a loose end, he would go and see whether Harry was around. They'd talk about rainfall or the absence of skylarks or what a disaster the railways were — anything, really. Emma called him "Parsons". "Morning, Parsons," she would say, and he would tip the brim of his flat cap.

"You been keeping well?" Phil said.

"Fine thanks, sarge."

"Sue all right?"

"She's fine." Billy paused. "The winter always gets her down a bit."

Phil nodded, as if he, too, found winter difficult. "And your little girl? How's your little girl?"

"She's eight now."

"Is she really?"

"It's still hard work, though. We have to watch her all the time."

Phil nodded, his eyes on the ground. "Sorry about the seven-to-seven, Billy," he said. "There wasn't anyone else I could call on, not just at the moment."

"That's OK."

Or it would have been, Billy thought, if only Sue had let him have his nap. After their argument at lunchtime, he had gone back upstairs, hoping to get another couple of hours' sleep, but he had been in bed for less

18

than ten minutes when Sue walked in on him, and even with his eyes closed, he'd had a clear picture of the inside of her head, all sparks and broken china.

"You don't care about us," he heard her say. "That's what it comes down to. You just don't care."

"That's not true," he murmured into his pillow.

"You don't care about me and Emma. The way you walked out when she was born —"

"Don't bring that up again. And anyway, I didn't 'walk out' . . ."

"What?" She was leaning over him now, her face only inches from his, and she was pushing at his shoulder. "*What* was that?"

Sometimes he had the distinct feeling that she was trying to goad him into violence. Then she would be able to stand back with a look of triumph on her face and say, *You see? I knew it. I knew it all along.*

"Oh, for Christ's sake!"

He hurled the bedclothes away from him, brushing her aside. Out of the corner of his eye he saw her stagger — a little theatrically, he thought — then press herself against the wall. Once on his feet, he didn't know what to do. In his T-shirt and underpants, he went and stared out of the window. The garden lay below him, with the allotments just beyond, the various plots forming a kind of patchwork that sloped gently uphill to the woods. Away to his right, a cornfield shifted and swirled as if governed by mysterious tides, hidden currents. When he first viewed the house it had been summer, and the corn was high, its yellow randomly sown with poppies. He'd rarely seen anything so beautiful. Today, though, its beauty seemed inappropriate, if not actually malicious. To think that their marriage had started there. To think that he had taken Sue by the hand and led her out into the middle of that field — Susie as she was then . . . And now, a decade later, here they were, bound together by little more than arguments and tears, by vicious words, by things they didn't even mean. *I might as well go to work right now*, he thought, *for all the peace I'm going to get.*

Phil began to talk again, this time about the woman whose body they were guarding. Since she had already been hospitalised on a number of occasions during the past two or three years — first for osteoporosis, then for a cerebral aneurysm, and, most recently, for respiratory problems — the police had been able to develop procedures for dealing with her when she left the confines of prison. Now that she was dead it was no different. The police were duty bound to protect her from anyone who might want to take revenge on her or do her harm — and there were plenty of those, as a glance at the Internet would tell you — but, equally, they had to see that the other patients and their families were not upset or disturbed. He had worked intensively with hospital staff to make the place secure while simultaneously attempting to keep disruption to a minimum. There were police stationed at the rear of the building, and in many of the corridors. There were police patrolling the grounds as well. Every entrance and exit had been covered.

A door clicked open somewhere behind them, and Billy heard rapid footsteps. Phil turned sharply, but it was only a nurse hurrying off in the opposite direction. Soon she was fifty yards away, her reflection a smudgy, swaying blur in the bright mirror of the floor.

"We have to make sure nothing happens," Phil said, his eyes still on the nurse. "If we manage that, we will have been successful."

Billy nodded. It didn't surprise him that Phil was jumpy. Should anyone slip up, he would be held responsible — and, what's more, it would be splashed all over the front pages of tomorrow's papers. *Make sure nothing happens*: it wasn't as easy as it sounded.

Ahead of them, a pair of double doors swung outwards, their leading edges padded with black rubber, and two men in dark-blue Adidas emerged, both with a cocksure, slightly bow-legged gait that Billy recognised from estates like Gainsborough and Chantry. A soft thump as the doors swung back. "She don't want it done, though," one of the men was saying. "Don't she?" said the other. "No," the first man said. "She's frightened, isn't she."

Hospitals, Billy thought. It was a world you tended to forget about, *wanted* to forget about, but it was always there, and most people passed through it in the end. Lives turned down so low that you wondered if it was worth it. No actual flames any more, just pilot lights. Then all the agony and mess of dying . . .

The colour of the corridors had altered. All trace of white was gone. Gone, too, were the gardens and the copies of *Good Housekeeping* and the bright framed prints. Only those who truly belonged would venture this far in, and there was less need now for tact and reassurance. Everything was green. Sombre. Medical. The green was in the walls and in the air. In the pouches under Phil Shaw's eyes. This was the business end of things. The autopsy, the coroner's report. Bodies opened up like bags, then fastened shut again, their contents not as tidy as before. A gruesome customs house. One last border to be crossed, one final journey.

To Billy, it suddenly felt colder. The length of the corridors, the endless labelled rooms, the hush: he was approaching something huge, oppressive, even dangerous . . . But this line of thinking would only unsettle him, and he had too much experience to let that happen. He kept his thoughts ordinary, prosaic. *Seven-to-seven. A twelve-hour shift. Still, at least there'll be some overtime in it.* And then, *I hope I didn't forget my sandwiches.* And then, *It's just a job.* Those words again. Though this time he was trying to convince himself.

CHAPTER
FIVE

The double doors that led to the mortuary were pale-green and set deep into the wall. To their left was a notice that said FOR ENTRY PLEASE PUSH BELL ONCE. Another notice close by said STAFF ONLY. Fixed high up on the wall was a circular convex mirror in which both Billy and the sergeant featured as thinner, more alien versions of themselves. Bulbous heads, bodies tapering away to nothing. Like tadpoles. Behind him, Billy could see a wide passage or ramp that sloped up to a large, cavernous area. Parked at the top, and motionless amid the constant, low-level grinding of generators, were several small-scale fork-lift trucks that were known as tugs. Phil told him they were used for ferrying the patients' dirty linen to the back of the hospital. The woman's bedding had been brought here too, though it had been treated not as laundry but as non-chemical waste. The moment her body was wheeled out of the private ward where she had spent her last days, her sheets and pillowcases had been disposed of, as had anything else that she had come into contact with. All such items would inevitably be viewed as souvenirs, he said, and that sort of temptation had to be removed.

Billy watched as Phil pressed the mortuary bell. The door opened from the inside, and a young blonde constable let them in. Billy didn't know her. They were using officers from a number of different stations. Whoever they could get hold of, really.

"You next, is it?" she said, looking at Billy.

He nodded.

"It's all right." Her face angled back into the room. "Just boring, that's all."

Billy followed Phil through the doorway. Putting his bag down on a chair, he noted the bank of fridges that reached from floor to ceiling.

"Is there anything I should know about?" he asked the constable.

She thought for a moment, her small mouth twisting to one side. "If the phone rings in the office," she said, "it's best to answer it. Otherwise it starts making a weird beeping sound that'll end up getting on your nerves."

"Anything else?"

"It smells a bit."

"That's death," Phil said. "Nothing you can do about that."

Billy watched the constable bend over the scene log and sign herself out. If he had been asked to guess her age, he would have put it somewhere between twenty-eight and thirty-one. When the murders happened, in other words, she wouldn't have been born, or even thought of.

She straightened up and ran one hand through her short blonde hair. "Well, that's me done."

"Have you got far to go?" Billy asked her.

"I live near Cambridge."

"That shouldn't take you too long."

"Seen me drive, have you?" She grinned at him, then reached for her belongings.

When she had gone, Phil called Billy over. Billy recorded the fact that he was now the loggist, and that Detective Sergeant Shaw was present, then he wrote the date and time in the left-hand column, signed the entry, and leaned back against the radiator, which was only faintly warm.

"Where is she?" he said. "Just so I know."

"That one." Phil pointed to the fridges marked POLICE BODIES, just to the right of the door that led to the postmortem room. "It's locked."

"Who's got the key?"

"The woman you met by the main entrance. Eileen Evans."

"Are there any others?"

"No."

Prompted by Billy's questioning, no doubt, Phil went over and tested the door of the fridge he had just identified. It didn't budge.

"You've seen her, haven't you?" Billy said. "Dead, I mean."

Phil spoke with his back still turned. "Yes, I've seen her."

"What did she look like?"

Now Phil's head swung round — he suspected Billy of being ghoulish, perhaps — but obviously he saw nothing in Billy's face to warrant such suspicions because he went ahead and answered. "She looked like she smoked too much," he said. "She looked old. Older than sixty."

"You ever think about what she did?"

"No. To me she's just another sudden death."

Billy nodded. "All the same," he said. He wasn't sure exactly what he was driving at, and yet he couldn't seem to let the subject drop.

Phil walked over to another fridge, one that had a brown envelope taped to it, and inspected the names of the deceased. Once again, he spoke without looking at Billy. "Put it like this. When people die, I reckon they deserve a bit of respect — no matter what they've done."

Billy thought Phil might have a point, though there would be many who would disagree. In this particular case, at least.

"And anyway," Phil went on, still studying the names, "I think something goes out of people when they die, even someone like her. They stop being who they were."

"I hadn't thought of that," Billy said, "but yes, I suppose that makes sense."

"In the end, she's just another code two-nine, you know?" Phil turned to face him.

Billy nodded, then opened his hold-all and took out a plastic folder. Behind with his reports, he had seen the twelve-hour shift as an opportunity to do some catching up.

"No chance of you getting bored," Phil said.

Billy gave him a steady look, then the two men smiled at each other. Most police officers hated all the paperwork that came with the job — and there was so much more of it than there used to be. A lot had changed since 1984, when the Police and Criminal Evidence Act was introduced, and none of it for the better.

"Brought any refs with you?" Phil asked.

Billy reached into his bag again, producing a large package wrapped in silver foil. "Wiltshire ham," he said, "with plenty of Colman's."

"If you need anything else," Phil said, "there's a cafeteria near the front entrance. You'll get your first break at midnight and another one at about four."

"OK, sarge. Thanks."

Phil took one last look round the room, then left.

CHAPTER
SIX

Once Billy had secured the double doors and made a note of Phil's departure in the scene log, he sat down and stretched out his legs, one ankle crossed over the other, the heel of his left boot resting on the drain in the middle of the floor. He flipped the folder open and began to leaf through his paperwork. The third form he came to had the words MISSING CHILD/YOUTH printed in bold black type across the top. His throat tightened, and he let the folder fall shut. He had spent most of Sunday afternoon in a council house out near Cherry Tree Road, interviewing a couple whose daughter, Rebecca, had been missing since the day before. Thankfully, Rebecca had called home as Billy was driving back to the station that evening, but since he felt a follow-up enquiry might be in order he had held on to his report, and he now needed to complete the continuation sheets, which would prove invaluable if she were to go missing again. "Misper" forms took time — they were exceptionally detailed — and they always filled him with foreboding. Even though seven years had gone by, the memory of Shena Coates still haunted him. One summer morning, while her parents were out shopping, Shena had left her house by the back door.

She was wearing a velvet dress and a pair of high heels, and carrying her brand-new vanity set. She locked herself in the garden shed, applied lipstick, rouge, eye-shadow and mascara, and then hanged herself. She was eleven years old. You could see her hand-prints on the window where she had tried to clean the glass. She had needed more light, in order to do her make-up properly ... You'd think a seasoned police officer would have got used to occurrences like these, tragic though they were, but, if anything, the opposite was true: they seemed to affect him more as time went by, the way an allergy might, so much so that he began to wonder whether they might not actually kill him in the end. One of the reasons why he'd put in for a transfer to Stowmarket at the beginning of the year was because it was such a sleepy little town, and the crime would be gentler, more trivial. That was the theory, anyway. Rebecca's story might be over — for the time being, at least — but the bad associations were still there. He would deal with the report later on, he told himself, when he had the stomach for it.

As he set the folder aside, he became aware of a smell — or not so much a smell, maybe, as a prickling in his nostrils, a slight sense of irritation — and he remembered what Phil Shaw had said. *That's death.* Turning in his chair, Billy stared at the fridge Phil had pointed out for him. Like the others, it was white, but the wipe-clean board where the identity of the deceased would normally be recorded had been left blank. There was nothing to indicate that anyone was there at all.

A name came floating into his mind. *Trevor Lydgate*. It had been surfacing ever since he heard the news on Friday afternoon. Once again, he had to push it away. He didn't want to think about Trevor, not now.

He stared at the blank space on the fridge until he too began to feel blank.

No names, no thoughts . . .

The inside of his head felt hollow, scooped out, smooth as an empty eggshell.

CHAPTER
SEVEN

A couple of years ago, in that sluggish, soporific time between Christmas and New Year, Billy had driven to the place where the murderers had buried their victims. He had left Sue and Emma with his mother, saying that he was going to visit his friend, Neil, in Widnes. Snow had fallen overnight in Yorkshire and Humberside, but Cheshire was bright and sunny when he started out, and his spirits lifted, as if he were embarking on an adventure. As the M60 curved through Manchester, though, he caught his first glimpse of the moors, a looming shoulder of high ground to the east, treeless and primitive, and he felt something sink inside him, and a slow burning around his heart. It was all he could do not to drive straight back to his mother's house.

Soon after turning on to the A635, he became aware that he was now following in the murderers' footsteps. This was the road they would have taken — there was no other — and he doubted very much had changed since the sixties. Chinese restaurants probably wouldn't have existed then, not in the small towns, nor would shops that sold computers, but everything else looked at least a century old. The rows of terraced housing, the factories, the stations, the churches: he was seeing what the two murderers would have seen. And the moors always there above the rooftops, their brooding presence softened that day by a sprinkling of snow . . .

On the high street in Mossley he passed a car coming the other way. The driver was a woman with blonde hair, the top half of her face hidden by a lowered sunshield. Only the blunt curve of her chin was visible, and a hard mouth made even harder by her bright-red lipstick. That scorched sensation round his heart again. The urge to hurry home.

After Greenfield, the road began to climb, and in no time at all he was up on the moor, the land stretching away on either side, wild and deserted. The air thickened, and turned white. Sometimes the sun pressed through the murk — a silver disc, sharp-edged but misty, dull. He parked in a lay-by, then put on gloves, a woolly hat and wellingtons. He stood quite still beside the car. A silence that was eerily alive, like the silence when you answer the phone and there's someone on the other end not talking. He set off down a track, making for an outcrop of rocks known as the Standing Stones. One of the victim's bodies had been found near by.

Before long the track narrowed, and he struck out across open country, thinking it would be more direct, but the yellow grass was coarse and wiry, which slowed him down, and the light covering of snow hid lethal troughs and hollows. He could sprain an ankle if he wasn't careful, or even break it. As he walked, he noticed that he kept looking over his shoulder. He needed to be able to see his car, he realised, and the further he went, the greater this need became. He felt nervous, almost distressed. In these icy conditions, the countless slabs of rock that pushed up through the moor looked black. His car was black too, and merged with the landscape perfectly. Once, as he glanced behind him, he trod in a boggy hole, and his right leg sank in up to the knee. He had to tug to get it out.

Not until he was returning from the Standing Stones did he feel easier in himself. The fog had thinned. A weak sun shone. He began to think about the boy whose body was still missing, and fell into such a strange, trance-like state that when the ground seemed to leap up in front of him, he let out a cry and jumped backwards. He watched, startled, as a huge, ash-grey hare bounded away, its black ears showing clearly against the frost-encrusted grass. When the hare had vanished, he studied the place where it had been crouching, a patch of crumbly, peat-dark earth beneath an overhang. Before he knew it, he was scraping at the soil with his boot. The hare was a marker, he felt, like a cross on a map: if he dug here, something might come to light — a pair of spectacles, a shoe . . . He stood back. What was he thinking? The moor had been searched again and again, by hundreds of people. Besides, the top layer had shifted over the years; areas of peat that had been exposed in the sixties would now be thoroughly grassed over. But a miraculous discovery, he realised, was what he had been hoping for. That, in part, was why he'd come.

Before he left the moor, he crossed the road and climbed up to Hollin Brown Knoll, another of the murderers' favourite spots. Stopping for breath, he saw three men with rifles striding towards the Standing Stones, a black dog with them. He thought of the hare and hoped that it was safe. On the knoll itself was a rock that was the same height as a chair, and slightly concave too, but when he sat down on it he had such a powerful sense of the woman's presence that he instantly got up again and moved away.

Further on, the land levelled out, and he came across several shallow gullies that meandered off in a northerly direction. The streams had frozen over; black water squirmed through narrow channels beneath the ice. While up there, he saw a tree, its twisted trunk growing along the ground as if seeking shelter, then veering up into the air, the thin grey branches trembling. Once again, he had the feeling there was something to be discovered, but it was like having a word on the tip of your tongue and knowing you would never remember it. There were things here that couldn't be grasped or squared away — not by him, in any case. He stared off into a gully, imagining a man leading a small boy by the hand. After a minute, only the man's head and shoulders showed above the bank, and the boy wasn't visible at all . . .

The snow had blown in from the east the night before, and now it was coming again, the air closing in, surrounding him, a whirl of tiny flakes.

He turned and started back towards the car.

CHAPTER
EIGHT

Glancing at his mobile on the table, Billy was reminded of the text Sue had sent. Sometimes, when she bombarded him with messages, each one more desperate and abbreviated than the last, or when she asked the impossible of him, as she had that afternoon, he would wonder why he put up with it. Where had Susie Newman disappeared to? And when? *Don't go travelling*, he had said, and she hadn't. She had got a job with a firm of marketing consultants, and later, in October of that year, she had moved in with him. They'd lived in his little two-room flat on Frederick Street, just round the corner from the police station. Christ, the sex they'd had back then. The love they'd had. He used to run home from work to see her. Actually run. But he had never taken her to India or Thailand; he hadn't paid enough attention to her dreams. Fourteen years had passed, and certain possibilities had slipped through their fingers, and now she was turning into somebody he didn't recognise. He would get flashes of how she used to be, but it was as if he were trying to tune into a foreign radio station with a weak signal; mostly all he received was interference, static, nothing he could make any sense of. What about the feeling of familiarity he'd had, though, when he stood in Murphy's garage on that sunny morning in 1988? Had that been an illusion, some sort of trick? Or had he failed to look after what he'd been given? And if it was gone, was it gone for ever, or could it be recovered?

He was going round in circles.

He saw her again, standing by the front door in the cold, her face lowered, her arms folded tightly across her chest. There were days when he couldn't seem to please her, no matter what he did or didn't do, and it would occur to him that she might simply have grown tired of him, that he might be less than she had imagined him to be, less than she'd wanted. Certainly there were those who took that view. Her father, for one. Peter Newman never missed an opportunity to let Billy know that she deserved better. Not that Newman was such a great advertisement for marriage: he had left Susie's mother when Susie was just thirteen.

Billy first met Peter Newman in a wine bar in Manchester in the summer of 1989. Though wine bars were no longer a novelty — they had started appearing in the north-west at least five years earlier — Billy had never set foot in one before, a fact that Newman seemed to intuit almost immediately. Newman had a couple of business associates with him. The three men wore double-breasted suits with padded shoulders, which made them look American, and Billy was painfully aware of his cheap black shoes and the soiled bandage on his right hand, an injury sustained while arresting a drunk at a rugby-league game the previous Saturday.

When the waitress came over, Newman and his colleagues ordered glasses of wine. So did Susie. Billy said he would have wine too.

"Really?" Newman said. "You wouldn't rather have a pint?"

"No, I'll have some wine," Billy said. When, actually, a beer was what he wanted. But he felt clumsy in the company of these business people; he felt the way he'd felt when he failed his sergeant's exam.

To begin with, Newman talked about a project he was investing in — a luxury resort on a Greek island — but gradually he steered the conversation round to Susie, and the fact that she was going out with a policeman.

"'Scruffy Tyler', they call him," Newman told his colleagues.

The two men laughed softly and nodded. This piece of information didn't seem to surprise them in the least.

"It's 'Scruff'," Billy said, "not 'Scruffy'."

"I still don't get it," Newman said. "How on earth did you two meet?"

Billy did his best to ignore the slight. "Susie was working in a garage in Widnes," he said. "It's a place I often call in at when I'm —"

Newman talked right over him. "Of course, I've seen her with all sorts," he said, addressing his business associates again. "I mean, she's not exactly particular."

Newman's cronies leered at Susie, as if they, too, might be in with a chance of having her. Susie was staring down into her glass.

For a few moments, Billy couldn't quite believe what he had just heard. Then he took hold of his wine-glass, which was still half-full, and pushed it away from him into the middle of the table.

"You ought to watch your mouth," he said.

"Oh dear" — Newman was talking to the two men, but his eyes were on Billy — "I think we could be looking at another case of police brutality."

A smirk on his face. On the faces of his colleagues too. One of them took a long, slow mouthful of wine, watching Billy over the rim of his glass.

Billy reached for Susie's hand. "Come on. It's getting late."

Outside, he stood on the pavement, trembling. A cold wind, streets all red and grey. Manchester.

"Sorry about that, Billy," Susie said.

He turned to her with a kind of desperation. "How could you just sit there?"

She smiled at the ground. "That was nothing. You should hear some of the —"

"No, don't. Please. I don't want to know."

Later, on the train, he said, "It's not true, is it?"

Susie was staring out of the window. "No," she said. But she had put no effort into her answer, as if she wasn't sure, or didn't care.

"Susie?" He leaned closer.

When she turned to him, she looked desolate, her skin stretched thin and drained of all its colour. "No,

Billy," she said. "It's not true." She held his gaze for a moment longer, and then, finally, some humour crept back. "I'm not exactly a virgin, though, either . . ."

The mortuary radiator clanked once, then gurgled. Billy reached out and put a hand on it, but it was no warmer than the last time. He shifted in his chair. After that awkward evening in Manchester, he had refused to have anything to do with Susie's father. The man was only interested in making what they had seem grubby. If Newman ever rang up to suggest a drink or dinner — though based in the South of France, he was always travelling to England, it seemed, on business — Billy would claim to be working. "But you go," he would say to Susie. "You go." When she was offered a job in Suffolk and asked Billy whether he'd consider leaving the north-west, he surprised her by saying yes. He surprised himself too — he had never seen himself living anywhere else — but perhaps, in the back of his mind, he thought a move to the other side of the country would put them out of Newman's reach. He worried about his mother being on her own — his older brother, Charlie, had moved to America the year before — but she made light of it, telling him that, after all, there were such things as cars and he could always drive up and see her now and then. Once Susie had accepted the offer, Billy requested a transfer to the Suffolk Constabulary — luckily, they had a vacancy for an officer with his experience — and by the spring of 1990 he and Susie were renting a neat modern flat in the centre of Ipswich.

At first he missed the buzz of Widnes, the muck and stink of it. The huddled red-brick terraces and the towering, tangled heaps of scrap metal. The bloody fights that broke out every five minutes for no good reason. Sometimes you'd find teeth in the gutter, or a clump of hair. When Widnes played arch-rivals Warrington at Naughton Park, the coaches bringing in the visitors would have to run a gauntlet of stones and bottles, and the police took dogs along to keep the two sets of fans apart. Then the game itself, with half the players on amphetamines, the tackling so brutal that Billy's bones would shudder — and he was only watching . . . Afterwards, he and a few other bobbies would call in at the pie shop, pork-and-apple fillings or hamburger-and-baked-beans. You'd get stomach-ache just looking at those pies, but you'd still have two, and you'd wash them down with tea that had brewed so long you could have used it to stain furniture. Later, there would be trouble at one of the nightclubs, the Landmark or Big Jim's, and they'd go down there mob-handed to sort it out. The women were even more ferocious than the men, especially if they'd had a drink. "Don't let them get you on the floor," a sergeant told him early on. "You won't get up again." There was the night three pubs spilled out at the same time, and an almighty punch-up started in front of the chip shop on Victoria Road. Billy tried to nick somebody in a black shirt who was only about half his height. The bloke turned out to be some sort of martial-arts expert, and Billy came away with one side of his face swollen up like a melon and his left arm fractured in two places.

But the way the bobbies pulled together, Neil and Terry and Vomit Molloy and the Perv and Dad, even Light Duties Livermore, everybody looking out for everybody else, that was really something . . . Ipswich felt tame by comparison, less vivid. If asked, though, Susie could explain exactly what was better about their lives. She seemed happier, and that was Billy's one great wish, to make her happy.

But before the year was out, Susie began to feel that something was missing. She wasn't homesick for the north; it was more like a kind of restlessness or hollowness, the sense that she hadn't fully occupied the space around her. The space inside her too: in early 1991, she'd had a miscarriage, and she was frightened she might not be able to have children. Words like "security" and "the future" crept into her conversation; she worried about what she called "missing the boat". These were things that mattered to her, and he considered it his duty to provide them. After months of searching, they found a property a few miles out of town. It was a small place, semi-detached, the end house in a row of eight, and there was noise from the railway line on the far side of the road, but it would be their first real home. Billy waited until they had settled in — the house had needed painting inside and out, and it took weeks to clear the garden — and then, on a cloudy, drowsy afternoon in late July, he reached for Susie's hand and led her out into the field. "Where are you taking me?" He wouldn't say. Only when they got to the middle did he stop. The corn waist-high, and seeming to whisper, even though there wasn't any wind.

Then, holding Susie's hand in both of his, he knelt in front of her and asked her to marry him. She looked away into the sky, and a dreamy smile rose on to her face, as if he'd reminded her of something that had happened a long time ago, in her childhood. When she said, "Yes, I'd love to," he was still on his knees, invisible to everybody in the world but her. Anyone watching would have thought she was talking to herself.

They didn't invite Susie's father to the wedding. Billy wouldn't allow it. "He'd ruin everything," Billy said, and then added, somewhat hysterically, "It's him or me," which made Susie laugh. "My father won't be coming either," Billy told her. He didn't know where his father was living, or even if he was still alive. "Let's invite Harry Parsons instead," he said. The wedding took place in Stockport, and Susie's stepfather, the car-dealer, paid for everything. They'd been married for less than a year when Susie became pregnant again, and this time she didn't lose the baby.

In the coroner's office the phone started ringing, and the sound brought Billy swiftly out of his chair. Stepping into the cramped room, he picked up the receiver.

"PC Tyler," he said.

The woman on the other end told him that her name was Marjorie Church, and that she was the charge-hand porter. "We've got a body to bring down," she said.

Five minutes later, Billy heard a knock, and when he opened the mortuary doors a short, solid woman in a blue shirt and dark trousers was standing in front of him.

"Marjorie?" he said.

"That's me."

Behind her were two men with a trolley. One of the porters was middle-aged and bald, with clownish tufts of hair protruding from both sides of his head; the other one was younger, in his twenties.

Billy stood aside to let them in, making sure the doors were properly bolted after them. He would have to write their names down in the scene log, he said.

The younger porter blew some air out of his mouth. "Is that really necessary? We're only going to be a moment."

"It's standard procedure," Billy said. "It applies to everyone, me included."

"You like your job, do you?"

The number of times Billy had heard that.

He looked at the porter. "You can take it up with the sergeant if you want."

"There's other people dying round here," the porter said, "not just her."

"His name's Peter Baines," said the porter with the clown's hair. "I'm Colin Wilson."

The young porter scowled at him.

"Thanks, Colin." Glancing at Billy, Marjorie raised both her eyebrows, then she moved over to the bank of fridges and opened one of the doors.

Using his right foot, Wilson pumped up the trolley until it was on a level with an empty compartment, then Baines helped him slide the body on to a steel shelf. The body was wrapped in a whitish shroud, but the head was uncovered, and Billy glimpsed the crown of an old man's head, the scalp mottled and waxy.

Marjorie closed the fridge door. "No need to lock this one in," she said.

Billy smiled faintly. He watched as she took a black marker pen out of her pocket and wrote the dead man's name on the fridge door, then he returned to the log and recorded what had just occurred.

Moments later, Wilson wheeled the trolley off down the corridor, with Baines walking behind, still grumbling. Marjorie went to follow them. On reaching the doorway, though, she paused and then turned round.

"It's that woman," she said. "She upsets people."

"I understand that," Billy said.

"It'll be good when she's gone. When things are back to normal."

Billy nodded.

Her face brightened suddenly, as if whatever had been awkward or difficult was now over. "Anything I can get you?" she said. "A cup of tea?"

"No thanks, Marjorie," he said. "I'm fine."

CHAPTER
NINE

Alone again, Billy noticed something on the floor under the table. Bending down, he picked up a metal nail file with a handle of pearly white plastic. He doubted that Marjorie would have brought a nail file to the mortuary — and besides, the iridescent handle didn't seem in character — so he could only assume that it belonged to the young blonde constable who had preceded him. He turned the nail file slowly in his hand. If he had asked the constable what she thought of the woman in the fridge, what would she have said? What would she have made of it all, born as she undoubtedly had been in the early seventies? Would she have wanted to try and understand how it was possible for a woman who had once been a trusted babysitter to become involved in the torture and murder of children? Or would she simply have repeated what the tabloids were telling her, and what most people in the country appeared to believe, namely that the woman was inhuman, evil, a monster?

In the autumn of 1999, Billy had spent some time in a newspaper library, reading up about the murders, and one story in particular had stayed with him. When the woman was a girl of fifteen, she'd been friends with a boy two years her junior. He was delicate, apparently, and she'd taken it upon herself to protect him. One day he asked her if she would come swimming. She told him she couldn't. That afternoon he went up to the local reservoir on his own and drowned. For weeks afterwards, she was inconsolable. She wore nothing but black. The boy had always been a weak swimmer, and yet she had refused to go with him. She was to blame for his death. She couldn't forgive herself. Some people said it was then that she first turned to the Catholic Church. There are moments in your life when something's taken from you, and once you've lost it you don't get it back. What you were before is neither here nor there. You're different now.

Billy didn't pretend to be an expert — what did he know, really, except for what he had picked up on the streets? — but he couldn't help wondering whether that boy's death by drowning wasn't a defining moment, a kind of turning-point. Supposing somewhere deep down in her there was the feeling that she had killed, and not a stranger either, but somebody who was dear to her, somebody who had — and this detail always sent a shiver through him — *the same initials as she did?* If that was the case, if that was how she had felt, did the psychopath from Glasgow see that abyss in her, that bottomless pit, the belief that she had nothing left to lose? Could that be what had attracted him? She'd done it once. She could do it again. What difference would it make? She was already guilty. And having more experience than he did, she could even, maybe, guide him, show him the way . . . It wasn't an apology or an excuse. It might just be a fact, though. And that eerie coincidence with the initials . . . When the boy died in the reservoir, did part of her die with him?

CHAPTER
TEN

The image of Baines, the young porter, lingered — his gelled hair, his slouch, his barely concealed sneer. *Like your job, do you?* There were certain people who couldn't resist having a go at you, and though Billy was used to it — after twenty-three years, how could he not be? — he was closer to losing control these days than at any other stage in his career. But he was acutely conscious of what had happened to his friend, Neil Batty. A couple of years ago, Neil had beaten a suspect so badly that the man had ended up in hospital, and in spite of an exemplary record, Neil had been thrown out of the force. Billy couldn't help but sympathise. There had been moments when he, too, had been tempted: a Friday night in the mid-nineties, for instance.

He had come home from work to find an unfamiliar car parked outside his house. It was exactly the sort of car that Sue's stepfather, Tony, would put on his showroom forecourt — long, sleek, unnecessarily fast. But as Billy pulled up behind it he saw a chauffeur behind the wheel — he could make out the shape of a peaked cap above the head-rest — and, knowing only one man who'd be likely to have a chauffeur, he almost drove away again. At that moment, Newman came round the side of the house and moved languidly across the pavement. He was wearing a dark-blue suit and light-brown shoes, and his hands were in his pockets. His face was tanned. In the seven years that had passed since their first and only encounter, Newman didn't appear to have aged at all.

Billy slowly opened his car door and got out.

"Still a constable, I see," Newman said.

Billy locked the door, then straightened up.

Newman was standing on the narrow strip of grass next to the kerb, hands still in his pockets. "Failed our sergeant's exam, did we?"

"I failed that before I even met you," Billy said.

Newman shook his head.

Billy glanced at the house. It was after ten o'clock at night, but there wasn't a light on anywhere. "No one here," he said, half to himself.

"No." Newman's expression was expectant, sly, even faintly humorous, as if Billy was about to deliver the punchline to a joke.

"Well, you'd better come in, I suppose," Billy said eventually.

Newman had a word with his driver, then followed Billy up the short drive. At the front door Billy paused, fumbling in his pocket for his keys.

Once through into the hall, he stood still for a moment, listening. When he came home from work, he usually walked in on some kind of disaster; it was almost never calm or tidy. He wondered if Newman could sense that. He was aware of the man behind him, alert, quiet, mocking. Like an assassin.

"Sue?" His voice sounded thin, plaintive, and he wished he hadn't opened his mouth.

There was no reply.

He was angry with her for not being home to deal with her father — but perhaps she hadn't known he was coming. It was probably Newman's style to spring surprises.

He showed Newman into the lounge. Newman picked up a framed photograph of Emma as a one-year-old, and then put it down again almost immediately.

"Your granddaughter," Billy said.

Newman looked at him steadily, but didn't speak. Billy watched Newman's gaze shift to the wedding pictures on the sideboard. There was Billy, with his top hat and his toothy smile — *I can't believe my luck* — and there was Sue, in cream satin, a bunch of white and yellow flowers held at waist-level. She had the flushed, exultant look of somebody who had been proved right. *I always knew this day would come, and now it has.* Billy wondered how Newman had felt about not having been invited.

Newman turned and sat down on the sofa, one arm stretched along the back. "So where's Sue?"

Like most successful people, he gave you the feeling that you lived too slowly, without sufficient clarity or focus. He didn't waste any time on subjects that didn't interest him.

"I've no idea," Billy said. "Do you want to wait?"

"If you don't mind."

"Would you like something to drink?"

"What have you got?"

"Tea, coffee. Beer." Billy moved towards the kitchen. "I'm going to have a beer."

"I'll have beer too."

Billy fetched two cans of Heineken from the fridge, then walked back into the lounge and handed one of them to Newman.

"Do you have a glass?" Newman said.

Billy hesitated, then went out to the kitchen again. The cupboard where the glasses were kept was empty — they would be in the dishwasher, which Sue never ran until last thing at night — so he chose a plastic beaker with Pooh and Piglet on the side. One of Emma's. He took it into the lounge and handed it to Newman. Newman looked at the beaker, and Billy saw him decide not to comment. Opening his beer, Billy dropped heavily into the armchair by the fire. It had been a long day: a wife beaten by her husband, a stolen motorbike, two drunk builders fighting in a pub . . .

"I thought your house might look a bit like this," Newman said after a while.

"Not what you're used to, I imagine."

Newman laughed unpleasantly.

Lose your temper, and you lose, Billy thought. It was a lesson he had learned over the years. Another lesson: don't say any more than you have to. He raised his can to his lips and drank.

"Actually, to be honest," Newman said, "I thought it might be even worse. You know, more depressing . . ."

Through the closed window Billy heard the clank of a bicycle. That would be Harry Parsons, riding home from the allotments. Harry had recovered from the fall he'd had not long after Billy and Sue moved in, and he was up there most days, whatever the weather. The last time they had spoken, Harry had told him that he was thinking of growing delphiniums. A beautiful flower, Harry had said. Beautiful colour. Not blue, but not purple either. Somewhere in between.

"I'm sure you do your best," Newman was saying. "It's just that she wants more from life. More than you can offer, anyway."

"Did she tell you that?"

"She didn't have to. I'm her father."

"You left her when she was thirteen."

"I left her mother."

Billy shrugged. "Same thing."

Newman watched him from the sofa.

"You know, when I first knew Sue," Billy said, "she never mentioned you at all. I used to think her father must be dead. He must have died when she was very young, I thought — or maybe he died before she was even born —"

"Are they teaching you psychology now? Is that what they're teaching on those training courses?" Newman studied his beer. He still hadn't taken so much as a sip.

In that moment, a curious vibration went through Billy, a sort of flutter or crackle, as though his body were full of tiny people clapping. He had just realised that Newman was a man he could kill, and he would feel no qualms about it. He could use the onyx clock Sue's mother had given them when they got married. He could see Newman on the carpet, one arm trapped beneath his body, the other pointing at the door. Battered to death with a present from his ex-wife. There was a nice symmetry to that.

"I'm not sure I get the joke," Newman said.

This would be one of the very few times that Billy managed to turn the tables on Sue's father, and he wanted to make it last. No qualms, he thought, and no remorse. None whatsoever.

Standing up, he stepped over to the mantelpiece and adjusted the position of the clock, not because it needed adjusting, but because he wanted to feel the weight of it, the heft. Oh, this would do, he said to himself. This would be perfect.

Not exactly the perfect murder, though.

As he put the clock down and turned away, he caught a glimpse of himself in the mirror that hung opposite the fireplace. For several seconds he stood quite still, struck by a thought he'd never had before. In Ipswich there was a man — a local character — who'd had his entire face tattooed in an attempt to stop himself committing crimes. Billy would see him sometimes, on Westgate Street or Norwich Road, his eyes appearing to stare out from behind a jungle of Celtic swirls and flourishes. Granted the man was mentally ill, but the measure did have a certain logic to it. If he ever broke the law, there would be no problem identifying the culprit. *It was the bloke with the tattoos. He did it*. Looking at himself in the mirror, it occurred to Billy that he might have joined the police for the same reason, to prevent himself from doing wrong. Not to protect other people, then, but to protect himself.

His uniform was a same version of the tattooed face. It hadn't worked, though, had it? Even with his uniform on, he had done things he shouldn't have; if anything, in fact, the uniform had helped. He thought of Venetia's father, and the memory came to him so forcefully that the wet-hay smell of the old man's breath seemed present in the room.

"You know, a few years ago —" Billy checked himself. This wasn't something he should ever talk about, and least of all with Newman listening.

"A few years ago what?" Newman said softly.

Billy shook his head. "Another drink?"

Newman looked at his plastic beaker. "I've got plenty."

When Billy returned from the kitchen with a second beer, he went and stood by the window. He saw Newman's chauffeur fold a newspaper and place it on the dashboard. He wondered how the chauffeur felt about his employer. He imagined walking outside and telling him Newman was dead. *I killed him. Just now. With a clock.* And the chauffeur nodding, smiling, maybe even patting him on the back —

"It's not that you're stupid exactly," Newman said.

To the west, the sky was streaked with violet and gold. Summer nights — the way the light never seems to go . . .

"It's just that you lack drive."

Billy watched as a car came into view further down the road.

"You'd rather avoid things," Newman said, "than really take them on."

When the car pulled up level with the house, Billy saw that it belonged to one of Sue's friends from the school gates.

"You're frightened," Newman said.

Above the car's roof was a row of trees, arranged along the horizon. Billy knew that they were poplars, and that they grew in the field beyond the railway line, but in the slowly fading light they looked like an ancient curse written in a language he could not decipher. They had the same qualities as Newman's words: spiteful, insidious — black as the wrong kind of magic.

The car door opened, and Sue got out with Emma in her arms. Emma's legs hung straight down, which meant she was probably asleep. Sue glanced at her father's car, then turned back and watched her friend drive off, freeing one hand so she could wave. She hadn't noticed Billy in the window, and somehow he felt she ought to have done. That lack of awareness, that apparent self-sufficiency didn't say much for their relationship — or rather, it said everything.

"What do you think, Scruffy?" came Newman's voice. "Do you think that's unfair?"

CHAPTER
ELEVEN

Billy stood up suddenly and walked down to the far end of the mortuary. He would have liked some air, a change of scene, but it was still hours until his break. Newman's voice had been so gentle and considered, as if he were dispensing valuable advice, each sentence carefully shaped and weighted so as to lodge in Billy's memory. Billy rubbed at his face with both hands. Had he avoided things? He didn't think he had. Sue had wanted security, and he had done his utmost to provide it. He had worked unceasingly to try and build a life that seemed worth living, and now, after fourteen years together, they had more or less everything they were supposed to have — a house, a child, a car, a job, a pension — but nothing felt secure at all, and nothing felt quite real either.

In the last few months he had stopped going straight home after work. The first time it happened, in February, it had been an accident. He knew the roundabout well — he used it most days — so there was no reason why he should have taken the first exit instead of the second, and even once he'd made the mistake he could easily have pulled into the side of the road and turned round. But he didn't. He carried on. And there was a distinct lightness about the way he drove after that, a detached quality, as though the decision was not only one that had been made for him, but also one that he didn't have the power either to challenge or to overturn. He wondered if that was how his father, Glenn Tyler, had felt when he walked out on his pregnant wife in 1956. That lightness, that detachment. Things shaken off — for ever, in his father's case.

From that day on, even after his transfer to Stowmarket had come through, Billy would go back to that same roundabout, and he would follow the road that curved under the Orwell bridge and out along the river. He would always park in the same lay-by. If it was raining, he would listen to the radio, or read the local paper. From time to time, he would switch the wipers on and peer through the windscreen, but there was nothing much to see, just the dark twist of the road ahead of him, and the grass verge to his left and, beyond that, the river's dull grey surface. If the weather was fine, though, and the tide was out, he would walk across the mud-flats, eyes lowered, as if searching the ground for something he had lost. He only engaged with what lay directly in front of him — seaweed, nails, bones, feathers, shells. The rest of his life he was able, for a while, to keep at bay. He saw all sorts of people. Lonely types mostly. There was a man who carried a white bucket and a long stick with a spoon taped to the end of it. Employed by a nearby farm, he had taken it upon himself to poison the rats that were breeding on the riverbank. There was also a man who dug up ragworms and razorfish, which he would use as bait. Like most keen fishermen, he didn't have too much to say. And there was a frizzy-haired woman who fed the swans — with biscuits, usually, or stale buns. Another woman, older, would stare out over the water, one hand pressed against her collarbone, as if waiting for a lover to arrive by boat. They would exchange a few words, or nod at each other, but that was about it. Nobody came down to the estuary to make new friends. Sometimes he would read the notice that had been erected on the grass verge. He learned about the various birds that visited the area — the godwit, the redshank, the dunlin. They would spend the summer in Norway or Greenland or Russia, and then, when the temperature began to drop, they would fly south. Those names, though: they sounded like characters from myth or legend. Redshank the warrior, soaked in blood. Godwit the jester, the holy fool . . . And beyond the notice, of course, there was always the view. There were two cargo ships moored against the far bank, their hulls rusted ginger and listing in the water. There were yachts too, tacking upriver, their sails paunchy with the wind. Behind them lay the Nacton foreshore, where people often went to have sex or smoke dope, and away to his left, the bridge itself, its giant concrete span so high that it looked precarious, almost unsafe. Only the westbound lane was visible from where he stood, the cars and lorries sliding endlessly and steadily from right to left like targets in a fairground rifle-range. Above all, though, there was a sudden immense resource of space and light. It had sufficient power to absorb him, he felt.

58

It was something he could vanish into if he wanted, and that notion gave him solace, making it possible for him, after a while, to turn his car round and drive back home.

Billy sat down again, then leaned forwards, the points of his elbows on his knees. Placing the palms of his hands on his forehead, with his fingers reaching up into his hair, he stared down at the metal grating that covered the drain. He was aware of the pulse beating on the inside of his right wrist. Years ago, when he was sixteen or seventeen, he had imagined all kinds of scenarios, but never anything so obvious or so difficult. He had met people here and there, people who could make things happen. Somehow none of it had quite come off. Life could surge away from you at great speed, leaving you bobbing dumbly in its wake. His friend, Raymond Percival, for instance, who had tried to persuade him to move down south, to London. *We could get a squat. Go on the dole. There'll be parties, girls . . .* Raymond who always said he wanted to be an arms dealer — where was Raymond now? And what about Venetia? He would have married her in two seconds flat, but marriage had been the last thing on her mind. Venetia with her hair flowing over her shoulders, like black treacle poured out of a tin . . .

He last saw Raymond in Cheshire. It was October 1993, and he had driven up to the north-west to visit his mother who'd just celebrated her sixty-eighth birthday. Sue was three months pregnant with Emma, and Billy's father, Glenn Tyler, had died a few weeks earlier, in Germany. It was a strange time, full of events that were enormous but concealed, remote. He found it hard to work out what he was feeling. He just kept going, without thinking too much, and tried to do the ordinary things as efficiently as he could. On the Saturday night he took his mother out to dinner in a country pub where the food was supposed to be good, and as he went up to the bar for the second time, to fetch more drinks, somebody called his name. He glanced over his shoulder, and there, unbelievably, was Raymond Percival, sitting at a candlelit table with a girl.

"Billy Tyler," Raymond said, not getting up. He was wearing a fawn leather jacket that looked expensive, and his skin was lightly tanned.

"Raymond! What are you doing here? I thought you'd be in London."

"Oh, you know," Raymond said. "I get around."

He had the same mocking smile that he'd had as a teenager. It had been amusing then, even necessary, as much a part of his image as his haircut or his flared trousers, but in a man approaching forty it looked much more like provocation. It didn't seem as if Raymond knew that, though — or perhaps he just didn't care.

"So," Billy said, "how are you?"

"Could be worse. What about you?"

"Not bad."

"I almost drowned him once," Raymond told the girl, his eyes still moving over Billy's face. The girl's mouth opened a fraction, then she laughed quickly and reached for her champagne.

For a moment Billy saw the water, almost black, and seeming to slope uphill, away from him.

"I suppose you're running Scotland Yard by now," Raymond said.

Billy smiled faintly. "Something like that."

So Raymond knew what he did. He was sure Raymond found it not only ludicrous but incomprehensible. After everything they had been through together, he would be bound to see it as a betrayal too. But that was years ago, all that . . .

Raymond introduced him to the girl. Her name was Henry, Raymond said. When Billy stared at her, she smiled and told him it was short for Henrietta. They shook hands, hers cocked slightly at the wrist, and bright with rings. She had a pair of sunglasses in her hair. Billy thought she was probably a model.

He turned back to Raymond, his eyes dropping briefly to Raymond's jacket. "You look as if you're doing all right for yourself," he said. "Nothing illegal, I hope."

Raymond laughed. "You want to join us, Billy? You want to pull up a chair?"

"I'm afraid I can't. I'm with someone."

Raymond looked past him. "Who's the lucky girl?"

"My mother," Billy said.

They both smiled, but their smiles didn't reach their eyes.

"Well, anyway," Raymond said, brisker now, "good to see you." You'd think they ran into each other all the time. It had been twenty years, though. Maybe more.

"Take it easy, Raymond," Billy said, then he turned to Henrietta. "Nice to have met you."

He walked over to the bar. As he ordered the drinks, he heard Raymond and the girl start laughing. On his way back, he passed their table again and nodded, but he didn't stop, focusing instead on the two glasses he was carrying, as if worried they might spill.

Sometime later, he looked through the window and saw Raymond standing near a low-slung sports car. The girl was with him. Though it was already dark, she had her sunglasses on. Out of habit, he made a mental note of Raymond's number plate. BOY 1DA. If Raymond wanted to, he could drive to London tonight with that beautiful girl beside him. Or Paris. He could do anything.

"Are they friends of yours?" Billy's mother asked.

"That's Raymond," Billy said. "Raymond Percival."

"You were at school with him, weren't you?"

Billy nodded. "I went on holiday with him as well. We travelled all round Europe."

"I remember." His mother's eyes lingered on Raymond as he climbed into the car. "Good-looking boy."

Billy smiled to himself.

"Your father had something of that about him," she said.

"Really?"

"He was glamorous." She took a sip of wine, then put the glass back on the table. She kept her hand on it, though, and twisted it from time to time. "Imagine falling for a musician . . ."

They both watched through the window as the sports car moved noisily out on to the road.

"Was he ever violent?" Billy asked.

"He got drunk sometimes. I was frightened of him then." She looked across at Billy. "He never hit me, if that's what you mean."

Billy stared at the table. His father had been drinking the night he died, apparently. A tram had knocked him down. In Hamburg. When Billy thought about the death, all he could see was a saxophone lying on a cobbled street, the bell tinted red by strip-club neon, the octave key bent out of shape. His father, the musician . . . Had he been playing live that night? Where had he been living, and who with? What had happened to the saxophone? The questions came to him in a leisurely, almost sluggish way, as though aware that answers were unlikely to materialise. They had more to do with a kind of nostalgia than with any real curiosity. He had seen his father just twice in his entire life.

"Why do you ask?" his mother said, and he could sense her eyes on him.

"No reason," he said, still staring at the table.

"You're not in trouble, Billy, are you?"

"No." And he wasn't. But he felt as if he was.

CHAPTER
TWELVE

He couldn't remember actually meeting Raymond
Percival. There had been no fanfare, no shaft of light,
no thin blade through his heart — nothing to let him
know how deeply he would fall under Raymond's spell.
He thought they must have been in the same year at
school, but it wasn't the classroom that Billy saw when
he brought Raymond to mind. He didn't see a uniform
either. Somehow Raymond always appeared in the
clothes he put on after school, or at weekends. It was
the late sixties, and Raymond dressed in long-sleeved
T-shirts that were too tight under the arms, usually with
a picture of an album cover or a group on the front. He
wore flared jeans too, often with a triangle of fabric
sewn into the lower leg to make them wider still. His
hair was cut shorter than everybody else's, a style that
only came into fashion more than twenty years later, in
the early nineties. Ahead of his time, Raymond was.
Naturally.

The first conversation Billy remembered had to do
with fathers. As a boy, Billy would never admit that his
father had walked out — he had invented an alternative
reality involving things he didn't understand, like
record deals and gigs — so when Raymond asked him

whether it was true that his father was a musician, Billy gave his standard reply:

"He plays jazz. I don't see much of him, though. He's always away, on tour."

Raymond sent him a look that tilted through the air towards him like a flying roof-tile in a gale. "I heard he left before you were even born."

Perhaps because he was so shocked, Billy reverted to the truth. "So what? Have you got a dad?"

"He's a nobody," Raymond said. "I'm never going to be like him." He kicked a stone into the gutter, then said, "Anyway, he's dead."

"I think my dad might be dead too, actually." Billy had no reason to say that. It just came out.

"Do you care?" Raymond asked.

Billy shook his head. "No."

Raymond seemed to approve of Billy's answer. The speed of it. The frankness.

Raymond's father had died of cancer, but Raymond wouldn't talk about it except to say that he'd like to fucking blow up ICI. His father had worked at ICI for thirty years. His uncle still did, and now he had cancer too. One evening Raymond took Billy into a field that overlooked the plant. A few horses stood about, tearing at the grass with big stained teeth; against the mass of spotlit pipes and tanks, they looked incongruous, primitive, oddly out of date. Coming to a halt in the middle of the field, with Castner Kellner and Rocksavage glittering below him and the River Mersey in the distance, Raymond threw his arms out wide and made a loud exploding sound. The horses scattered, eyes rolling, their hooves thudding across the lumpy turf. One of them almost ran Billy down. He murmured in protest, but Raymond was hunched over with his hands wrapped around his head, and Billy understood that debris from the dynamited factories was falling from the sky. If you said ICI had brought jobs to the area, Raymond would tell you it had brought pollution too. If you mentioned the recreation club and the sports facilities, he would smile sourly. "That's just guilt," he'd say. He was unshakeable. Raymond always slept with his windows shut on account of the toxic gases that were released into the atmosphere at night. He didn't trust anything that was produced locally. He only ever drank soda water, which he stole from the Co-op, and he refused to eat fruit and vegetables unless they came from somewhere far away like Israel or Costa Rica.

One particular afternoon from that time stood out in Billy's memory. He would have been about fourteen. It had been a hot, sticky couple of days in an otherwise dismal summer, and when Raymond turned up at Billy's house, he didn't have a shirt on, only a pair of mulberry-coloured loon pants, the backs frayed where they dragged along the ground. Raymond's dogs swirled about on Billy's small front lawn, growling and snapping at each other. One of them was called Cabal, which had been the name of King Arthur's dog. The other one was John. John the dog. Raymond thought that was funny. When Billy answered the door, Raymond held up a plastic bag and swung it from side to side. The contents clinked. Billy knew then that they would be getting drunk together. Raymond would have conned somebody into buying alcohol for him, or maybe he'd been shoplifting again. If you stole something and got away with it, you were innocent. That was Raymond's philosophy. You were only guilty if you got caught, and Raymond never got caught: people would look into his face and see nothing but honesty in it.

"I'm going out for a bit," Billy called back into the darkness of the house. He heard his mother's voice, but Raymond was already turning away, so he shouted, "See you later," and then slammed the front door shut. Once on the pavement, he glanced up and saw a bent head in the upstairs window. His brother Charlie, reading. Charlie's A level results were due any day now, and they were all expecting great things.

That afternoon Raymond and Billy did what they usually did. To get to the park, most people would have walked along the road, a distance of less than a mile, but Raymond and Billy would cut across the open fields, which took them past the brine reservoir. Billy was fascinated by the warning signs — DROWNING HAZARD, CORROSIVE LIQUID — and he was drawn, too, by the mysterious square brick huts. As for Raymond, he had his own personal agenda. The reservoir belonged to the company he held responsible for his father's death, and he would be muttering threats and curses as they approached the padlocked gates. He seemed to like this route to the park. It kept his hatred fresh.

There was a place where the path narrowed, and they had to walk in single file. Raymond went first, the dogs running on ahead. A high hedge shielded them from the sun; the air cooled suddenly. As he followed Raymond, he noticed the paleness of Raymond's back, more like the inside of something than the outside, as if the skin had already been peeled away and this was the fruit, the goodness, the part that you could eat. He felt himself blushing, and he lagged behind, feigning interest in a discarded cigarette packet.

Later, they lay side by side on the warm grass. They started with barley wine. There was a kind of thickness to the liquid in those small brown bottles; you could taste how strong it was. Drink three and you'd see double. They drank two each, then switched to vodka.

"You want to do something?" Raymond said.

Billy was staring up into a sky that was so smoothly blue, so absolutely free of clouds, that it made him feel dizzy, and when he heard the words "do something", his heart turned over.

"Sure," he said. "Why not?"

And then, when Raymond didn't speak, he said, "Like what?"

"Come on." Raymond got to his feet. Two fingers in his mouth, he whistled to the dogs, then he began to walk.

"Where are we going?" Billy asked.

Raymond didn't answer.

They circled back past the brine reservoir and ducked through a wire fence, coming out on to the footpath that led to Raymond's house. When they arrived, his sister, Amanda, was lying on her stomach in the front garden, reading a comic. She was wearing a lime-green bikini and sunglasses with pink plastic frames. She was only eleven, but she already had breasts.

"You're burning," Raymond said as he passed her.

Amanda gave him a V-sign without even lifting her eyes off the page.

Billy grinned, but she didn't notice. They were all the same, he thought, these Percivals . . .

Once they had locked the dogs in the back yard, they got two bikes out of the shed and cycled down the hill to Weston Point. They had to wait at the level crossing while a train laboured past. Billy counted eighteen wagons, each one filled with chemicals. The gates lifted, and the two boys cycled on. The village streets were deserted. All the shops looked shut, even though they weren't. You could feel the heat rising off the tarmac in ghostly waves.

They hid their bikes in the gap between a fence of concrete slats and an old free-standing garage, then they scaled a wall and dropped down into a jungle of bindweed, lavender and nettles. Billy had climbed into other people's gardens before, with Trevor Lydgate, when he was younger, but this felt different. There was something driven about Raymond, something merciless. Billy looked towards the house, with its black windows and its untended garden, and wondered what Raymond had in mind.

Crouching low, they crossed the lawn, and when they reached the house they flattened themselves against the wall, their palms and shoulder blades pressed against sun-toasted brick. They must look as if they'd been caught in an invisible force field, Billy thought. Like people in a science-fiction programme. Turning his head sideways, he met Raymond's gaze, and they both began to laugh. And once they'd started, they couldn't stop. They bent double, gasping, trying not to make a sound. *What if someone comes?* Billy kept thinking, but that only made it worse. In the end, Raymond brought out the vodka. He took a long swig, then offered it to Billy. Billy swallowed some. It was warm and slightly oily, and he shivered as it went down.

Just along from the back door, they found an open transom window. The frosted glass told them that it was a lavatory. Raymond heaved himself up on to the window ledge and slithered in head first, his legs wriggling comically for a few moments before they disappeared. *I hope no one's having a crap in there,* Billy thought, and he had to pinch his arm hard to prevent himself from having the hysterics again. He glanced round quickly to see if anyone was watching, then followed Raymond through the narrow gap. He was stockier than Raymond, which made it more difficult; one of his trouser pockets snagged on the window-catch and ripped. Using both hands, he managed to manoeuvre himself down from the closed lid of the toilet seat on to the floor, landing in a heap at Raymond's feet. He stood up. The room was only just big enough for the two of them, and he could smell the alcohol on Raymond's breath.

"What are we doing here?" he said.

Raymond shook his head, then opened the door. They stepped out into a long, thin corridor with brown walls and a floor of cracked linoleum. There was a rack of musty raincoats, and a metal Hoover with a torn dust-bag. From somewhere near by came the squeaky chipmunk voice of a cartoon character.

"'Sexton's have solved the mystery of elegant living,'" Raymond said.

Billy stared at him.

"I saw it above a furniture shop," Raymond said, "in Widnes."

Later in his life, as a policeman, Billy would often walk or drive past that very sign, and it always reminded him of Raymond. It was as if, in saying the words out loud when they were fourteen, Raymond had erected a memorial to himself.

They crept along the passageway, with Raymond leading. To the right was a parlour that gave on to the back garden. No sooner had Raymond entered the room than he was lifting a silver tankard off the bookshelf and forcing it into his trouser pocket. Billy wandered over to the window. Lying on the table was a black-leather handbag, half-open, with two five-pound notes visible inside. There was some loose change too. Billy held the handbag out to Raymond, showing him the contents, but Raymond was busy peeling a banana. As Raymond came and took the bag, the door behind him swung outwards and an old man shuffled into view. Though it was hard to believe, the old man didn't seem to realise anyone was there. Seen sideways-on, the top half of his back was curved, like the shell on a tortoise;

were he to walk up to a wall, his forehead would reach it first. Billy and Raymond kept perfectly still. If they didn't move, perhaps the old man wouldn't notice them at all. In any case, it was too late to hide.

Arms dangling, the man hung in front of a sideboard. His head wobbled slightly, as though mounted on a spring, and he was mumbling to himself. Billy couldn't make out any of the words. Then, after what felt like an age, the man turned and saw them. His eyes widened behind his spectacles; his mouth fell open.

"Time to leave," Raymond said.

But somehow they couldn't even take a step. It was as if they were being told a story, and they wanted to hear more.

The old man staggered towards them. He was shouting, but all the sounds that came out of him were slurred and nasal, and both his ears were full of hair. It was horrible. Just then, a wailing started up, very loud yet strangely forlorn, and it took Billy a moment to realise that it was a siren at one of the chemical plants. They would go off as part of a practice drill, or when a shift ended, but sometimes it meant that an accident had happened. If there was a leak, you had to run as fast as you could into the wind. Raymond had told him that, and he'd got it from his father. Billy wondered which way you were supposed to run if there wasn't any wind.

The noise seemed to trigger something in the old man. He grabbed a walking stick from the back of a chair and began to lash out in all directions. *Swish — swish — swish.* He didn't appear to be attacking anything in particular, unless it was the air itself — or perhaps he was signalling his outrage at the presence of intruders. In any case, he was destroying the room. First a chintzy table-lamp went flying, then a shelf of bric-à-brac. The head snapped off a prancing china horse. A shell-shaped ashtray shattered. Billy watched, half-enthralled, as the stick's black rubber tip arced through the centre light. The shade exploded, and bits of cloudy glass bounced like hail on the carpet.

By now, Raymond had slipped out of the room. Eluding the stick's wild orbits, Billy followed. Through a half-open door he saw an old woman with thick glasses and very little hair. She was watching *Wacky Races*. When she spotted Billy in the doorway, she waved, not with her whole hand, just with her fingers.

Raymond and Billy cycled back over the level crossing and up the hill, not stopping at all until they reached the park. One foot on the ground and the other on a pedal, Billy could taste blood in his mouth, and his right side ached, but it felt good to be outside again. There had been almost no air in the house, and what there was had smelt unpleasantly sweet, like stale cake.

When they had got their breath back, Raymond offered Billy one of the fivers.

Billy shook his head. "You're all right."

"Sure?" Raymond said.

Billy was looking back over his shoulder. "They were mad."

"They were just old," Raymond said.

That night, when Billy was cleaning his teeth, a tiny triangle of misty glass fell out of his hair and landed in the sink. He kept it in a matchbox for a while, not because it was precious, but as a reminder of something. He couldn't have said what exactly.

He didn't see Raymond after that, not for several weeks, and when school started again they both avoided each other. That year Raymond went around with an older boy called Derek Forbes. Billy took up judo.

He dreamt about Raymond, though. All the time.

CHAPTER
THIRTEEN

On first arriving in the mortuary, Billy had had the impression of an orderly, efficient space, but the longer he spent in the room, the more damage and neglect he noticed. The pale-green doors were set in a plain wooden frame that was badly scarred, especially at a point about three feet off the floor. The doors themselves were marked as well: there were dozens of little dents, all in a cluster, and all roughly the same diameter. There were similar marks on the fridge doors, and at a similar height. He thought he knew why, and a brief inspection of the trolley at the far end of the room confirmed his suspicions. Its leading edge and sharp corners lined up perfectly with most of the marks and dents. Clearly the porters were none too careful when it came to wheeling bodies about. The work wouldn't exactly be well paid, of course, but that was only part of the story. If you had a job in a hospital, you couldn't allow yourself to be disturbed by all the illness and disease surrounding you. You had to go to the other extreme, affecting indifference at the very least, and, from the outside, that could look insensitive or even callous. Similar strategies came into play if you worked for the police. Walking back to the entrance, Billy touched the dents in one of the doors. Maybe, after all, he had something in common with that surly young porter. He still felt like thumping him, though.

He moved to his left, passing shelves of neatly folded shrouds. In the gap between the main bank of fridges and a fridge marked POLICE BODIES he found a mop, a bucket, two rolls of pale-blue paper towels, and a yellow-plastic pyramid that said WET FLOOR. There were also a couple of empty cardboard boxes, one of which had the words RETURN TO MORTUARY scrawled across it. Here, too, there was evidence of carelessness or haste. All the various items had been piled on top of each other, higgledy-piggledy, and Billy imagined, for a moment, that his neighbours, the Gibsons, had been involved somehow. Their back patio was always a jumble of toys, most of them broken. In the garden a swing lay on its side, grass growing over it; the sandpit was half-full of rain-water, and green with mould. The Gibson family: they weren't actually criminal, but they didn't seem to know how to clear up after themselves, and they never showed any respect for anything — and then they went and got their knickers in a twist about a windchime . . .

Rounding a pillar, Billy found himself facing the fridge where the woman's body was being kept. At some subconscious level, perhaps, this had been his intended destination all along. Now that he had arrived, though, he didn't know why he was there, or what it was that he wanted to do. At last, he reached out and tested the handle, just as the sergeant had done a few hours earlier. It was still locked, of course. How could it not be? All the same, a flicker of disappointment went through him. *She looked old. Older than sixty.* Was he becoming morbid, voyeuristic, or was it his own sense of dislocation that he was grappling with? Ever since he had been left by himself in the mortuary, he had felt a little as if he were guarding a phantom, or the figment of someone's imagination. He didn't quite believe she was there. Perhaps he needed something that would anchor him in the experience, make it tangible. But wasn't that exactly what all those journalists outside were saying? In the end, he didn't think his urge to look in the fridge would bear too much examination. *Do your job*, he told himself. *Just do your job*. With the murderer's head behind that sheet of metal, only inches from his knuckles ... He remained motionless for several seconds, and then stepped back, the cold shape of the door-handle imprinted on the inside of his fingers.

CHAPTER
FOURTEEN

Billy passed the narrow door that led to the toilet and shower room. On the wall was a cooling control panel and a boxed first-aid kit. Someone had added an "s" on to the end of the word "aid". There was nothing precious about a mortuary. The only concession to feeling was the chapel of rest. Directly linked to the mortuary through the bare wooden doors behind his chair, it could also be accessed from the corridor outside, which allowed members of the public to avoid the unsightliness, the ruthless practicality, of death. He pushed the doors open and peered in. A simple icon hung near the bed where the deceased would be laid out. Close by was an orange settee with arms of pale wood. The walls were orange too, though lighter. For all its warm colours, the chapel of rest was as functional as any other part of the mortuary. You came here to pay your last respects, or sometimes, even more distress-ingly, to identify your next of kin. In this room people's worst fears would become a reality, and the air was petrified, stale, glassy with shock. For many, this would be where the suffering began.

As he shut the doors, Billy noticed the clock. Nine-thirty-three. Was that all? He sat down on his chair again. His left arm ached where that vicious dwarf had fractured it with a karate kick back in the early eighties; if he felt the chill of the mortuary anywhere, it would be there. Unscrewing his Thermos, he poured himself a cup of coffee. It was strong, with plenty of milk and sugar. He took a sip and let out a sigh of satisfaction. Ah, that was good. Now for some paperwork. He picked up his pocketbook and leafed through the pages until he found his notes on the community-centre break-in that had happened the weekend before last. The culprits were two fourteen-year-olds, Darren Clark and Scott Wakefield. They hadn't stolen anything, but they had caused a fair amount of damage, smashing windows, covering the walls with graffiti, and urinating on a piano. Since it was a first offence, he thought it unlikely that they would go to court. Instead, they'd probably be cautioned by an inspector, in the presence of their families. All the same, there were at least three forms to be filled out. Drawing his chair up to the table, he began to compile his report.

It was just a laugh, really, Darren had said at one point. *Something to do, you know? We didn't mean nothing by it.* When Billy first started out in Widnes, in 1979, he might have thought he could steer a boy like Darren back on to the straight and narrow, but from long experience he now knew that very little could be done. In all his time as a police officer, there were only one or two teenagers whose lives he could honestly claim to have changed for the better. It wasn't much of a return on twenty-three years' work.

How many more times in his life would Darren Clark get into trouble and then try and make light of it? Pen poised above the paper, Billy stared into space, reminded once again of the afternoon when he and Raymond broke into the old couple's house. He would have been Darren's age, give or take a few months. Was that what he had thought — that it had all been a bit of fun? Before, perhaps, but not when it was over. No, from his point of view it had left a sour aftertaste. Something so exciting at the beginning — the hot weather, the walk up to the park, the vodka — and then something he wished he hadn't been part of, something he would rather have forgotten.

There was a sudden, prolonged buzz from the door-bell. Billy glanced at the clock — nine-forty-five — then went over and undid the locks. Standing in the corridor was the constable who had been on duty by the main entrance.

"Your wife's here," he said.

Billy stared at him. "What?"

"Your wife, Sue. She's in reception."

"Is she all right?" Billy said.

"I don't know. She just asked if she could see you." The man stepped into the room and stood by the stainless-steel sink in the corner. He rubbed his hands together. "Cold in here."

"Would you mind taking over?" Billy said.

"No problem."

Billy signed himself out, making a note of the time, then watched as the constable signed himself in. His name was Fowler.

"I shouldn't be more than a few minutes," Billy said. "That's if I don't get lost."

"Bloody corridors," Fowler said.

CHAPTER
FIFTEEN

After eight o'clock at night the main entrance was locked, and the only access to the hospital was through Accident and Emergency. As Billy followed the signs, hurrying now, he was still thinking about that afternoon in Weston Point. They had cycled back along the brow of the hill, a dense yellow haze hanging over the Mersey. The river had a sweaty gleam to it, more like skin than water. Billy had hoped Amanda might still be sunbathing in the garden, but when they got to Raymond's house she'd gone indoors. On his way home, Billy ate some grass to disguise the smell of alcohol, and Mrs Parks, their neighbour, saw him do it. He'd felt bad about the break-in. At least he hadn't taken any of the money, though.

When Billy reached A and E, Sue was sitting on a chair with a copy of the *News of the World* lying unopened on her lap. Inwardly, he was already groaning. What had happened this time? What was so urgent that it couldn't wait till morning?

As soon as she saw him, she stood up, the newspaper splashing to the floor.

"What is it, Sue?" he said. "Is something wrong?"

He watched her pick up the paper and put it on a small formica table. Looking away, he caught the eye of a constable stationed by the entrance. The man's expression was one of mild commiseration.

Billy turned back to Sue. "How did you get here?" he said. "Where's Emma?" He stepped past Sue and peered through the glass door, as if his daughter might be out there somewhere, in the dark. She could never be left alone, not even for a moment. She was always wandering off. She had no sense.

"She's asleep," Sue said. "Jan came over."

Janet Crook lived two doors down, next to the Gibsons. Her husband had left her three years ago. There had been talk of a younger woman.

"I borrowed Jan's car," Sue said.

Billy was aware that both the constable and the two volunteers behind reception were listening to their conversation, though they were pretending not to.

"Let's go outside," he said.

His arm round Sue's shoulders, he ushered her through the sliding door. Reporters instantly closed in, their faces blank, insistent, and Billy had to remind himself of one of Phil Shaw's directives: as regards the press, he should do his best to be patient and friendly.

"Could you leave us alone, please?" Billy said. "This is a private matter." He spoke more bluntly than he'd intended to, but his annoyance had spread rapidly and would now, he felt, include almost anyone he came across.

He walked Sue to the left, past the locked main entrance, then down the slope towards the building where the nurses lived. They found a picnic table set in among some trees and sat down side by side, facing out, like people on a bus. Though there was no moon, the tree-trunks glinted. Silver birches. He stared upwards through a tangle of bare branches. The yellow car-park lights made the pieces of sky that were visible look blue.

"Do you love me, Billy?"

Billy sighed. "Is that what you drove out here for?" Leaning forwards, with his elbows on his knees, he looked straight ahead. He wasn't sure he had the energy for this. "For God's sake, Sue, I'm working."

"I was worried," she said. "I don't know. I just got worried." Lines appeared on her forehead. "Will we be all right, do you think?"

His voice softened a little. "Of course we will."

"I don't know. Sometimes it seems so difficult."

"I know," he said. "I know it does."

"Maybe we could go away for a bit."

"You mean a holiday?"

"We could get a ferry over to Holland. We could drive around like we used to — stay in places . . ."

He lifted his head again and looked at the silver birches, the bark peeling back in delicate scrolls to reveal dark patches underneath. *We could drive around.* With Emma, though? In late November? Sue's wishes were becoming more and more fanciful. It was as if, in having failed to take her to India or Thailand when she was young, in having persuaded her into a different life, one that was more pedestrian, he had accrued a debt. The tasks she set him now would be

84

harder to fulfil — and yet he owed it to her, didn't he, to try?

"I'll be home in the morning," he said. "We'll talk about it then."

Sue was reaching into her pocket. "I nearly forgot." She took out a black stone on a thin leather cord and passed it to him. He held it in the palm of his hand. The stone gave off a dull, dark gleam, but seemed oddly difficult to see. Like a piece of the night itself. "It's jet," she said. "It will protect you."

"What am I supposed to do with it?"

"Wear it. You can put it round your neck, under your uniform." She smiled at him. "No one will know it's there."

"All right." He passed the cord over his head.

"It doesn't absorb the bad things," Sue said, "it repels them. It doesn't let them get too close."

"OK," he said.

As he tucked the stone down inside his collar, he was reminded of something he had read about the early years of the woman's imprisonment, in Holloway. Apparently, the guards used to argue over who was going to take her meals in to her. No one wanted to do it. They didn't like the idea of being near her. They weren't physically afraid of her; the fear was spiritual.

"One more thing." Sue brought a second stone out of her pocket. "You'll need to carry this as well."

He took it from her. It was lighter in colour, and much smoother. More pleasing. "What's this one?"

"Celestine. It complements the jet. It will put you in touch with the purest part of yourself."

He slipped the crystal into his breast pocket. "I hope you haven't got any more," he said. "I'll never be able to get up off this bench otherwise."

"No," she said, almost jaunty now, "that's it."

He checked his watch. "You should get back, or Jan will worry." He took his mobile out. "Why don't you give her a call and let her know you're on your way?" Punching in the number, he handed her the phone. The moment she said, "Jan? It's me," he stopped listening.

The wind picked up; trees shifted overhead. He thought about the guards, and how they were believed, at times, to have drawn lots outside the woman's cell. He wondered what they'd used. Matches, perhaps — or keys. Yes, keys. And the tray set down on the floor, the food going cold . . . Had the woman known what effect she'd had on those around her? What would it be like to know that?

Once Sue had finished with the phone, he walked her back to Janet's car. Even in the short time it had been standing there, condensation had formed on all the windows, and he went round with a packet of tissues, making sure that Sue would be able to see out. Ever since her accident, he worried when she got behind the wheel. She had crashed into the playground wall at Emma's school, knocking down a twenty-foot section, the car rolling over and then sliding, upside-down, on to the road again. Only when he saw the car the next day, in the scrapyard, its roof savagely gouged and crushed almost to the level of the steering-column, did he realise how lucky she had been, not just to have escaped uninjured, but to have survived at all.

"Take care on the road," Billy said. "I should be home around eight."

She looked up at him through the half-open window, her lips black in the dim light. "Sorry to be such a nuisance," she said, then her face seemed to clear and she gave him a mischievous grin. "At least I can still surprise you."

"I love you," he said. "Drive carefully."

He watched the tail-lights until they disappeared behind the trees, then started back towards the hospital. He had been firm with her. At the same time, he had tried to tell her what she needed to hear, and she had gone away happier. But he should take her somewhere. She had a birthday coming up. Maybe then.

Will we be all right?

There are things you don't forget. You can't wipe them out, or pretend they never happened. You wish you could, though. God, how you wish you could. Some of them seem fairly innocuous, and yet they stick — Newman's jibe about him lacking commitment, for instance — but others take place at the very centre of your life and alter every atom, every thought. Like the spring evening when he held his baby daughter's hand for the first time.

Looking at her tiny red palm, he noticed a line that ran across it from one side to the other. He wasn't sure what he was seeing, but he knew enough to suspect it wasn't normal. Then the doctor told them.

A slow smile spread over Sue's face. "Oh, that's a shame," she murmured. "What a shame."

Almost before he was aware of it, Billy had risen to his feet and turned away. *How can you be so fucking stupid?* Sue, he meant. And for a moment he was afraid that he had said the words out loud. Just to have had the thought was shocking enough, though, and he stared blindly into the corner of the room. He was feeling so many things at once. Most of all, he wanted desperately to be somewhere else. A pub where no one would talk to him, or even realise that he was there. A pub where he wasn't a regular.

"Billy?" The doctor laid a hand on his shoulder.

The air blurring around him, Billy muttered "toilet", then he left the room.

But he hurried straight past the toilet and down the stairs. One flight, then another, legs chattering like teeth. A wonder he could walk at all. He didn't stop until he reached the road outside the hospital. He stood on the kerb; a cold wind cut through his shirt. April the 4th. He looked at the brown sky and saw a plane up there, bits of cloud sucked into its landing lights like flung rags. He could hear the uneven rumble of the engines. "Don't let this happen," he was whispering to himself. "Oh God, don't let it happen."

He was behaving as if it were all just a remote possibility. He was acting as though he had a choice. But the world had already made up its mind. *Here. This is yours.* He was thirty-seven, almost thirty-eight. Sue was thirty. They'd been trying to have a baby for years.

A bus went past, its wheels surging through a deep puddle. Dirty water splashed across his trousers.

Standing at the edge of the main road, he watched the water dripping off him and began to laugh.

When he walked back into the delivery room, he made sure there was a smile on his face.

"That's better," he said.

He leaned over Sue and kissed her. Her forehead was clammy, sour.

The doctor spoke about the baby's heart. Billy kept on smiling. It was as if he were being photographed. Not just once, though. Again and again.

During the days that followed — and they were long days, the longest he had ever known — he thought that it was all his fault. There was something not quite right about him. A lack of clarity or definition. He locked the bathroom door and put his face close to the mirror. He studied himself for minutes on end, trying to catch a glimpse of it. The weakness, the ugliness. The fatal flaw. It must always have been there, he thought. Other people had seen it, perhaps. If they had, they'd said nothing: it wasn't the kind of thing you could talk about. It had taken the birth of a child to establish it beyond all doubt. To bring it out into the open.

After a while, though, the blame spread sideways, and he began to see the damaged baby as a verdict on their marriage. They couldn't have been intended for each other. They had made a terrible mistake. They'd flown in the face of nature. The sense of familiarity that he had felt at the outset had been a trick after all, a trap, and he had walked right into it, fool that he was. Or perhaps he was being punished for all the things that he had done and hadn't done . . . He would wake in the night, and the heat coming off him was unbelievable. On his side of the bed, the sheets would be soaked through.

It was Sue who put an end to these morbid imaginings. Not that she said anything. No, it was all in her manner, her behaviour: the way she knuckled down. *We've been chosen to look after this little girl*, she seemed to be telling him, *so we might as well get on with it*. This was a side of Sue he hadn't seen before, this practicality, this grit. Full of admiration, humbled by her, in fact, he began to try and follow her example. Still, there were times when he wished it was just a bad dream and he could wake up and it would all be over. No baby — or a different baby. A baby that was ordinary, not special. *Oh Billy, Billy*, he would whisper to himself in some damp church.

During this time, he became more than usually sensitive to his surroundings, and everything he noticed appeared to be commenting on his predicament, not only songs on the radio, but newspaper headlines, fragments of overheard conversation, even the names of racehorses. It was, ironically, like being in love. Once, scrawled on a wall in a nightclub toilet, he saw a piece of graffiti that said simply LAMENTATIONS 3:7. Lamentations — well, that, too, was obviously for him. The word was enough in itself, but when he got home he couldn't resist looking up the reference. *He hath fenced me about, that I cannot go forth; he hath made my chain heavy.*

He was determined not to leave, though. He didn't want to do what his father had done, even if it was in his blood. He had felt the urge, not in the delivery room, but on the road outside the hospital. To run, and keep on running. To hide. To die, even. Every muscle in his body braced for flight. But he remembered the promises that he had made. For better or for worse.

For worse, he thought.

He had drawn the short straw. The chickens had come home to roost. It was a bitter pill to swallow. There were a hundred little phrases to describe him now, and none of them were cheerful.

What he dreaded most were visitors. The way they went all soft and holy when they saw the child. Fake soft, though. Fake holy. And the way they looked at him — with sympathy, or with a kind of heartiness, as if they wanted to jolly him along. He knew it was difficult for them, but he just couldn't take it. He told black jokes — the blacker, the better — and watched their body language change. They weren't sure whether to laugh or disapprove. *It's all right for you*, he wanted to shout, his spit landing on their faces. *You don't have to live with it.*

What a relief when Neil Batty came to stay. Neil waited until Sue had left the room, then he turned to Billy and said, "Well, this is a right fucking mess, isn't it?" He could have hugged Neil for that. Neil who had joined the force at the same time as he had. Neil who had been his best man the year before . . .

It *was* a mess, and it would probably get messier. It wasn't going to go away, that was for sure.

And that was all he knew, when it came down to it.

Those were the facts.

Turning down the corridor that led to the mortuary, he thought of the crystals Sue had given him. He reached into his breast pocket and took out the pale-blue stone. It would connect him with the purest part of himself, Sue had said, but how much purity did he have in him after everything that he had been through?

CHAPTER
SIXTEEN

When Billy pressed the mortuary bell, Fowler opened the door and then looked past him, into the corridor, as if he expected Billy to have brought his wife with him.

"Everything all right?" he said.

Billy nodded. "Everything's fine."

"You took your time."

"Sorry. Nothing I could do."

"Don't worry about it," Fowler said. "She wasn't any trouble."

Billy suspected that this line had been rehearsed, but he gave Fowler the obligatory smile. To most people, a bobby's sense of humour would seem tasteless, if not actually sick, but then most people didn't have to cope with what bobbies had to cope with. Billy thought of the time Neil gave the kiss of life to a man who had been thrown through a windscreen. Thanks to Neil, the man survived, though his entire face had to be reconstructed. Neil won a commendation from the Chief Superintendent, and his name appeared in the local paper. He didn't make a big song and dance about it. In fact, he only mentioned it once, and that was later that night, in the equipment room. "I don't know much about that bloke," Neil said, "but I can tell you one thing: he'd had an Indian." Neil paused to allow the laughter to die down. "Chicken Madras, I think it was." A sense of humour. You wouldn't be able to carry on without one. It's how you protect yourself.

Taking over as loggist, Billy saw that he'd been gone for more than half an hour. Fowler had been right to draw his attention to it. He would have to tell Sue not to turn up like that again. It made him look unprofessional. It was humiliating too.

"Well," Fowler said, "back to those corridors."

"Thanks very much for filling in," Billy said. "I appreciate it."

Fowler looked at his feet and nodded, then he lifted his head again and gave Billy a lopsided grin.

When the constable had left, Billy sat down at the table. It was still almost two hours until his first real break, but he didn't feel like doing any paperwork. He poured himself another coffee. Half a cup. The lights on the ceiling gave off a faint mechanical sound, somewhere between a whine and a buzz, and a regular but spaced-out *beep-beep-beep* was coming from the coroner's office, which meant that Fowler had failed to answer the phone, and somebody had left a message. The noise didn't irritate Billy, as his young blonde colleague had assumed it would; if anything, he found it comforting, like a heartbeat, a vital sign. Sue would be on the A14 by now, he thought. The road would be quiet. Just the occasional lorry heading east to catch the night ferry.

He took out his mobile. If he sent Sue a text, it would seal the rare good note on which they had

94

parted. *Hope u got home safely*, he wrote. *Lets have b/fast 2gether. Billyx.* He hoped she had finally resigned herself to the fact that he had gone to work, as ludicrous as that sounded. After all, he was a policeman; he couldn't pick and choose between assignments. And certainly, when they sat side by side at the picnic table, she had seemed contrite, realising, perhaps, that she had overstepped the mark. But these recent, wild mood-swings troubled him. Following the birth of Emma, she had shown such courage, such application, and he had drawn strength from her example. He'd come to rely on her to keep things stable. Now, though, he wasn't sure if she was so reliable . . .

Last spring, he had returned to the house at midnight to find her sitting in the kitchen. He could see from her eyes that she'd been crying. A bottle of wine stood on the table, half of it already gone. She had smoked a cigarette too, which was unlike her. He should have been home much earlier — his shift had ended at ten — but he had driven down to the estuary. He had sat in the dark with the heater on and listened to jazz. He'd been thinking about his father. The usual unfinished thoughts. Looking at Sue's tear-stained face, he felt a certain guilt — or a sense of regret, at least — but he knew he would do the same again. He hung in the kitchen doorway, his arms held slightly away from his sides, as if he had fallen in the river and his uniform was wet.

"I'm terrible," Sue said.

"What do you mean?"

She glanced at him, and then away again. "I think there's something wrong with me."

Though tired, he pulled up a chair. "Tell me about it."

She shook her head. "I can't. Really."

He poured some wine into her glass and drank it. "Tell me, Sue," he said. "It can't be as bad as some of the things I've done."

She looked at him wide-eyed, but dubious as well, then lowered her head again.

"Just tell me what's troubling you," he said. *Then we can go to bed* was the rest of the sentence, but he left it unspoken.

She put both hands up to her face, using the middle finger of each hand to smooth the tears from beneath her eyes. "You remember when I went to Whitby last year?"

"Yes. You took Emma with you."

"I almost killed her." Sue kept quite still, her hands in her lap now, not daring to look at him. "I don't mean accidentally."

He stared at her lowered head, the white line of her parting.

"I didn't plan it," she went on. "At least, I don't think I did. It was a spur-of-the-moment thing." She glanced at him quickly, through her hair, then let out a short, oddly resonant laugh.

He wasn't sure what to say to her, but he also realised that he couldn't leave too long a silence, and he knew he couldn't judge.

"Tell me what happened," he said quietly.

96

The journey north took longer than she'd expected, Sue told him, but it was only when they arrived at their hotel that Emma started playing up.

"She would have been tired by then," Billy said.

Sue nodded. "You know how she gets."

She was in the car-park, trying to unload the car, and Emma kept wandering out into the road. She spoke to Emma calmly, warning her, then she tried to bribe her, then she shouted. None of it worked. In the end, she had to half carry, half drag Emma up to their room, with Emma bellowing the whole way, that awful, almost inhuman bellowing she did, and all in front of the other guests, who were watching from the lounge.

"Sometimes you want to punch her on the jaw," Sue said. "Just knock her out. Like they do in films."

"It's not that easy," Billy said.

"Well," Sue said, "you'd know, I suppose."

They stayed in their room that evening and ate the sandwiches and chocolate that were left over from the journey; she couldn't face the dining-room, not with all those people staring. Next morning, the weather was bright and clear. She stood at the window in her pyjamas, trying to shut the jabber of cartoons out of her head. Sun slanted across the hotel car-park. They would climb up to East Cliff, she decided. Visit the ruined abbey.

As they crossed the swing-bridge, Emma walked with her head tilted back and her mouth open, watching the seagulls as they wheeled, shrieking, above the harbour. The path to East Cliff was steep, and paved with slippery flagstones, but the two of them took it slowly, holding hands. By the time they reached the top, a cold wind was blowing in off the sea. It was a weekday, out of season; they were the only people there.

When Emma saw the abbey, she turned to Sue, her eyes glinting behind her spectacles. "Like Hunchback," she said.

Billy grinned. "She loves that video."

Later, as they explored the graveyard, Sue told Emma the story of Count Dracula. This was where he'd landed, she said, here in Whitby, during a ferocious storm. She led Emma towards the cliff-edge, thinking they might be able to work out where the vampire's ship had run aground. Leaning forwards from the waist, hands clenched and pressed against her hips, Emma peered down — she was imagining how Dracula had changed into a great black dog and leapt ashore, perhaps, or else she was simply hypnotised by the rhythmic creasing and folding of the waves — and in that moment, as they stood next to each other, no more than twelve inches from the edge, Sue thought, *She could fall*, and then, without a beat, *I could push her*. It was a drop of at least two hundred feet. She wouldn't have survived. Couldn't have. *I could push her now*, Sue thought, *and that would be the end of it*. She hesitated for several seconds, then she took a step backwards. She was behind Emma now, but near enough to be partly covered by her shadow. *All our troubles would be over.* She stood in her daughter's shadow, and she came so close to reaching out that her hands seemed to throb.

A terrible accident. A tragedy.

And since they were alone on that bleak cliff-top, who would have been able to prove otherwise?

She stepped back so abruptly that she bruised her leg on a gravestone. "Emma," she said, "I think we should leave now."

"Leave," Emma said. "Go down."

"That's right, my darling. It's lunchtime." Sue reached for Emma's hand and gripped it tightly.

"Fish and chips."

Sue smiled. "If you like."

In half an hour they were sitting in a restaurant on the waterfront, their cheeks glowing from the wind.

Sue's eyes fixed on Billy's face. "I came that close." She measured a gap with her thumb and forefinger. A very narrow gap.

"It's not just you," Billy said. "I've thought the same thing."

She pulled away from him. "You have?"

He poured another glass of wine. "Not exactly the same," he said. "I just used to wish that she hadn't been born."

Except no, he thought, as soon as he had spoken, that wasn't entirely accurate. Emma never came into it, not as a person. It was much more abstract than that. What he wished was that they'd been dealt a different hand. But Sue's eyes had already drifted to the kitchen wall. She looked infinitely sad, and he knew that she was thinking about her only child — her brightness, and her burden. If Sue was ever out for very long, he would find Emma sitting by the window in the lounge, watching the road. *Waiting for Mummy*, she would say, and her voice would have something of the goose's honk about it, as always. *But Mummy's going to be late*, he'd say. She would glare malevolently at him through her thick spectacles. *Put you in the tower.*

"It hasn't exactly been easy," he said. "If we didn't have thoughts like that sometimes, we wouldn't be human."

He wasn't sure he was right, actually. It was just something to say. But at least they were equally at fault.

"The main thing is, you didn't do it," he said.

"I could have," she said. "I almost did."

She didn't want him to dismiss the urge she had felt as a one-off, an aberration — the exception to the rule. It was serious, and real, and it was there all the time. That was what she was trying to tell him. *It's there all the time.*

"You didn't, though," he said again, more gently. "You haven't." He left a silence, and then he took a risk. "You won't."

Getting up off his chair, Billy shivered suddenly and rubbed his arms. He thought he understood why Sue had begged him not to go to work that evening. She was aware of the fragility of things. Their life together. Their foothold in the world. She might feel neglected, undermined as well. She might even suspect him. Not that he was driving down to the Orwell estuary and sitting in a parked car on his own — though that was bad enough, maybe — but simply that there was often an hour in his schedule that wasn't accounted for. Perhaps she imagined he was seeing someone . . . And now this job with so much grief and terror surrounding it, and so much rage — the way that could eat into your thoughts without you knowing. Something might give, something might crumple or blow, and then all the horrors would descend. She was afraid for him, for herself — for the whole family. The wall protecting them was so very thin. In fact, it was a miracle that it had held for as long as it had.

CHAPTER
SEVENTEEN

There was half an inch of coffee in the bottom of his cup, and though he knew it would have gone cold ages ago he drank it down, then leaned back in his chair and stretched, a loud, creaky sigh coming out of him, the kind of sound you don't make unless you're alone. It had taken him forty minutes to complete Rebecca's continuation sheets — *Nickname(s)/Alias(es)* . . . Becky, Becca — and it had only confirmed his anxieties.

When Billy walked into the Williams' house on Sunday afternoon, the radiators were icy, and there was dirt everywhere. On his way to the lounge, he glanced into the kitchen. Food had been thrown on the floor, and the sink was piled high with washing-up. Rubbish hung from the door-handles in Asda bags. There was something rotting in the microwave. It looked like part of a pizza.

The mother's boyfriend, Gary Fletcher, objected when Billy announced that he would have to search all the rooms in the house, but Billy told him that he was required to do so under Section 17 of the Police and Criminal Evidence Act. It wasn't that he didn't believe them; it was the law. When children were reported missing, he said, they often turned out to be at home, or else somewhere in the vicinity, at the house of a neighbour, or a friend. He told them the story he always told, how once, a few years ago, a boy of four had been found hiding inside a sofa in his own front room. If Rebecca had really disappeared, though, a search was crucial, since it might offer some clue as to her intentions or her whereabouts. Had she left a note? Were any of her clothes missing? Had she taken a coat with her? Also — and this he didn't say, for obvious reasons — a search would give the police a picture of the family: what type of people they were, how they lived.

After he had been through every room, Billy had talked to the couple in the lounge. During the interview Fletcher drank three cans of Special Brew. He used to work at B & Q, he said, but he'd been fired. One of the supervisors had stitched him up. Karen Williams was nodding, but Billy didn't think she had heard a single word; the gesture was just a reflex, a habit, a way of taking part without attracting attention to herself or having to make a real contribution. He wondered if she was on drugs. She had the brittle, washed-out look of someone who was barely coping. There were two other children, a nine-year-old boy called Dwight, and a girl of two. Neither of them was anything to do with Fletcher. Nor, presumably, was Rebecca. The toddler — Chantelle — had a nappy on, and nothing else. In an unheated house. In November.

Sitting in the mortuary, Billy leant over the misper form and studied the school photo that he had glued into the space provided. Rebecca had a plucky air about her, but he saw a certain apprehension too. Her lips were pale-mauve, and her teeth had a greyish cast to them. Her smile was forced and unconvincing; she'd had very little to put into it. Her hair hadn't been brushed. She was close to being at the end of her resources.

Some of her classmates had been picking on her, Karen revealed, late on in the interview, as if she had only just remembered. Once, Rebecca had been tied to a tree and left there. Another time, two boys had whipped her. They'd used a car aerial, apparently. *Marks/Scars/ Tattoos/Body Piercings* . . . Scars on legs and buttocks. Two-three inches long. Billy asked whether they had lodged a formal complaint with the school authorities. They'd gone down there, Fletcher said, but the head teacher wouldn't see them. Bastard. Fletcher was one of those people who think of themselves as permanently wronged: he took no responsibility for anything, and nothing was ever his fault. The dynamic between him and Karen was tense but lacklustre. There was almost no eye contact, and Karen deferred to Fletcher constantly in a way that made Billy wonder whether Fletcher hit her. On another day, he might have been taking Fletcher down to the station to be charged. Different paperwork in that case, of course. A Domestic Violence/Incident report.

Billy asked if there was anything that Rebecca particularly liked doing. Shrugging, Fletcher reached for another can, opened it and tossed the ring-pull on the table.

"Karen?" Billy said.

"She's always on at us to take her to the zoo," Karen said, "but we can't afford it, can we." She sent a wary, hunted look in Fletcher's direction, which he affected not to notice, then she lit a cigarette.

From the back of the house came the sound of glass shattering. Fletcher jerked upright in his chair. "Dwight?" he shouted. "Come here!" Billy looked at the doorway, but the boy didn't appear.

Ash from the end of Karen's cigarette landed on the carpet. Fletcher sank back, scowling, and lifted his can towards his mouth. "Little fucker," he muttered, and then drank.

Back at the station that evening, the phone rang. It was Karen Williams, calling to tell him that she had spoken to Rebecca.

"So, you know," Karen said in her sloppy, distant voice, "no need to do anything."

"Where was she?" Billy asked.

"At her cousin's — I think . . ."

Leafing through his report again, Billy checked that he had ticked the *High Risk* box. A few moments later, he took the piece of jet from around his neck and placed it on the photo of Rebecca, just below the V-neck of her school jersey. *It will protect you.* After work on Sunday he had driven straight home, needing company, distraction, but he had forgotten that Sue was going to the cinema with friends, and that he had agreed to babysit. When he walked in through the front door, she was facing him across the hall, one arm already in her coat, the other bent behind her and searching blindly for the opening.

"Don't forget that Emma needs a bath," she said, "and I haven't given her any supper yet."

That night, when he had sung Emma to sleep, he poured himself a large vodka and sat down at the table in the kitchen. He kept returning to the section on the form that said *Other unlisted factors the officer believes should influence the level at which this assessment is weighted*. Rebecca had been missing for most of Saturday, but Karen hadn't bothered to call the police until late on Sunday morning. She said she thought Rebecca was in her room. She hadn't checked, though. If a girl Rebecca's age went missing, and she had wild friends or a history of truancy, the police would start worrying only when she had been gone for two days, but with a quiet girl like Rebecca, you'd start worrying much sooner. In the end, he wasn't sure he believed what Fletcher and Karen had told him. Who was to say that the abuse they'd described hadn't taken place at home? Fletcher unemployed, frustrated, drinking; Karen on drugs, or in denial . . . They could easily have made up that story about the two boys and the aerial. It would be interesting to find out if there was any record of their visit to the school.

The following day, the Monday, when the phone-call turned out to be for him, Billy thought it might be the community officer — he had left a message for her outlining his concerns — but it was Phil Shaw, about another job entirely . . .

Though Billy had put the report away, the look Rebecca had in the photograph still haunted him. *I've tried*, her face seemed to be saying, *I really have, but it's no use.* He let his mind wander in the hope that it might offer him a strategy, a course of action that would guarantee her safety. It depressed him to think that he might already have done everything he could, just as it had depressed him on Sunday night. When Sue got back from the cinema, she found him sitting in the kitchen with his head in his hands, the vodka bottle nearly empty.

CHAPTER
EIGHTEEN

"I was planning to look in earlier," Phil said when Billy opened the door, "but things kept coming up."

Stepping into the mortuary, he seemed to scour the air with his nose, as if he relied on his sense of smell for a reading of the situation. There was a distinctly feral aspect to the sergeant, now Billy thought about it. There always had been.

Phil put both hands flat on the table, on either side of the scene log, and studied the recent entries. "I heard Sue was here."

Billy swore under his breath. He'd been hoping to keep that from Phil. "She stopped in about an hour ago," he said. "There was a problem with Emma."

"It's sorted now, though?"

"Yes."

Still bent over the scene log, Phil looked at Billy across one shoulder, and Billy saw a question form: *Is everything all right at home?* He also knew this was a question that Phil probably wouldn't ask. The last time he'd had Phil over to the house, they had got drunk in the garden, and when Sue went to bed, Phil had started talking about his life — his wife had walked out, no children luckily — and there had been no bitterness in him, just a wistful quality, a kind of disbelief: that it should happen to him . . . On that occasion Billy hadn't pried, or pressed for details; he had simply waited until Phil had finished, then murmured, *Fuck* and poured Phil another drink. There was nothing else to say. If you were in the police, you rarely asked about each other's marriages because you knew what the answer was going to be. All right? It was almost never all right. Police officers worked anti-social hours. They drank too much and slept too little. They ate junk. They were society's dustmen, always cleaning up, dealing with the rubbish that no one else wanted to deal with. Most of them had gone into the job with good intentions, thinking they could be of use, but they soon realised that the task was well nigh impossible. If you closed one crack house down, a new one sprang up somewhere else. Book one prostitute, and three more would be doing business round the corner. As for burglary, forget it. Recently, a constable in his fifties had told Billy that he was now arresting the sons and grandsons of people he had arrested when he first started out. The crime figures might go up or down, but nothing changed, not really. The pressure on police officers was immense, and their home lives suffered. Phil knew that better than anyone.

"You need a break, Billy?" Phil said. "You want to go outside and stretch your legs?"

With those words, Billy understood that, as far as Phil was concerned, the matter was closed.

"I'll wait till midnight, sarge," he said. "It's not long now." He watched Phil yawn, then rub his eyes. "You're probably the one who needs a break."

"When this is over, I'm going to sleep for a week."

"A week? They'll never give you a week."

"Right." Jaw clenched tight, Phil smiled another of his grim smiles.

When Phil had gone, Billy returned to his chair. Yes, the pressures were immense. It wasn't just the long hours, the bad food and the lack of sleep. It was all the temptations that came your way as well. Women often threw themselves at police officers. Was it because police officers were confident, decisive characters who knew how to handle themselves? Or was it because they were supposed to represent the straight and narrow, and there was a kind of thrill in leading them astray? Or was it just the uniform? He didn't know. It definitely happened, though. On Saturday nights, when he parked outside a club like Pals at closing time, women would dance in front of the police van, taking off half their clothes. The previous summer, a dark-haired girl in a short skirt had leaned over the bonnet and given the windscreen a long, slow kiss. Tongue and everything. Sooner or later, most policemen weakened. They had one-night stands, quick flings — full-blown affairs. They would bring their lovers to parties in the police station and leave their girlfriends or their wives at home. They would claim to be on a training course and all the while they'd be on holiday with another woman. If you met a bobby who told you he'd never been over the side you didn't entirely trust him. Nobody could be that bloody perfect.

Once, in the mid-nineties, Billy had been called to Sir Alf Ramsay Way on a grade-one response. A prostitute had thrown a brick through the plate-glass window of a car showroom. Jade was known to the Ipswich police; she was a good-looking girl when she wasn't on the smack. Poor old Sir Alf, Billy thought as he drove across town; he'd turn in his grave if he knew that the street named after him was now a red-light area. By the time he arrived at the scene, Jade had a friend with her. The friend's name was Carly, and she caught Billy's eye the moment he stepped on to the pavement. He wasn't making excuses, but Shena Coates had killed herself a week or two before, and then, a few days later, in a hostel, a dead baby had been found at the bottom of a bed. As a policeman, there were times when your life was so sickening and brutal that you felt you'd earned whatever came along, and Carly had such a cheeky, dirty look about her . . . For the six weeks it lasted, she always wanted him to do it the same way — from behind. By the end, he knew the back of her head like the back of his own hand. The soft groove that ran vertically from the top of her spine into her dyed blonde hair, the smooth curve of bone behind each ear. The smell of her neck: Anais Anais and the sweat of guilty fucking . . . "You're rubbish, you are. You should be at home, with your wife." Though she had been wearing very little when she said that. She'd been sitting on the bed and she'd given him a steady look that came up at him through her eyelashes, and then she'd moved her knees apart ever so slightly, not so he could see anything, but so he thought about it, what was there. Carly. Seven years on, he could still remember the taste of her earlobes, faintly metallic where they'd been pierced . . .

But infidelity could be subtler than that, and more contaminating. Though he was in the mortuary, he could no longer smell formaldehyde or disinfectant; now it was jasmine suddenly, a heady, cloying cloud of jasmine shot through with the much keener scent of lemons, and he found himself remembering the holiday he'd had with Sue and Emma in Newman's villa in the hills above Cannes, and in particular the night when he met Newman's girlfriend — if that was the word . . .

Billy had only agreed to go because Newman wasn't there, but Newman called halfway through their holiday to say that he would be returning earlier than expected, and though Billy tried to reassure himself — in the five years since Newman's surprise visit to the house, perhaps he would have mellowed — the thought of spending forty-eight hours in Newman's company filled him with unease, if not with dread. "We should have left the moment we heard," he told Sue later. "We should have booked into a hotel." Sue thought he was overreacting. It hadn't been that bad, she said. She didn't know, though, did she?

Billy was in their bedroom high up in the house when Newman arrived. Through the open window he heard the murmur of a car on the drive, and then voices, Newman's to start with, silky but authoritative, followed by a woman's. Hers had a blur to it, and he sensed right away that English wasn't her first language.

He didn't meet her until shortly before dinner. He was sitting on the terrace with Emma, drinking a beer, when a young woman appeared in the doorway. She had long black hair, and wore a sheer black dress that clung to her body. She was from somewhere like Japan, he thought. As she was about to venture out on to the terrace, Emma sprang forwards, blocking the doorway with one arm.

"Password," she said sternly.

"Emma, it's all right," Billy said. "I think you can let her through."

Emma grudgingly lowered her arm.

When the woman came over, Billy explained that Emma was just playing a game. If you didn't know the secret password, it meant you were the enemy. You would have to be locked up. Put in the tower. The woman had been watching Emma, but now she turned her depthless black eyes on Billy, giving him a look that was somehow both startled and intrigued, and seemed to bear little or no relation to what she'd just been told. Her name was Lulu, he learned when they sat down, and she was Korean. She worked in a casino.

Emma had never met anyone like Lulu before — Ipswich had a fair number of Bengalis and Iranians, Iraqis too, but very few people from South-East Asia — and she was utterly besotted. Perhaps that was why the evening went so smoothly. Newman seemed relaxed, almost benign, chuckling over Emma's sudden infatuation.

After dinner, Lulu let Emma brush her hair.

"Beautiful." Standing behind Lulu, brush in hand, Emma's whole face appeared to be radiating light.

"No, you're beautiful," Lulu said over her shoulder.

"No, *you!*" Emma boomed. She'd never been able to stand being contradicted.

Later, when it was time for bed, Emma took Lulu by the hand and led her away. After a while, Billy went upstairs to help Lulu out, only to meet her on the landing. She had started telling Emma a story, she said, but Emma had fallen asleep almost immediately.

"She gets very tired," Billy said.

"How do you call it," Lulu said, "what she has?"

"Down's syndrome."

"She's very different . . ."

"There isn't a cell in her body that's the same as yours or mine." The moment the words had left his mouth, Billy felt as if he'd said something oddly intimate.

Lulu only nodded. "Like a dolphin," she said, then glanced at him quickly.

"It's all right." Billy grinned. "I think I know what you mean."

When they returned to the dining-room, there was a CD playing, some French singer Billy had never heard of, but Sue and her father were nowhere to be seen. Lulu poured Billy a glass of champagne, and they sat out on the terrace. The warm air shifted; the leaves of a palm tree scraped against each other. He asked Lulu about her job. It paid well, she told him, but the hours were long. The dresses they wore didn't have pockets, which was supposed to stop them stealing chips, but

114

one girl had a special technique; though Lulu didn't go into any detail, Billy was left in little doubt as to what this might involve. She said she wasn't allowed to give out her phone number, or even accept tips. Men were always hitting on her — that was the phrase she used — sometimes women too, but fraternisation with the patrons was strictly forbidden.

"So Peter's not a gambler, then," Billy said slyly.

Lulu sipped her champagne. "I met him at a party," she said. "On a yacht."

As they were talking, Newman appeared in the garden below, stepping backwards, then sideways, a woman in his arms. It took Billy a few moments to realise that it was Sue, and he felt an instant surge of resentment. There was no reason why they shouldn't dance together, of course — for all he knew, it was a ritual of theirs — and yet, somehow, everything Newman did seemed calculated to exclude him. No, it was more pointed than that. He behaved as though he was quite unaware of Billy — as though Billy didn't actually exist.

"Fathers and daughters," Lulu said, following his gaze. "Always special."

Billy looked at her smooth face — the wide cheekbones, the eyes that seemed so bottomless, the luscious crushed rose of a mouth.

"Why are you smiling?" she asked.

"You're lovely," he told her.

He was speaking as an older man, and not one who wanted anything from her, and she understood this perfectly.

"Thank you," she said. "Would you like to dance as well?"

He shook his head. "I'd only tread on your toes."

"Maybe I should open more champagne."

"Now you're talking."

He was smiling now. The same smile. Apart from that one flash of jealousy, which Lulu had extinguished with just five words, the evening had been marked by a rare innocence, an utter lack of subterfuge. Something so unusually pure about the whole experience.

It didn't last.

In the morning he woke when Sue got up, but lulled by the crisp, plump sound of a tennis ball being knocked about on the court next door he dropped back into a deep sleep, and by the time he dressed and went downstairs, Sue and Emma had gone out. In the dining-room, Newman and Lulu were having breakfast.

Newman waited until Billy was seated, then fixed him with a gloating look. "You ever had a Korean?"

Billy glanced across the table at Lulu, but she was paying close attention to the kiwi fruit on her plate. Slicing the end off, she carefully peeled the rough brown skin. The sleeve of her robe had fallen back on her right forearm, and he could see a raw red mark encircling her wrist.

"You don't know what you're missing," Newman said.

Gazing out into the garden, Lulu placed a segment of fruit in her mouth. She gave the impression that she was alone at the table — or that she didn't understand the language that was being spoken.

"If you're interested," Newman went on, "I'm sure I could set something up . . ."

There are certain people who have to be treated with extreme caution, or else avoided altogether. They're like toadstools, or coral snakes — all bright colours on the surface, and poison underneath.

Billy wanted to apologise to Lulu, but he didn't have the chance to speak to her again. She left that morning, and didn't say goodbye — not even to Emma, whose face crumpled when she was told. She stood all alone on the drive in the brilliant sunlight, head thrown forwards, fingers splayed. "Lulu," she bellowed. "Want Lulu."

It took most of the day to console her.

The following evening they flew back to England.

Afterwards, Billy would often wonder if Lulu had been coerced. Could she have been drugged, for instance, or blackmailed? Or had she been a willing participant? She could have been trying to please Newman, he supposed, she could have done it out of love for him — though she didn't have the look, at breakfast, of somebody in love . . . It was always possible, of course, that she'd been paid. How much would that cost, he wondered, on the Côte d'Azur? Then again, what if it was something Lulu had specifically requested? It was what excited her. She *needed* it. The situation was so ripe with ambiguity that Billy never felt he got any closer to a definitive interpretation. In the end, all he could be sure of was the extent of Newman's corruption, and the ambivalent, insidious nature of the world he inhabited, how it could both repel you and seduce you.

He glanced at his watch. Only twenty minutes to go, and then he'd have an hour off. He was nearly halfway through his shift. He could afford to relax a little.

CHAPTER
NINETEEN

He couldn't remember leaving the hospital, but clearly he was no longer there. He didn't panic, though. He wasn't even anxious. Instead, he seemed to give himself up to his new surroundings. He was sitting at a wooden table. In front of him was a tin ashtray and a lighted candle in a red glass dish. Near the ashtray was a small dark ring where somebody had put a drink down. The brightly coloured paper-chains that looped above his head told him that it would soon be Christmas. People stood in groups all round him, talking and laughing. It was the saloon bar in a pub, he thought, or the private-function room in a hotel. Or, possibly, it was the back room in a working-men's club. What had he come here for? And who with? He didn't know; he had no memory of having arrived. There was a loud crackling sound, then an early Beatles number blared out of the speakers that were mounted on brackets halfway up the wall. He recognised the song. He even knew some of the words. A young woman in a floral print dress leaned down and spoke to him, but he couldn't hear what she was saying. Was she asking him to dance? He watched as she stubbed her cigarette out in the ashtray and turned away from him.

As he sat there, enjoying the music — it was years since he had listened to the Beatles — a couple stepped out on to the dance floor. They were young, no more than twenty or twenty-one. The man wore a grey suit with wide lapels. His complexion was pasty, and there was something loose and twisted about his mouth. The girl's hair was a bright-blonde beehive, and she was dressed in a pink sleeveless blouse, a white skirt decorated with small pink squares, and white-leather boots that almost reached her knees. They danced rock-and-roll-style. The man held the girl at arm's length, bringing her in close and twirling her round, then allowing the gap between them to open up again, but no matter how fast they moved, no matter how recklessly they whirled and spun, his right hand never let go of hers. The contact was always there.

Once, though, halfway through a song, the girl spoke into the man's ear, then broke away from him. Walking to the edge of the dance floor, she picked up a cigarette that was already alight, tapped a length of ash off the end of it and brought it to her lips. The man watched her from where he was, feet shifting in time to the music, loosely clenched hands held close to his chest. A lock of hair fell across his forehead. He reached up to push it back. The girl took a long, slow drag from her cigarette and blew the smoke in his direction. Almost immediately, she inhaled again, the tip of the cigarette a vivid red now. She lit a new cigarette from the old one, which she crushed out beneath the heel of her boot, then she rested the new cigarette on the rim of an ashtray and moved back towards her partner, smoke pouring from her nostrils. They went on dancing as before, stepping close to each other, then stepping back, the distance between them tense and yet elastic, the connection plain for all to see . . .

Then, without any warning, there was a shriek as the needle was roughly snatched from the record. Someone switched the house lights on. The young couple came to a standstill, his right hand gripping hers, their faces motionless, and bleached of all expression by the harsh white glare. It was so quiet that Billy thought he could hear them panting. Smoke lifted casually from the cigarette she'd balanced on the ashtray.

Billy half rose out of his chair, unable to work out where he was or what had happened. The green of the mortuary doors, the smudged white of the fridges. The intermittent beeping of the answer-machine . . . Ah yes. Yes, of course. He grinned almost foolishly, then blinked and rubbed his eyes. What time was it? Three minutes to midnight. Lowering himself back down into his chair, he waited for somebody to come and relieve him.

CHAPTER
TWENTY

Billy zipped up his anorak, then walked out on to the road that ran past the front of the hospital. There were fewer reporters now, and they ignored him. They knew he wasn't authorised to speak to them — and besides, he didn't have anything to say. Since Friday afternoon the body of Britain's most notorious woman had been lying under police guard in the West Suffolk hospital. That was all the news there was. In the morning Phil would brief the press on the details and timing of the funeral. He would inform them that he had arranged for the hearse to slow down on one particular bend in the hospital grounds so they could get the photographs they needed. In return for this concession, he hoped they would agree not to disrupt or in any way interfere with the progress of the cortège.

Passing Rheumatology, Billy followed the road down to the picnic area where he and Sue had had their conversation earlier. It was colder now, and the treetops stirred in the wind. He sat on the same bench, facing out into the dark. He had dozed off, perhaps only for a minute, but he had seen the two lovers. The two murderers. He had gatecrashed a Christmas party that was being held by the chemical firm that had employed them, the party at which they were supposed to have met properly for the first time, and the Beatles song that had been playing in his dream had stayed with him — its bright voices and its crisp, slightly gawky guitar:

When your bird is broken
Will it —

At that point, the needle had skidded across the record, and the music had cut out. In his dream he had imagined that someone had collided with the turntable. A moment of clumsiness or tipsiness. Now, though, half an hour later, he saw it differently. He thought it more likely that part of him had needed to stop the couple before they could go any further. He'd brought the whole thing to an end while they were still free of guilt. It was as if he couldn't bear to see any more.

He leaned back, the edge of the picnic table pressing against his spine.

"It wasn't like that," came a voice.

He turned slowly. At first, there was only the table's splintered surface, and the slender trunks of silver birches, and an unlit building just beyond . . . But then he saw a figure standing twenty feet away, half-hidden by the trees, a red dot glowing at about head height. Glowing, then fading. Glowing again.

"It wasn't that dramatic."

Oddly enough, he didn't feel frightened, or even surprised. At some level, perhaps, he had been prepared for something like this — or else he was still in the dream's soft grip, and normal reactions had no purchase. He looked back towards the hospital. Lights shone in the windows; a group of reporters huddled by the entrance to A and E. He thought about calling the control room on his radio. What would he have said, though?

"Do you like my suit?" came the voice again. "I got it from a catalogue."

A Manchester accent — even after all these years . . .

He turned round again. She had left the shadows, and was standing on the pavement, under a streetlamp. The suit was a lilac colour, and her blouse was white with a scalloped collar. Her hair was a dull dyed brown.

"You must be cold," he said.

She seemed to look at him steadily, then she began to laugh.

Rising to his feet, he moved off in the opposite direction, up the slope. The bones in his legs felt spongy. There was the smell of pine needles and damp bark. He took a deep breath. As he let it out, he heard her speak again.

"Everyone was dancing, not just us."

When he reached the path that would take him down the west side of the hospital, he hesitated, then glanced over his shoulder. There was nobody under the streetlamp, or in among the trees.

There never had been.

There couldn't have been.

CHAPTER
TWENTY-ONE

The wind eased. In the silence a firework burst softly, gold sparks dropping through the darkness to his right. But November the 5th was more than a fortnight ago . . . Strange how people cling to things. That woman under the streetlamp. The murderer. A trick of the mind, of course — he had been talking to himself — and yet there had been a kind of authenticity about the experience. An attention to detail. The lilac suit, the dull brown hair. She'd even had a cigarette with her. He could hear her speaking, the voice flat, curiously deep, and coarsened by years of heavy smoking.

It wasn't like that.

Well, of course not. How could he possibly have known what it was like? And anyway, it had been a dream. He was exhausted, under pressure. He was not himself. If only Sue had let him have his nap . . . Instead, they had argued. Again. And nothing had been resolved.

He circled round behind the hospital. Parked cars, draughty doorways. To his left was the administration block where Eileen Evans had an office. Most of the windows were showing lights. Nobody was sleeping tonight — or not for too long, anyway.

Everyone was dancing, not just us.

In a brick bicycle shed opposite the Day Surgery Unit, he found some shelter from the wind, and taking out his mobile, he pressed "Contacts" and then "Neil". When Neil answered, Billy could hear people shouting in the background. Gunshots too.

"Hold on," Neil said, "I'll turn it down."

From the slur in his voice, it sounded as if Neil was drinking again. When he was thrown out of the force, he had lost everything, even his pension. "I gave them half my life," he had said when Billy visited. "All those fucking years, and for what?" The last Billy heard, Neil was on the books of a firm that supplied security guards.

"Not working tonight?" Billy said.

"No. You?"

Billy told Neil where he was.

"Christ!" Neil said. Billy imagined him sitting up a little straighter on his lumpy sofa. "What's it like? What's happening?"

"Actually," Billy said, "it's pretty quiet."

He could sense Neil's disappointment. Neil was one of those bobbies who like there to be something always going on. He would have wanted scuffles and clashes at the very least, if not a full-scale riot. He would have wanted batons, long shields. Water cannon. Stepping out of the bike shed, Billy turned into the wind. It roared across the mobile's mouthpiece, which gave him an excuse not to speak for a moment. He had rung Neil, his best friend, because he needed to talk to somebody about what he had seen, but now he had the chance he didn't think he could do it. He didn't know how to describe what had happened without sounding a bit unhinged. He wasn't even sure he could describe it at all. It occurred to him that he might be able to tell his brother — Charlie was a good listener — but it was mid-afternoon in San Francisco, and Charlie would be at work. Besides, he didn't have enough credit on his phone for an international call.

"Are you outside?" Neil said.

"I'm on my break," Billy said, shielding the phone again. "How's Linda?"

"She left me," Neil said. "She didn't like me being a security guard. 'What's the matter?' I said. 'Don't you feel safe?' She didn't think that was very funny."

They talked for another five minutes, then Billy said he should be getting back.

"Hang on in there, Billy," Neil said. "Don't blow it." And then, with some of his old sharpness, "What were you calling about, anyway?"

"Nothing, really," Billy said. "I just wanted to say hello. It's been a while."

"Maybe I'll come down and see you sometime."

"That'd be good."

"I'll do it," Neil said. "I'll come and see you."

Just before Neil hung up, the voices and the shooting came back, even louder than before.

Billy put his mobile away and started walking. In the distance he could hear a siren. It seemed to be drawing closer, and then, quite suddenly, it faded. The wind lifted again. Leaves shook on their branches. Feeling the cold now, Billy quickened his pace. *Hang on in*

127

there. Neil had given him the encouragement he needed without even being asked. Friends could do that.

CHAPTER
TWENTY-TWO

Back in A and E, everything was peaceful, just the lowlevel droning of the hospital itself, the sense of being inside a vast, benevolent machine. He nodded at Fowler, who was guarding the entrance, then walked on through reception. The cafeteria was closed — a security grille had been lowered over the counter — but there were still plenty of places to sit. He removed his anorak and hung it over the back of a chair, then sat down facing the corridor. Opening his bag, he looked for his sandwiches. To be on the safe side, he had made himself four rounds. He always got hungry on night-shifts. It was the boredom. As he took his first bite, he remembered an evening in Paris when he was seventeen, Raymond handing him one small tomato and a toe-end of stale French bread.

Following the break-in at Weston Point, he had avoided Raymond, and Raymond, too, had turned his attention elsewhere. For the next three years, Billy only ever saw Raymond from a distance, and always in the company of older boys, but then, inevitably, the chain that seemed to bind them tightened again. A few days after O levels, he was standing outside the school gates when Raymond sauntered over.

"Any plans for the summer, Billy?"

Lighting a cigarette, Raymond tossed the match into the gutter.

"No," Billy said warily. "Not really."

He did have plans, though. He was all lined up to work at the animal-feed business his uncle ran. Later, in the autumn, he wanted to take an HGV test. You could make decent money driving lorries. Or he might even apply to the police. His friend, Neil, was thinking of applying too. Their reasons were the usual ones. They thought they might be able to make a difference. Do some good. But these weren't the kind of things that you could say to somebody like Raymond.

"Why don't we go travelling," Raymond said, "in Europe?"

Billy stared at him. "Europe?"

"There's no need to worry about money," Raymond said. "I've got enough for both of us."

Billy remembered the fiver Raymond had offered him. It came back so vividly that he could almost feel the stitch he'd had from cycling up the hill without stopping.

"Athens, Venice, Copenhagen." Raymond's arms opened wide, as if he might actually conjure one of those great cities out of the air. "Monte Carlo . . ."

On the last day of July they crossed the Channel by ferry, then caught a train to Paris, and it was there, in a park called Buttes-Chaumont, that Billy began to understand what he had let himself in for. He looked over at Raymond, who was stretched out on his back under a tree. Raymond wore a dark-blue suit with chalk pinstripes — it had once belonged to a drug dealer from Moss Side, or so Raymond claimed — and tipped down over his eyes was the grey fedora he'd found in a flea market the day before. Beside him, on the grass, lay a small leather suitcase with gold catches. Raymond wouldn't have been seen dead with a rucksack. Rucksacks were for students. Billy had a rucksack, of course. His mother had bought it for him when he told her about the trip. She couldn't afford to buy him presents, especially now Charlie had gone to medical school, but she had wanted to please him. *It's a good one, Billy.* He could still hear her saying that. And yet, in Raymond's presence, the rucksack was an embarrassment, and he took no care of it. Sometimes, as he threw it on to a hostel floor, or kicked it across a railway station concourse, he imagined his mother watching, and shame would sweep over him. He felt an awful, nameless sadness about the way people treat each other.

"Let's go and eat, Raymond," he said.

They'd had nothing since breakfast, and it was already early evening.

Raymond pushed the brim of his hat up with one finger. "Did you say something?"

"What are we going to eat tonight?"

"I bought a couple of tomatoes," Raymond said, "and there's half a baguette left over from yesterday. That should do us."

So that was supper.

Afterwards, Raymond declared himself quite full — "replete" was the word he used — and Billy couldn't bring himself to disagree.

Over the next few days, as they journeyed south, Raymond subjected Billy to a series of lectures on food. It was his belief that food both dulled perception and extinguished desire. Raising his voice above the clatter of the train, he recited lines from Baudelaire, then he talked about how Jean Genet had written most of his books while hungry. He quoted a letter in which William Burroughs describes finding an inch of fat on his stomach and being repulsed by it. He quoted some Chinese poets as well. The only image Billy could remember later was that of an old man surviving on the leaves that fall from a locust tree. He hoped to God there were no locust trees in Monte Carlo. Food breeds laziness, Raymond said. It breeds complacency. Food's dangerous. If the trip they were making was to be worthwhile, if they wanted to see things, really *see things*, they should be careful not to eat too much.

"Dangerous?" Billy said in a quiet voice. "Food?"

"Oh yes," Raymond said. "The danger cannot be over-estimated."

Billy watched a field of vivid lavender float by. "So we have to starve?"

"Think of Rimbaud in Ethiopia," Raymond said. "Think of St Francis in that cave outside Assisi."

In part, Billy brought it on himself, since he deferred to Raymond constantly. It was Raymond who decided where they stayed — doss-houses every time, for their "atmosphere" — and it was Raymond who came up with the itinerary. But then the whole trip had been Raymond's idea in the first place, so what was Billy to do? Although he did have a little money of his own, he

132

felt awkward using it — and besides, it wouldn't have been enough to make a real difference. He was dependent on Raymond, in more ways than one, and Raymond knew it.

In a spirit of defiance, Billy walked over to the snack bar's vending-machines and bought a packet of crisps and an orange Fanta. He imagined Raymond's lip curling at this display of weakness. The conversations in the park and on the train had happened at the beginning of their holiday, and it wasn't until the last night that Billy finally rebelled. It was late afternoon when they arrived in Ostend, and the ferry didn't leave until eleven. Billy had already imagined a farewell dinner — nothing fancy, just some fried fish and a bottle of local wine — but Raymond had other ideas. He thought they should eat on the boat, or else wait till morning.

Before Raymond could finish outlining his plan for the evening, Billy interrupted. "I need a bit of money."

Raymond gave him a look that was both baffled and sly, and then took a step backwards. It was possible that he had known Billy would react in this way; in fact, maybe this was the effect he'd been after.

"Please give me some money, Raymond," Billy said. "I'm starving."

Before Raymond could walk away, Billy reached out and grabbed him by the collar. As Raymond tried to jerk himself free, his suit jacket split right down the back. Letting out a string of swear words, he hit Billy on the side of the head with the back of his hand. Billy felt a flicker of triumph: Raymond so rarely lost control. He still needed money, though. As they wrestled on the quay, Raymond's ankle turned on the cobbles, and he fell over. One knee on Raymond's chest, Billy pinned him to the ground. Raymond stopped struggling and closed his eyes. Billy found Raymond's wallet and removed a few notes, then stood up quickly and dropped the wallet next to Raymond's out-stretched hand.

Raymond lay quite still for a few seconds, then opened his eyes and shouted, "Thief!"

At first Billy thought he must be joking — it was Raymond's sense of humour exactly — but then he saw the fear and hostility in Raymond's eyes, and in that moment he had the feeling that he didn't know Raymond at all, that the two of them had never met before, and that he had, in fact, attacked and robbed a total stranger.

Raymond shouted the word again, in French this time, and Billy stared in disbelief as Raymond sat up and pointed an accusing finger. Passers-by were looking at Billy now, and at the money in his hand; some of them seemed to be about to intervene. Snatching up his rucksack, Billy started running.

That night he ate by himself, and the old couple who owned the bistro let him sleep in a small room next to the kitchen. The following morning he caught the ferry to Dover. He was home by midnight. He didn't see Raymond again for years.

CHAPTER
TWENTY-THREE

For the last few minutes he'd had the sense that he was being watched. A light sweat broke out on his forehead as he remembered the figure in the hospital grounds, and how her gaze had seemed to linger on him even after he had moved away, into the trees; there had been a kind of weight to it, as if her eyes were thumbs and they were being pressed into his back. Warily, he glanced over his shoulder. Sitting behind him, two tables away, was an Asian man in a dark-grey suit and an open-necked blue-and-white-striped shirt. Although the man appeared to be staring downwards at his hands, which were resting on the table, Billy still felt as if he was being scrutinised. Facing the corridor again, he started on another sandwich. He now knew what he should have said to Raymond in that pub in Cheshire. *I still owe you forty francs.* That might have put paid to his irritating smile.

A staff nurse walked past, jingling a bunch of keys. Billy was about to open his newspaper when the Asian man finally spoke.

"You're guarding that woman, I suppose . . ."

The man's voice was genial, and a little careworn, but it had no false notes in it. Clearly, he was no threat to security. Billy turned in his chair. The man was still looking at his hands.

Billy adopted the same innocuous tone. "That's right. I'm on duty all night. A twelve-hour shift."

Only now did the man look up. There was a pale cast across one of his eyes, as if candlewax had been smeared over the iris. "You work hard," he said.

"Pretty hard. What line of business are you in?"

"Hi-fi. I own a couple of shops."

"I've had the same system for twenty years. Ever since I joined the force."

"Come to me," the man said. "I'll upgrade you."

"I probably wouldn't be able to afford it."

"I'll give you a special price."

The two men smiled at each other.

Billy raised his can of Fanta to his lips and drained it. "So what brings you here?"

"My wife's having an operation tonight."

"Nothing too serious, I hope."

The man looked away for the first time, his eyes moving across the cafeteria. "I don't know. Something to do with her bowel."

"I hope she comes through it all right," Billy said.

"Thank you," the man said. "Me too."

There was a silence during which he appeared to be trying to decide whether or not to go further, and Billy glanced down at his paper. In interviews he often used this technique. If you stepped back, it had the effect of allowing the other person to come forwards, almost involuntarily, and occupy the space you'd just vacated. It was one of the more subtle methods of eliciting a confession.

"I have been listening to Mozart," the man said.

Billy sat sideways on his chair, one forearm resting on the back. This wasn't what he had expected.

"Do you listen to classical music?" the man asked.

"Not much."

"I listen to Mozart," the man went on, "and I have trouble understanding how someone could have thought of something so beautiful. I try to imagine the world before that music came into being, and then I try to imagine someone creating it from nothing — all those sounds . . . Impossible." He shook his head and then allowed himself a brief sad smile. "And yet it's just as impossible to imagine the world without that music in it."

Billy watched the man carefully, but said nothing. One of the vending-machines behind him shuddered and then fell silent.

"If something should happen to my wife . . ." Forearms still lying flat on the table, the man's hands lifted off the surface and then dropped back again. He had come as close as he dared to saying what he wanted to say.

Billy looked up as an elderly woman in a pink dressing-gown hobbled past. Noticing him, she raised one fragile fist and shook it in the air beside her ear. *I'm giving it everything I've got*, she was telling him. *I'm not bloody going quietly.*

"There are things we don't understand," the man said, staring at his hands again. "This woman that you're guarding, for instance. The things she did . . ."

Billy made sure that the wariness he now felt didn't reach his face.

"What do you think about that?" the man asked.

"I try not to think. I just do my job."

"But thoughts still occur to you," the man said seductively, "despite yourself."

Rather than express an opinion of his own, Billy fell back on the conversation he'd had with Phil a few hours earlier. "I never met the woman," he said. "A colleague of mine met her, though, on several occasions, and he told me that it was difficult to connect the things she did then with the woman he saw in front of him."

The man nodded slowly. "Perhaps it was difficult for her too." He paused. "Even at the time it was difficult, perhaps . . ."

"Yes, perhaps," Billy said. "But you or I would never go so far."

"Wouldn't we?" The man's good eye seemed gentle, as though it were contemplating another, far more selfless world, while his damaged eye, by contrast, had a critical, even accusatory gleam to it. "Who really knows how far we would go," he said, "if the circumstances were right?"

They both fell quiet again. In a nearby ward a man laughed — or it could have been a cough.

"If you were in love, for example," the man said. "Not ordinary love. A love that takes you over, turns you upside-down. An absolute dependency. A kind of trance."

Billy thought of Venetia and her father, their two faces overlapping, merging into one. He felt unsteady, giddy. He felt as if the world was accelerating away from him in all directions. At the same time, everything had remained exactly where it was.

"The things she did," the Asian man went on, "they weren't natural to her — not at the beginning, anyway. They *became* natural, though."

"You don't know that," Billy said. "You're just guessing."

He had assumed that the man would argue the point, but the man just looked at him and said, "Of course."

At that moment, Phil appeared with two other men, one of whom was a detective inspector. They were so deep in conversation that they didn't notice Billy, but the mere fact of their presence prompted him to glance at his watch. Eight minutes to one.

Rising to his feet, he wrapped his last remaining sandwich in silver foil and tucked it into his bag. "I have to get back to work, I'm afraid."

The man reached into his jacket pocket, brought out a card and handed it to Billy. "My name is Vijay Prabhu. If you're ever looking for some new equipment . . ." His smile told Billy that he needn't take the offer too seriously: he had simply wanted something tangible to pass between them.

Billy pocketed the card, then leaned across and shook the man's hand. "I'm Billy Tyler."

"PC Tyler," Mr Prabhu said, as if correcting him. "A pleasure to have met you."

"I hope everything turns out well for your wife."

The man inclined his head in thanks.

Billy gathered up the crisp bag and the can of Fanta, both empty now, and dropped them in the rubbish bin, then he started back towards the mortuary. The small hours. It was so quiet that he could hear his own footsteps. They had a measured, dependable sound, and contrasted strangely with his thoughts, which kept flitting from one subject to another. It could be fatigue, or it could be the eerie suggestibility of a hospital at night. It could even be the influence of Mr Prabhu. The good eye, dark and gentle. The other with its lavish swirl of white. A little like being looked at by two people at once. That subdued, intriguing way of talking around a subject, then closing in on it and capturing it with elegant precision. At some fundamental level, Billy felt they had understood each other perfectly. Mr Prabhu had implied that he was there for his wife, as any caring husband would be, and that was almost certainly true, but Billy knew that Mr Prabhu was also there for himself. There was a tremendous fear in you at times like that. There was the need to stay close to whatever was going on. You had to try and hold things together, even though it seemed to be their natural tendency to fall apart.

He thought of how he had rushed to A and E the year before, having just been told about Sue's crash. He found her behind a curtain, on a high, hard bed. She looked so young that he knew she must have been through something violent, but the only mark on her was a small scratch at the base of her thumb: she'd cut herself when she crawled out through the shattered window. On the right side of her head, behind her ear, her hair looked as though someone had furiously back-combed it, and the fine, spun-sugar tangles were studded with bits of broken glass. The fact that she'd escaped without injury staggered everybody. It also made them suspicious. There had to be damage *somewhere*, surely . . . The doctor who examined her described how organs could get twisted in certain types of accident. If the car rolled, for instance, as it had in her case, there was always a possibility of internal bleeding. Sue should stay in bed, he said. She had to keep quiet. Rest. During those long, tense days, Billy turned on the TV and saw a plane slide slowly into one of the Twin Towers. He wasn't able to process the images at all. They had no effect on him except as an illustration of his own private catastrophe. The demolished skyscrapers stood in for the car that Sue had reduced to a pile of scrap. The three thousand casualties symbolised her brush with death. It was his own story, written large, yet it all felt curiously stilted and obscure. It was a time when things seemed hard to believe, and hard to sustain. He dressed Emma in the mornings, and drove her to school. He cooked her meals. "Mummy resting," she said once, at breakfast — and then, looking him full in the face, "Mummy all right." She wanted him to reassure her, but she might also have been prompting him, or even coaching him. The future could be talked into existence. He took one of her hands in both of his. "Yes," he said. "Mummy's fine." At night, though, when Sue was sleeping, he would tiptoe into the room and hover uselessly next to the bed, her bitter breath clouding the air below him, or he would leave the house and stand on the grass track, shivering. What did he think as he stared out over the field? Did he pray?

If something should happen to my wife . . .

He turned the corner into the corridor that led to the mortuary. At first, he didn't notice the woman, partly because he hadn't expected anyone to be there, and partly because she was leaning against the wall in one of the shadowy areas between two lights. She was wearing the same lilac suit, and she was smoking, as before.

"How did you —?" He broke off, uncertain as to what question he should be asking.

She didn't look at him. Instead, she simply lifted her cigarette up to her mouth. When she inhaled, a row of fine vertical lines showed on her upper lip. She took the smoke deep into her body and didn't exhale at all. The smoke was just absorbed.

"Did you believe him?" she said.

She sounded the same as she had when he saw her in the hospital grounds, her vowels harsh and flat, her accent recognisably Mancunian.

"That Indian bloke," she said. "Do you think he got it right?"

Billy couldn't take his eyes off her. His forehead felt cold, his ears too. A steady industrial hum came from the ramp beyond her.

142

"Don't worry. I won't bite." She tapped half an inch of ash into the cupped palm of her left hand. "I spent a lot of time in this place." She looked past him, down the corridor. "I have to say, they were pretty good to me, actually."

And now Billy saw that she wasn't alone. Behind her, standing close to the wall, was a frail, dark-haired boy of about thirteen. He wore a pair of black swimming-trunks, and his body was the colour of cement.

As Billy watched, the boy stepped out of the shadows, into a pool of light. Bending suddenly, he vomited on the floor. It was just water, Billy realised. Water from the reservoir. The boy stayed doubled up, hugging himself as though he'd caught a chill.

"What can I do for him?" the woman said. "There's nothing I can do." She rounded on Billy, her voice losing its note of resignation, becoming harder. "You don't say much, do you?" She looked straight at him, with her cigarette held just to one side of her mouth. "Most people want to ask me questions. Why did I do it? What was I thinking? How can I live with myself?"

She reeled off the various expressions of other people's curiosity in a bored monotone that Billy found repellent. Yes, the questions were predictable, and she had probably heard them a hundred times, but she was talking about torture, murder . . . Then again, she'd never been known for her tact, had she?

"What are you doing here?" he said. "What do you want?"

"Surely you can do better than that." She was still staring at him. The swollen eyelids, the narrow mouth. One hand full of ash. "Come on, Billy," she said. "This is your big chance."

Take a deep breath. Look away.

A few feet to his left he saw a notice that said PATHOLOGY. There was a door with a small window in it, at head height. He peered through. There didn't seem to be anybody in the room, but all the lights were on. In the fluorescent glare he could see a row of white coats hanging on a rail, each one clean but shapeless, limp, like recently discarded skin. He felt a creeping sensation at the back of his neck, beneath his hair, a dread that he was quite unable to explain.

He had a question for the woman now, but when he turned to face her she was gone. She must have run out of patience. Lost interest. Or perhaps she had sensed what he was about to ask, and it had driven her away. He crossed to the place where she had been standing and moved the flat of one hand over the wall. It felt uniformly dry and cool. There was no evidence that anyone had been there, not the slightest vestige of human warmth or body heat. Kneeling quickly, he inspected the floor. No suggestion of any water either. Not a trace of ash.

"Did you drop something?"

Still on his knees, he glanced over his shoulder. A nurse stood at the end of the corridor. Though her eyes were fixed on him, her face was turned slightly away, as if she found it difficult to look straight at him.

"Yes," he said, getting to his feet. "Well, I thought I did."

"What was it?"

"It's all right. It was nothing." He gave her a smile that was supposed to be efficient and reassuring. "Thanks, anyway."

As he hurried off towards the mortuary, he was aware that the nurse was probably still watching him. Had she seen him running his hand over the wall? And if so, what sense could she possibly have made of it?

CHAPTER
TWENTY-FOUR

There was a name he could no longer avoid. It had come to him on Friday, when he sat in his car and listened to the news, and then again on Saturday, when he went walking in the woods. It had come even more strongly when Phil Shaw showed him the fridge where the woman's body was being kept. During the past few hours it had grown more and more powerful until it seemed that the name had a voice, and it was calling out to him, demanding his attention.

Four years ago, in the autumn of 1998, he had been summoned to Northampton to give evidence in a trial. He hadn't been able to leave Ipswich until the late afternoon, and after driving for about two hours he had checked into a Travel Inn at the junction of the A14 and the A1, not far from Huntingdon. His room was tidy and overheated, with a big double bed and a notice you could hang outside your door that said SSSSHHH . . . FAST ASLEEP. Like most Travel Inns, it made you feel as if you'd ended up in the middle of nowhere. Their locations seemed determined largely by the presence of a main road or a motorway; apart from that, they didn't appear to have any connection with real life at all. This would be a terrible place to die, he remembered thinking as he set his case down on the bed.

On the far side of the car-park was a large, partially timbered building that the brochure referred to as the "food barn". It had a restaurant and a bar, and on that particular night it was full of lorry-drivers, travelling salesmen, and a party of high-spirited golfers from a club in Warwickshire. Billy was halfway through his Chicken Kiev when a man in a grey suit jerked to a standstill in front of his table.

"Billy Tyler?"

Billy stared up into the man's face. "My God," he said. "Trevor? Is that you?"

He rose quickly to his feet, and the two men shook hands.

"Billy Tyler," Trevor said again, but in a tone of wonderment this time.

Billy was grinning now. "What a coincidence."

Trevor Lydgate had been in the year above Billy at primary school, but their mothers were friends so they had played in each other's houses from an early age. Their friendship hadn't lasted long, though, because the Lydgates moved away, to Manchester, and the two boys gradually lost touch.

"Look, you finish your meal," Trevor said, "then come and join me for a drink. I'm over there, in the corner."

Billy watched the thin, balding man move away across the bar — he remembered a slender boy with light-brown hair — then he sat down again. Picking up his fork, he smiled to himself and shook his head. So there was a reason for these out-of-the-way places after all . . .

A few minutes later, he was sitting in a booth with Trevor, drinking pints of Stella and catching up on the events of the last twenty-five or thirty years. They both drank fast, excited by the chance reunion, and determined to make the most of it. Every now and then, their conversation would reach into the distant past, as if for a point of reference, a touchstone; they wanted to emphasise the unlikely nature of their meeting — or to make sure that it was all true, perhaps, to prove that the things they remembered had actually happened, that they really were who they said they were.

Trevor was married, with four children. Three boys and a girl. He worked for a firm that manufactured pottery. Plates, mugs, bowls — that sort of stuff. The firm was downsizing, though, and he would soon be looking for another job. At his age, he didn't think it would be easy. "I'm in my forties now," he said. "Can you believe it?" Trevor sounded amazed, almost jubilant, and yet, at the same time, Billy saw anxiety pass over his face, as sudden and fleeting as the shadow of a cloud. In any case, Trevor went on quickly, he would cross that bridge when he came to it. He was living in Staffordshire, in a town called Stone. It was very handy for the M6.

"But tell me about you, Billy," Trevor said, leaning forwards over the table. "What have you been up to?"

Billy couldn't help smiling at Trevor's eagerness. He seemed so interested. As if any news of Billy's would delight him, just so long as Billy could manage to put it into words. It was a childlike quality, one not generally found in people who were middle-aged: either they had lost it along the way, or else they'd had it ground out of them.

"I'm in the police," Billy said.

"Really? I've never met a policeman. I mean, not socially."

"We're all right, you know. We're human."

Trevor beamed. "You know, I didn't used to trust the police. Back in the late seventies, I mean, when Thatcher first came in. Now, though, I think it would be a fascinating job. Who knows, if I get fired, I might even become one myself — or is it too late for me?"

"It's not exactly well paid," Billy said, "and you do have a large family . . ."

"That's true." Trevor nodded, then drank.

Though he appeared to be agreeing with Billy, he had by no means been put off the idea. Trevor seemed to be a man who was given to continual small enthusiasms. He would probably be exhausting to live with.

"Four children," Billy mused. "How do you do it?"

"Ask my wife." Trevor chuckled, shook his head. "What about you, Billy? Have you got kids?"

"I've got a daughter," Billy said. "Emma. She's got Down's."

This piece of information would have thrown most people. Not Trevor, though.

"How bad is it?" he said.

"We're lucky, really. On a scale of one to ten, she's probably seven or eight. I mean, she's fantastic, I love her to bits, but it's still difficult."

"You must worry . . ."

"She's four and a half, and she can't talk properly. She just makes sounds. Their tongues are bigger, you see." Billy swallowed some more lager. "Her eyes are bad too. She had to have an operation to tighten the muscles. And she has to wear special shoes to help her stand up . . ." Billy thought about mentioning her heart, but he just couldn't bear it.

"I expect you have to watch her all the time," Trevor said.

Billy nodded. "Yes. Non-stop."

It was his round. He went up to the bar and ordered two more pints. Before he could even sit down with the new drinks, Trevor was talking again.

"If you think about it, though, we all have to watch our children now, don't we? So many things can happen to them. When we were young, it was different." He reached for his new pint and took a gulp. "Back then, it was all woods and fields, and we'd be gone for the whole day, and no one even thought twice . . ."

Trevor's voice had started trembling halfway through the sentence, but then it gave out completely, and he put his face in his hands. Billy stared at Trevor's bald spot, unable for a moment to believe what was happening.

"Trevor?" he said. "What is it?"

150

But Trevor wouldn't answer. He sat in the booth with his hands covering his face, his whole body shaking.

"What's wrong, Trevor?"

People were beginning to look at them, wondering what was going on. *There's a bloke crying over there.*

Billy clambered to his feet and put an arm round Trevor's shoulders. "Come on, Trevor. Let's get you back to your room."

He picked Trevor's key up off the table, and they left the food barn together, with Billy taking most of Trevor's weight. Once outside, the cold air hit them. The wind was swooping in from the east, over the landscaped banks and mounds, and Billy thought he could smell snow. That keen, metallic edge. When he lifted his head, the cars bounced beneath the yellow lights. Their shiny surfaces swirled glassily about. How many pints had they had? Six? Seven?

Trevor's room was on the ground floor, behind reception. On opening the door, Billy saw that the room had been designed for people who were disabled, with pinkish-brown grab-rails everywhere, and a red string dangling between the toilet and the bath. IN THE EVENT OF AN EMERGENCY THE DUTY MANAGER CAN BE CALLED BY PULLING THE RED CORD. Billy hoped it wouldn't come to that.

"Asked for a non-smoking room," Trevor said, slurring his words, "and this's all they had." His head lurched on his neck as he looked around. "It's no different, really. Everything's a bit lower, that's all. The bed, door-handles . . ."

"It's fine," Billy said.

Trevor stumbled into the bathroom. Through the closed door, Billy heard the splash of urine, then a controlled roar as the toilet flushed.

When Trevor emerged again, he avoided Billy's gaze. "Sorry about all that," he said, wiping his face. "Sorry, Billy. God. Do you want a drink?"

He seemed to have pulled himself together. His speech was clearer. All the same, Billy didn't feel he could leave Trevor on his own.

"Go on, then," he said. "Just the one."

Trevor fetched two water-glasses from the bathroom, then opened his briefcase and took out some red wine and a corkscrew. "I always have a bottle on me," he said, "just in case I run into an old friend." He was trying to be funny, but his voice was too thin to carry it off. Too wobbly.

He poured the wine. Even as he held out a glass for Billy, he was gulping from his own. "So I never told you what happened to me?" he said.

Billy crossed the room and sat down in the armchair by the window. He had checked into the Travel Inn because he was tired, and here he was, staying up and getting drunk. "When are you talking about?" he said.

"When I was ten."

"I didn't know you then. You'd moved away."

"That's right." Trevor settled on the end of the bed. He drank some more wine, then reached out and placed his glass on the desk where the TV was. Only alcoholics put glasses down that carefully.

"So what happened?" Billy said.

Trevor began to talk about the old days again, what he called "back then" — children off playing by themselves, and no one giving them a thought. Had it ever really been like that? Maybe it had. What Billy remembered most, though, was the housing boom, and all that building going on. Stacks of bricks, cement-mixers. Scaffolding. He and Trevor would climb up inside the new houses and drop messages down between the walls: swearwords, or spells, or sometimes just their two names and the date. They were still there, probably . . . Only dimly aware of Trevor's voice, Billy was on the point of drifting off to sleep when a single sentence drew him right in close.

"But that day, for some reason, I was all alone . . ."

Billy roused himself. "Sorry. Where was this?"

"In Manchester. A place called Fallowfield."

A white car pulled alongside him, Trevor said, as he was walking. The driver was a woman, and she was on her own. She wound her window down, called out to him. He couldn't remember what she said, but he remembered that she had a hard voice, flinty and impatient; she sounded like someone who was bad-tempered, or in a hurry. She had black hair, with a headscarf tied over it. Though it was November, she dangled her right arm out of the window, and her painted nails showed up vividly against the door. Between the first and second fingers was a cigarette. There was a moment when she withdrew her arm and dragged on the cigarette, and the whole time she was inhaling she never took her eyes off him, then her arm returned to where it had been before, and the smoke soon followed in a thin blue stream.

His parents had told him that there were people called "strangers", and that they might offer him a bag of sweets, or a ride in their car, and that he should always say "No, thank you", but somehow, that afternoon, he forgot everything he'd been taught. Oddly enough, it was the woman's harshness that drew him across the pavement. She didn't make the slightest attempt to be friendly, let alone seductive. On the contrary. If he couldn't be of any use to her, she would have to find somebody else, and he could see that thought annoyed her.

"I wondered later," Trevor said, his eyes wide now, "whether she might have been nervous, you know?" He paused. "I mean, what if I was one of the first?"

At this point, Billy still wasn't quite sure what Trevor was talking about, but he decided not to interrupt.

Trevor went on. When he stopped at the kerb, the woman told him that she was lost. Did he know the area? He nodded. Good, she said. If he would just get into the car, maybe he could show her the way. Once again, there was no subtlety in her approach, nothing remotely clever or ingratiating. He asked her where she was going. He called her "Miss". Instead of answering, she cocked her head, appraising him, and then said something about him looking bright as a button: if he couldn't help her, she said, nobody could. Only then did he feel a flicker of misgiving. It was because she had flattered him. The hardness, the impatience — they were believable; they seemed real, and he trusted them.

154

But the flattery felt different, like something shiny that wasn't actually worth anything. So why did he get into the car? He didn't have an explanation. It still puzzled him, even today. Round the front he went, her made-up eyes tracking him across the windscreen. When he reached the passenger's side, the door was already open. All he had to do was climb in and pull it shut.

"Give it a good slam," the woman told him. "We don't want you falling out now, do we?"

Trevor looked away into the room. "Fuck," he murmured, then reached for his drink and finished it. He poured himself another glass, right up to the brim, and held the bottle out to Billy, but Billy shook his head. He'd had enough.

"It was so quiet," Trevor said. "I don't remember any noise at all." He paused again. "No, wait, that's wrong. Once, on a bend, I heard a motorbike. That was him, of course. He was following."

Only now did Billy understand what Trevor had been telling him, and he leaned forwards in his chair, clear-headed suddenly, as though all the alcohol had drained out of his body. "So you saw him too?" he said.

Trevor closed his eyes. "We haven't got to that bit yet."

They drove on for a while, and the woman kept her eyes fixed on the road. She braked, she indicated; everything was so normal that he forgot what he was doing there. Then he came to. She hadn't asked him for directions; she hadn't spoken to him at all, in fact. He glanced at her, and it wasn't her nails or her hair that he saw, but her blunt nose and her jutting chin. Any glamour there might have been had gone, and he was beginning to suspect that something might be wrong.

"I thought you were lost," he murmured.

The woman didn't seem to hear him.

Some time later, he said, "You haven't asked me which way to go."

"We're going to my gran's house first," she told him. "I forgot my gloves."

She parked in an area he didn't recognise. It looked poorer than where he lived. Rubbish was blowing about: bubble-gum wrappers, pages from the paper, plastic bags. On the roof of a nearby house a TV aerial quivered. It was windy out that day. He brought his eyes back down. A brown bottle rolled across the pavement, then stopped and rolled the other way. He remembered the sound of that bottle with such clarity that it might have happened half an hour ago. But it was thirty years now, thirty years . . .

"Come inside for a second," the woman said. "Come and help me find those gloves."

He knew what she was up to. She was trying to make something that was actually a chore sound like a game — grown-ups were always doing that — but she wasn't very good at it. There was no warmth in her voice, no sense of adventure or intrigue. He thought he'd better play along, though. If he didn't she would only get cross.

She came round to his side of the car and opened the door, then she took him by the hand and pulled him out. She hadn't used his name, he realised. She hadn't even asked him what he was called.

156

"My name's Trevor Lydgate," he said. "What's yours?"

"Imagine," Trevor said, putting a hand up to his forehead. "Imagine if she'd told me. Not that it would have meant anything to me. It wouldn't have meant anything to anyone, not then." He laughed a precarious laugh, high and thin, and then continued.

Her hand still gripping his, they walked along a path next to a white fence. Her gran's house was on the corner, at the end of the row. The woman opened the front door and pushed him into a narrow hallway. A cigarette-machine was fixed to the wall. He caught sight of his face in a chrome panel. He looked like someone pretending to be Trevor Lydgate, and had to turn away quickly because it made him feel strange. There was no sign of the woman's gran. Maybe she'd gone out. He heard the motorbike again, much louder this time, and glanced over his shoulder to see where it was, but the woman was blocking his view. She seemed bigger now she was standing up. She seemed to fill the hall. As he tried to look past her, she gave him another push.

"They're probably upstairs," she said.

The gloves, she meant.

Up they went. Him first, her following behind.

She took him to a small room at the back of the house. There was hardly any furniture, just a two-bar electric fire and a single bed with a bare mattress. There was no carpet. Only boards. On the mattress was a Kodak camera. The curtains were drawn, but light from outside filtered through the flowery material, enough to see by. On the floor were some magazines, with men and women doing things to each other.

The woman nodded when she saw that he had noticed them. "Have a look, if you like."

He shook his head.

She seemed to have forgotten all about the gloves. She was just staring at him, and there was greed on her face, and also a kind of pride, an expression that he didn't understand until much later.

The air in the room was motionless and stale, and smelled of something vaguely familiar, but private, secret. It was a smell he knew, but not too well, and he couldn't quite identify it. Mostly, he was trying not to look at the magazines.

"It's cold in here," the woman muttered, and she bent to plug in the electric fire.

A door opened and closed downstairs. He heard footsteps in the hall. The woman's back stiffened, as if she were anxious or fearful, and that was when he panicked.

The next few seconds were hard to piece together. What he saw wasn't continuous. It came to him in vivid fragments. Flashes and splinters. As though the film of his life had been slashed to ribbons and then taped back together. He didn't really know how he managed to get away. There were times when he found it impossible to believe. There were times when he thought he must have been in that room for longer, but part of him had shut down, blotting those bits out. There were times when he searched his body for traces of the things they must have done to him. There were times, too, when he felt that he might still be in there, and that all this — he waved a hand to indicate the room, the hotel, and everything outside and beyond — all this was just fantasy or wishful thinking.

The woman was bent over, by the fire. He moved suddenly and fast, slipping past her, even though she was between him and the door. She let out a cry, as if, in attempting to escape, he had hurt her. Her hand clawed at him, but he eluded it. Then he was on the landing. A yellow wall, music coming from below. Through the banisters, he saw somebody walking up the stairs. A man. Head lowered, the man hadn't noticed him. Trevor rounded the corner and hurled himself down the stairs so hard that he knocked the man off balance.

He reached the front door without seeming to have crossed the hall. The door flew inwards, hit the wall. Something shattered. He didn't look back, and yet he had a memory of the man in the doorway, mouth crooked, one hand bleeding.

He ran off down the street. The houses all looked the same. He had no idea where he was. An old lady came up the road towards him, but he was worried she might be the gran. He tore past her, as fast as he could go. He thought he heard the motorbike start up. *Quick. Hide.* He found a dustbin round the back of someone's house and climbed inside. Luckily, it was almost empty. It still stank, though. When he opened the lid again, it was dark, and the streetlights had come on. Standing on the pavement, he hesitated. Tried to guess which way was home. His stomach twisted, and he did some diarrhoea.

All down one leg. All runny. He stood there in his shorts, not knowing what to do.

Some time went by. A woman turned the corner with a shopping bag. She wanted to take him home and clean him up, but he said he wasn't allowed to go into strangers' houses. He asked if she could telephone his parents and tell them where he was. He recited his number for her, the number he had learned by heart, then he stood out on the street and waited.

When he saw them drive up in the car, he thought how innocent they looked. It was as if he was the parent and they were the children. He felt they needed to be protected. The fact that he had diarrhoea was useful because it gave them all something to talk about. He never told his parents the real story about that day. Not then, not ever. When they asked him what he was doing in Hattersley, he said he'd got on the wrong bus.

"Then you were scared," his mother said, "because you didn't know where you were."

He looked at her gratefully. "Yes," he said, and he was relieved that she had taken on the burden of thinking up a lie. He wasn't sure he could have done it on his own.

"Yes, I was scared," he said.

"You were lost," his mother said.

He nodded. He bit his bottom lip. "Yes," he said. "That's right."

Trevor wiped his face with one hand, then reached for his wine. "I was in that house." Unable to believe it, he shook his head, then glanced across at Billy. "The black hair. It was a wig, you see?" The skin on his face seemed to have tightened. "Do you understand what I'm saying?"

"I understand," Billy said, though he wasn't quite sure how to react.

Trevor finished his drink, but held on to the empty glass. "I've only told three people in my life," he said. "My brother, my wife — and now you."

Billy was staring at the carpet, but he could feel Trevor's eyes on him. Did Trevor expect something from him? If so, what? And why had Trevor told him, anyway? Because they'd got drunk together? Because he was a policeman? Because, once upon a time, they had been friends?

The silence lasted. Billy felt hot. Leaning sideways, he looked at the radiator on the wall. The dial was set to 5. He turned it down to 2.

"When did all this happen?" he asked eventually.

"1964," Trevor said. "November."

A child had been murdered at around that time, Billy thought, though he couldn't remember which one.

"I still think about that little boy," Trevor said, "you know, the boy who wasn't found."

Billy nodded.

"I think of him lying in that lonely place," Trevor said. "I just hope someone finds him one day. I'd hate to think he just stayed up there for ever, on the moors."

He fell silent again.

"Most of all, though, I feel guilty," he went on after a while, looking down into his empty glass. "Nothing happened to me. I got away."

"You were lucky —"

"That's not what I mean," Trevor said, cutting in with a kind of savagery. "I'm linked to them for ever, those children. The ones with the names we all know. Sometimes it's like I can sense their presence — somewhere near by . . ."

Billy watched as Trevor slowly lowered his face into his hands and began to cry again. There was another level to Trevor's guilt, he realised. Not only had Trevor survived, but he had also kept the fact of his survival to himself. If he had told his parents what had happened — the woman in the white car, the man on the motorbike — if he had identified the house, it was possible that lives could have been saved. Billy rather hoped this thought hadn't occurred to Trevor. It would be hard for him to bear.

Now Trevor had started crying, he couldn't stop. He was hunched over, only his hands separating his forehead from his knees. Billy sat beside him on the bed and put an arm round his shoulders. Trevor's body felt rigid, as though every muscle had been stretched to breaking-point.

Then, little by little, his breathing deepened. He had cried himself to sleep, just as a child might. Billy still had his arm round Trevor, though Trevor was leaning against him now. Trevor smelled of deodorant and alcohol. Once or twice, he jerked so violently that Billy was afraid they might both be thrown to the floor.

The next time Billy glanced at the clock on the TV, it said two-twenty-five. He must have dozed off for a while. Trevor was facing away from him now, lying across the bottom of the bed, the soles of his shoes pressed against Billy's thigh. One of his hands was curled into a fist and held close to his mouth. Billy did a quick calculation in his head. Northampton was still a good two hours' drive away, and he was due in court at ten. He would have to be up by seven — at the latest.

He took off Trevor's shoes and socks, then his trousers, and shifted him until he was lengthways on the bed. Trevor still hadn't stirred. Billy couldn't help noticing that Trevor's legs were smooth and white, and utterly without hair. Somehow this seemed in keeping with the story he had told, the horror he had so narrowly escaped. Gently, Billy drew the covers over him.

Ssshh . . . fast asleep.

Although he very much doubted that Trevor would wake, he still didn't feel he could leave. Not after what he'd heard. Switching off the lights, he loosened his tie and dropped into the chair by the window. It was a small modern armchair, with a low back, but he had slept in more uncomfortable places. Through the curtains behind him came a dim glow, citrus yellow, and Trevor's story came with it — the bare mattress, the camera, the dirty magazines. Billy emptied his mind, then folded his hands over his stomach and shut his eyes. In the sealed hush of the hotel room, he could hear Trevor's breathing, deep and ragged.

He woke what felt like moments later to see Trevor standing in front of the tall, thin mirror near the door. Though it was still dark, the spill of light from the bathroom allowed him to watch Trevor as he tied his tie. Trevor was wearing a suit and humming quietly to himself. He behaved as if he was on his own in the room.

Billy yawned and stretched, making more noise than was strictly necessary.

"I can't sleep sitting up," Trevor said. "I can never sleep on planes, for instance."

"In my job you get used to it." Billy yawned again. "What's the time?"

"Nearly seven."

Billy stood up and parted the curtains. The sky was a dull grey-blue. He could just make out a smooth grass bank and the section of main road that lay beyond. "I'm going back to my room," he said. "I need a shower."

"Yeah," Trevor said, then sighed.

He seemed the less embarrassed of the two. He had humiliated himself, and that gave him a kind of edge. As for Billy, he was keenly aware of the need to be delicate. He knew too much — more, he suspected, than Trevor had intended to tell him — and he had to imagine, for the time being, that what he'd heard was just a story. Certainly he had to forget how he had held Trevor in his arms while Trevor cried himself to sleep. They were two old friends who had run into each other by chance, and they'd had too much to drink, as old friends often do. That was all there was to it. Should they ever run into each other again, there would be nothing to say. They would probably act as if they hadn't seen each other. What had happened the

164

night before could never be repeated, or referred to, or even remembered — not out loud, anyway.

Billy moved towards the door. One hand on the handle, he turned and looked back into the room. Trevor was opening his briefcase. Billy watched as Trevor took out a sheet of paper and frowned at it. He had the distinct impression that Trevor was only pretending to be busy, and that, as soon as he was alone, he would sit down on the bed and simply stare into space.

"Maybe see you at breakfast," Billy said.

Trevor looked round quickly, as if he had forgotten Billy was there. "What?" he said. "Oh, sure. OK."

But Trevor would have finished his breakfast before Billy appeared in the food barn. Trevor would make certain of that. He might even skip the meal altogether. Just get in the car and drive.

"Take care," Billy said.

They both knew they would never see each other again.

Everything was silent in the mortuary. Billy realised that the answer-machine was no longer beeping; someone must have listened to the message while he was on his break. In the distance, on the very threshold of hearing, he thought he could detect the soothing hum of a floor-polisher — in hospitals, as in airports, cleaners nearly always worked at night — and he pictured a man with a blank look on his face guiding the machine from side to side, its brushes revolving briskly, smoothly, an endless series of tiny circles, each new circle covering a slightly different area from the

165

last, but all the circles overlapping, and the floor becoming shinier and shinier until it existed only as a perfect reflection of what surrounded it.

CHAPTER
TWENTY-FIVE

Whenever Billy thought about Trevor, he was overtaken by an intense feeling of regret. He couldn't help feeling there was more he could have done. He hadn't asked for Trevor's phone number, for instance, or his address — surely Trevor would've had business cards in that briefcase of his — nor, on returning home, had he tried to trace his old friend using the one piece of information that he'd picked up. After all, there couldn't have been too many people called Lydgate in a small town like Stone . . . They had parted at the door of room number 8, and just as Billy had predicted, Trevor didn't appear for breakfast. Their paths had crossed for the first time in thirty years, but they had chosen not to benefit from the coincidence.

Almost exactly a year later, in the autumn of 1999, a woman called Mary Betts left a message on Billy's answer-machine at home. She had some news for him, she said. Though he didn't recognise the name or the voice, he called her back that evening. She told him that she'd been a classmate of his at primary school. They hadn't known each other very well, she reassured him, so he didn't have to pretend he remembered her. He laughed.

"Before we go too far," she said, "it's not good news, I'm afraid. Trevor Lydgate's dead."

Standing in the lounge, next to the window, Billy thought of the brownish-pink grab-rails in Trevor's hotel room. In their colour and their smoothness, in their curiously glossy quality, they had reminded him of something you might find inside a body. Organs of some kind. Intestines.

It's no different, really.

"I just thought you might like to know," Mary Betts said, "since you were once a friend of his."

The funeral was in two days' time, she said. She was sorry not to have given him more notice. He told her he would do his best to be there. Later that night, he phoned Maureen, his mother. She hadn't seen Trevor since he was a little boy, she said, but she would try to attend the funeral, if only for Betty's sake, her dear Betty Lydgate who had died some years before. At work the next day Billy applied for compassionate leave, claiming that he and Trevor had been cousins.

It was a four-hour drive from Suffolk, and he arrived at the church a few minutes late, but he was able to slip into a pew at the back without anybody noticing. The church was less than half-full. When the service ended, he remained in his seat, watching the mourners file past. There was Trevor's wife, a big, dumpy woman with long hair and glasses, and there were the four children Trevor had talked about, at least three of them already in their teens. The church doors had been thrown open, and the faces of the bereaved were brutally exposed by the white autumn light. Billy could

168

see shock and lack of sleep, but he could also see the strange, self-conscious, almost narcissistic sense of loss that often accompanies an unexpected death in the family. They walked down the aisle as if dragging heavy weights, and the youngest child, a boy, was looking from side to side, embarrassed by all the attention, but fascinated too. The man supporting the widow was much stockier than Trevor, and had more hair, including a closely trimmed beard and moustache, yet he was clearly recognisable as Trevor's brother. These, then, were the other two bearers of the secret.

Outside, Billy caught up with his mother, who was searching in her handbag for a tissue.

"It's a mercy Betty's not here to see this," Maureen said. "She would have been heartbroken. Heartbroken."

The crematorium was only five minutes' drive away, and this time Billy sat near the front, watching as Trevor's coffin slid through a dark-blue curtain. The music played during its short and slightly jerky trip was a top-ten hit from the eighties:

Look at me standing
Here on my own again —

Billy remembered dancing to the song with Susie once, in a nightclub in Manchester, a slow shuffle of a dance during which they kissed non-stop. It had sounded oddly mournful even then, as though the singer was trying to convince people that he was happy when, actually, nothing could have been further from the

169

truth. Now, in the context of a funeral, his plaintive voice seemed almost too much to bear, and Billy's mother wasn't the only person in tears.

No need to run, and hide
It's a wonderful, wonderful life —

When the ceremony was over, the priest announced that refreshments were being served in a nearby hotel, and that everyone was welcome. Billy said goodbye to his mother outside the crematorium — she had to be getting home, she said, having always hated driving in the dark — and although he, too, had a long journey ahead of him, he decided to put in an appearance, if only to offer his condolences to Trevor's wife.

The room they'd booked had green flock wallpaper and windows that gave on to a stagnant pond. There were plates of sandwiches and cups of tea laid out on trestle tables. There was a bar too. Billy bought himself a pint, then turned and looked for Mrs Lydgate, but before he could single her out, the stocky man with the beard walked up to him.

"Billy Tyler?"

"That's right."

"You're the policeman."

"And you must be Trevor's brother."

"I'm Steve."

After shaking hands, Steve Lydgate turned his eyes to the window, then took a deep breath and blew the air out loudly.

"I'm very sorry," Billy said.

170

Steve looked at him again. "Did you come far?"

"I drove up from Ipswich."

Steve nodded, as if the strength of one's support could be measured by the distance travelled. "Listen, thanks for making the effort."

It was Billy's turn to avert his eyes. The room had filled up, with most people under fifty preferring alcohol to tea. You always get drunk fast at funerals. There's that inappropriate hilarity, that giddy feeling of relief. *It wasn't me this time. It wasn't me.*

"I take it you know about Trevor . . ."

Billy studied Steve across the rim of his glass. "Know what?"

"He killed himself." Steve took a gulp from his pint in exactly the same way that Trevor would have done, with a kind of ferocity, so much so that a speck of foam leapt up on to his cheek.

"Oh. I see." Billy nodded slowly, sadly.

Steve was staring at him. "You don't seem very surprised."

Lowering his voice, Billy started telling Steve about his encounter in Huntingdon the year before.

"Trevor got upset that night," Billy said. "He was haunted by what had happened to him, and he felt guilty too, but I didn't think it would drive him to —"

"Guilty?" Steve said. "What do you mean, guilty?"

"He survived — not like the others. He was lucky."

"Not that fucking lucky."

Biting his lip, Billy stared at the floor. "That was tactless of me. Sorry."

"If they ever let her out," Steve said, "I'm going to kill her, I swear to God. I'm going to hunt her down and kill her. I'll serve time for it. I don't care."

Only after his outburst did he seem to remember what Billy did for a living, and he mustered a defiant, self-righteous look, as if challenging Billy to arrest him there and then.

But Billy hardly noticed. An idea had just occurred to him for the first time. "Do you think Trevor was telling the truth?"

"What are you saying?" Steve said.

Had the woman — *that* woman — really taken Trevor home with her, Billy thought, or was there another interpretation?

"What are you on about?" Steve's face was suddenly closer than Billy would have liked, and his eyes had hardened. "Why would he lie?"

Billy thought it wise not to go any further. In fact, it was possible that he had already gone too far. Trevor's suicide only made sense to Steve if he believed the story his brother had told him, and believed it one hundred per cent. That was all he had to hold on to. For Billy to suggest that it might have been a fabrication, or even that Trevor might have been exaggerating, was disrespectful, if not downright insulting, especially on a day like today, and clearly Steve wouldn't hesitate to defend his brother's honour. Billy had already noticed Steve's knuckles. They were red and glossy, blurred-looking, and Billy knew what that meant: Steve was someone who liked to hit people. Even as Billy stood in front of him, he could feel the violence. It came off Steve in waves.

"There's Trevor's wife," Billy said.

Before Steve could speak or otherwise detain him, Billy moved away. Crossing the room, he introduced himself to Mrs Lydgate as Trevor's childhood friend and told her how sorry he was. He didn't live in the area, he said, but if there was anything he could do . . . He talked about his friendship with Trevor, and the adventures they used to have.

"Happier days," she said with a weak smile.

He nodded. "Yes." And then added, "For all of us," though he wasn't sure why he'd said that, or what he meant by it.

Soon afterwards he left.

Only when he was on the road did he realise that he had never got to meet Mary Betts.

Sitting up straighter in his chair, Billy rubbed his face quickly, then forced himself up on to his feet. The mint-green mortuary doors, the tube-lights fizzing softly overhead . . . Memories kept coming, and none of them gave him any respite. If only he could just switch off. *Christ.* What time was it?

CHAPTER
TWENTY-SIX

The smell of cigarettes first, then the smoke rising, grey-blue, in the corner of his eye. Then, finally, the voice: "I had nothing to do with it."

She sat across from him, a cigarette in her right hand, her left arm resting on the table. Britain's most hated woman. She was wearing a suit again, only this time it was darker. Maroon, he thought, or burgundy. In front of her was a packet of Embassy filter, with a box of matches on top. There were chocolates too. He remembered reading somewhere that she had a sweet tooth.

"That friend of yours," she said. "I never saw him before in my life."

As she shifted on her chair, the lights on the ceiling picked out coppery tints in her hair. According to one of the newspapers, she was so pampered while in Highpoint that she'd had her own crimpers. He watched as she carefully selected another cigarette. She acted as if each cigarette was slightly different and uniquely delicious. It wasn't the behaviour of someone who'd been pampered. She struck a match and lit the cigarette, then put the used match back in the box and placed the box on top of the cigarette packet. The years she had spent in prison were evident in every movement, no matter how small. When she touched ordinary objects, they seemed to acquire new value, greater substance.

"He was making the whole thing up," she said.

"Why, though?" Billy wasn't surprised by her denials; on the contrary, they were entirely consistent with the thought he'd had on the day of Trevor's funeral, a thought that had lingered in the back of his mind ever since, ghostly, unconfirmed. "Why would he do that?"

"How would I know?" Eyebrows raised, mouth a little pinched, she held the cigarette away from the table and tapped it twice with her index finger. Ash fell silently into the drain.

"Maybe he was having some kind of breakdown," Billy murmured.

In the excitement of that chance encounter, he had overlooked the most important factors: Trevor had a large family — four children — and was about to lose his job. He would have been under enormous strain.

The woman took another long drag and looked off into the distance, beyond the white doors of the fridges, beyond the hospital walls. "You want to know about breakdowns?" she said. "I'll tell you about breakdowns." She began to describe her life in Holloway, and then in Cookham — the insults, the beatings, the constant degradation. She talked about being kicked unconscious by a fellow inmate, and how her appearance had altered. Bones had been broken in her face. She wasn't asking for pity. She was just saying. Billy realised that he was only half listening.

"There's no way you'd ever admit to it," he said, bringing her back to the original subject. "You can't afford to."

"Oh?" she said. "And why's that?"

"If you own up to abducting Trevor, then it's like saying there were others — and that's my question, actually, since you wanted me to ask you a question: not 'Why did you do it?' but 'How many more?'"

"How many more?" she said.

"How many more," he said, "that we don't know about?"

She looked at him steadily, smoke rising in a thin spiral past her eyes. "You're quite a clever-clogs, aren't you?"

Even if she was in possession of certain knowledge, she wasn't about to share it with him. She wouldn't give him that satisfaction. She'd rather torture him by leaving all his accusations hanging in the air. But he had noticed a twitch in the skin under her right eye.

"You killed people," he said. "Children."

She held his gaze. The twitch became irregular, then vanished.

"Most of the time I wasn't even there," she said.

Most of the time. She had no idea how chilling those words sounded.

"Once, I sat on a rock," she said. "Another time I waited by the car. I wasn't there."

"That's what happens in a war," Billy said. "That's what generals do. They watch from a distance while their soldiers do the —"

Her expression hardened into one of thinly suppressed contempt. "So that's your theory, is it? You think I was in charge?"

Well, why not? he thought. *A female general. In her kneelength boots and her helmet of blonde hair.*

The people who spoke in her defence tended to claim that her lover was both evil and deranged, and that she had fallen under his influence. Had she never met him, they argued, she would have led a perfectly normal life. But supposing the opposite was true? Supposing *he* had fallen under *her* influence? What if her presence alone had been enough to unleash the wickedness in him, to spur him on to greater and greater acts of savagery? What if she not only allowed him, but encouraged him — no, *required* him — to explore that side of himself?

"Are you denying it?" he said.

Sighing, she stubbed out her cigarette in the lid of her cigarette packet. "I didn't have anything to do with your friend."

"I'm not sure I believe you." He leaned over the table, feeling that he had her now, that he was finally getting somewhere. "Why *should* I believe you?"

She, too, leaned over the table. He was aware of her hands, pale and plump, carefully manicured, and he thought of her lover, and what she was supposed to have said about him: *The first man I ever met who had clean fingernails.* Billy shuddered. Then she took what he'd been thinking and she put it into words:

"If he was in that house," she said, "you really think he would have got out again?"

CHAPTER
TWENTY-SEVEN

During the weeks that followed Trevor's death, and prompted at least in part by his unfinished conversation with Trevor's brother, Billy had found himself researching the murders, casually at first, but then with increasing vigour and intensity. He was curious to see whether there were any references to children who had got away — and, oddly enough, he found one: a boy called Sammy whose photograph had turned up among the murderers' possessions subsequent to their arrest. There was no mention of a Trevor Lydgate, however, nor was there any suggestion that other children had had narrow escapes. But if there had been one, then surely it was possible . . . As a result, Billy had to ask himself why he had doubted the story in the first place. Partly, he supposed, because it was so extraordinary. To fall into the clutches of two such dangerous people and yet live to tell the tale. To be lured into that house — actually *into the house* — and then to make a getaway. It sounded like a bizarre fantasy, or a much embroidered version of a far less terrifying event. Which brought him to the second reason for his scepticism. At some level he thought that what he had heard had all the trappings of a story that was being told to cover another story, one that had to remain secret. There might well be three stories, then: the story Trevor had told his parents — *I got lost* — the one he told his wife, his brother, and his childhood friend — *I was abducted* — and the one he kept to himself, or even, possibly, hid from himself. This third story had never been revealed, probably because it was too close to home. Perhaps it even involved members of his family. The advantage of the version he had told Billy was that it allowed him to unburden himself without actually giving anything away.

At the time, the details had seemed authentic enough, but Trevor could easily have invented them. Billy wouldn't have known the difference, nor would most people. Equally, Trevor could have gleaned certain facts from newspapers, or documentaries, or one of the innumerable books written on the subject, and then, over the years, he could have internalised those facts, made them his own. The motorbike, the wig — the cigarette-machine . . . If Billy's theory was correct, it showed how deeply that series of murders had embedded itself in the nation's psyche. No one who had been alive at the time could ever be entirely free of it. It was one of those rare news items against which you defined yourself.

When Billy visited the moors just before the millennium, he had been attempting to put Trevor's story into some sort of context — the very one that Trevor himself had claimed for it — but his journey had also been undertaken in a spirit of recognition. In a sense, he had been demonstrating solidarity, paying tribute. The pictures of the murdered children that appeared in the papers looked like the pictures his mother had taken of him and Charlie when they were little — the same dated black-and-white, all shadows and smudges, an eerily prophetic pattern of erasure and concealment. Those children belonged to the same generation as he did. They were his exact contemporaries. We were all damaged by what happened, he thought. We were all changed.

CHAPTER
TWENTY-EIGHT

Imagining he heard a sound outside, Billy moved across the mortuary and listened at the doors, then he undid the locks, pulled the right-hand door open and put his head into the gap. It was late now, after three in the morning, and the corridor had a deep stillness, an almost supernatural hush: if he had seen a fish sliding soundlessly through that watery green air, somehow he wouldn't have been surprised — or the boy in the black swimming-trunks, his skinny body doubled over, hair dripping . . . As Billy stood in the doorway, Raymond's voice came to him, Raymond in that pub in Cheshire, talking to the beautiful girl. *I almost drowned him once.*

There were people things happened to. Billy knew that because he'd been one of them himself — for a while, anyway. The boy in the swimming-trunks had been another. So, for that matter, had Trevor Lydgate. What was the quality they shared? Were they unlucky, or naive, or were they simply weak? He couldn't decide. Nowadays, of course, they would be called victims. Not a word you'd ever think of applying to Raymond.

Halfway through their European holiday, while they were exploring the chilly, urine-scented passageways of the Colosseum, Raymond started telling Billy about the next stop on their itinerary. There were some volcanic lakes to the north of the city, apparently, where Roman emperors used to bathe. He thought these lakes ought to be worth a visit.

They caught a train to Bracciano, then hitched a ride in a lorry that was loaded with gravel. The man behind the wheel had bloodshot eyes and stubble. As he drove he drank red wine from a huge, clear, pear-shaped bottle. A piece of rolled-up rag served as a cork. He offered Raymond and Billy the bottle, and because it seemed expected they had several large gulps each. The wine was inky and brackish; Billy was sure he could taste the man's saliva. "*Grazie tanto, signore,*" Raymond said as he handed the bottle back. "*Molto gentile.*" The lorry-driver grunted, then spat out of the window.

They had to walk the last two miles down a white track, and before too long their shoes were pale with dust. "*Una strada bianca,*" Raymond said, half to himself. Billy wondered where Raymond had learned the language. They didn't teach Italian at school.

The sky had clouded over, but it was hot, and the cicadas were so loud that Billy felt as if they were actually inside his head. He hurled a stone at the trees, and the chattering stopped abruptly. Just as he was about to congratulate himself, though, it all started up again, even louder and more grating than before. He glanced at Raymond, but Raymond seemed quite oblivious, his hands in his trouser pockets, his fedora

182

tilted jauntily over one eye. He had picked a purple flower, Billy noticed, and threaded it through his lapel.

After about an hour, they saw the lake below them, away to their left. From above, it looked circular, and hard as well, somehow. Like a lid. A path curved steeply down through dusty woods. At the top two cars were parked side by side. One had its headlights on, which Billy found slightly sinister.

Raymond set off down the path, and Billy followed, the trees offering some welcome coolness. Billy paused to remove his shoes and socks. After taking a few steps in bare feet, he called out to Raymond.

"It's so soft, like powder. You should try it."

Raymond glanced at him over his shoulder, but kept going.

At the bottom of the hill they came out on to a wide, pale-yellow beach. They appeared to be the only people there. Perhaps the weather was too cloudy for the locals, Billy thought — or perhaps they were all indoors, having siestas. He could see no houses, though, not even one. The place excited him, and he was glad Raymond had suggested it.

"This is great," he shouted.

He rolled up his trousers and walked slowly into the lake. The water seemed sensitive, as if every movement that he made could be felt out in the middle, and on the far shore too. At the same time, it had a stealthy quality, a kind of silkiness. Something to do with volcanic ash, no doubt. Or lava. Hearing a cry, he turned round. Raymond was waving from further along the beach. He was trying to drag a boat down to the water and needed Billy's help.

The boat was a miniature catamaran, with two moulded plastic seats and two sets of pedals. Though rusty, it looked as if it might still work. Taking one side each, they pushed it into the lake, then scrambled on board and started pedalling. The sky seemed lower now, and strangely green; the day had darkened. Billy wondered whether there was going to be a storm. What if lightning struck the water? Would they be killed? He wiped the sweat from his forehead.

"It's hot, isn't it?" he said.

Raymond took off his suit jacket and draped it over the back of his seat. "Why don't you have a dip?"

Billy eyed the surface of the lake, opaque, impenetrable. They were a long way from the shore. Though he was still sweating, a shiver passed through him. "I don't really like deep water," he said. "I never have."

"Just lower yourself over the side," Raymond said, "and then hold on. You'll be fine."

Billy wasn't sure.

"It'll cool you down, won't it?" Raymond said. "And when you've had enough, you can climb back into the boat."

Billy nodded slowly. "I suppose so."

As he undressed, he was aware of Raymond watching, and he felt embarrassed by his body, so big and white and clumsy. He hurriedly stowed his T-shirt and jeans behind his seat, then, wearing nothing but a pair of Y-fronts, lowered himself backwards into the lake. He gasped with shock and pleasure as the water took hold of him. It was colder out here in the middle, far colder than he'd imagined.

He gripped the side of the boat with both hands, as Raymond had suggested. It wasn't easy. The wet plastic was smooth, slippery.

"It's fantastic, Raymond," he said in a voice made thin and breathy by the cold. "You should come in too."

"Why don't you swim?" Raymond said. "That's what the Roman emperors did."

"All right."

As soon as Billy let go, Raymond began to pedal away from him.

"Raymond?" he called out. "What are you doing?" The gap between Billy and the pedalo was widening, and he knew he had no chance of closing it. He'd never been much of a swimmer. "Come back."

Raymond was looking at him over his shoulder, but he was still pedalling.

"Please," Billy said. "I'm not joking."

The water in front of him had a terrible blackness to it, and he couldn't allow himself to think about what might be under there, or how deep the lake might be. His chest had tightened: he couldn't breathe properly. He stopped trying to swim, but treading water felt worse. He saw his body dangling, as if from below. It was the point of view of something that lived on the bottom — or something that had died.

His legs were moving in slow-motion; they were slender, feeble, pale as roots.

"Raymond! Please!"

Water poured into his mouth.

Gradually, the pedalo swung round until Raymond was facing him again, but Raymond's eyes had no light in them, no feeling. They looked flat, like bits of paper; if you poked one with a finger it would tear, and there'd be nothing behind the hole, just darkness.

Choking, Billy sank below the surface, then rose again and found some air. Thirty feet away, the boat sat on the lake. It seemed higher than Billy, as if the water had a gradient to it, as if it sloped uphill. The splashing sounds that he was making took place in a vast, bored silence, and would soon be swallowed by it.

Then, with a certain reluctance, Raymond started pedalling towards him. At last, Billy was able to grab hold of the side and haul himself back into the boat. Wrapping his arms around himself, he hunched over in the seat. Despite the heat, he was shivering.

"You bastard," he said in a low voice.

But Raymond was staring at the trees on the far shore. He appeared not to have heard.

"Bastard," Billy said again.

Raymond reached behind the seat for Billy's T-shirt. "Here. Put this on."

"What did you do that for?" Billy said. "I could have drowned."

Raymond smiled. "Let's go and get something to drink." He glanced over his shoulder, back towards the beach. "There was a little bar there. Did you see?"

The moment when Billy could have hit him was already gone. Instead, he lapsed into a sullen silence, hardly bothering to pedal, which meant that Raymond had to do most of the work. After a while, Billy began to feel as if he was the one in the wrong. That was the thing about Raymond. He had this uncanny knack of turning everything on its head. And before Billy knew it, gratitude was lifting through him. He was grateful to have been included in Raymond's new initiative, and for the hint of affection that he had detected in Raymond's voice. *Did you see?*

Looking at the shore, he noticed a wooden hut or kiosk set back in the shadow of the trees. Above the open hatch was a faded Campari sign. At the front, on the sand, were several benches and trestle tables, the wood buckled, silver-grey. Once they had hauled the pedalo out of the water, Raymond and Billy walked over to the hut where a man in a soiled white vest sold them two bottles of lemon soda. They both drank thirstily.

When they turned to go, three other men were standing on the beach, no more than fifteen feet away. They wore shabby, colourless clothing, and their faces were dark from the sun.

Raymond started speaking in Italian, but one of the men talked over him. He kept his eyes fixed on Raymond, though he seemed to be addressing the men behind him, and his voice sounded dismissive, contemptuous. Every now and then, he would punctuate his speech with abrupt, violent gestures that Billy didn't understand. Perhaps he and Raymond were trespassing — or perhaps the men owned that little boat . . . Though the man was still talking, Raymond had moved off along the beach, making for the path that led back up the hill. He kept his head down and walked quickly. Billy took one last look at the three men, then hurried after him.

Halfway to the path, Billy heard a sound behind him and turned round.

"Raymond?" he said in a shaky voice.

The three men had surrounded the man in the dirty vest, and they were punching him. Though it was happening about a hundred yards away, Billy could hear the blows — solid, weighty, dull, like somebody beating a carpet. As he watched, the man in the vest dropped to his knees, but the other men kept hitting him, taking it in turns. It was all amazingly slow and deliberate.

"Keep going," Raymond said.

But Billy was still hesitating. "Shouldn't we do something?"

"Don't be a fool."

Once they had entered the woods, Raymond spoke again. "They thought we were queer."

"What?" Billy's voice was almost shrill. "That's ridiculous." They were both panting as they climbed the hill, the sandy soil working against them now. Billy glanced over his shoulder. "Do you think they'll come after us?"

Raymond didn't answer.

When they reached the top, the cars were still there. The one on the right had its lights on, as before. It was at least two miles to the road, but Billy and Raymond had no choice. They began to walk.

A white crack showed briefly above the high ground to the south. Lightning. Billy counted the seconds, bracing himself for thunder. None came. But the air seemed to have thickened all around them.

They had only been on the track for a few minutes when Billy heard the cars. First one engine started, then the other. He sent Raymond a wild look. "It's them!"

Raymond didn't react.

With a cry, Billy plunged down a bank of stiff yellow grass into the undergrowth. He lay on his stomach and covered his head with his hands. The cars slowed down, as he had known they would. He heard Raymond's voice, then another voice. A man's. A door slammed. The cars both revved savagely, and then drove on.

When the sound of their engines had died away, Billy climbed cautiously back up the grass bank. The track was empty. Raymond had gone.

Panic and helplessness prevented him from doing anything at all for quite some time. The sky seemed to heap itself on top of him. Sweat stuck his T-shirt to his back. In the end, he realised there was nothing for it but to carry on towards the road. Certainly he wasn't about to go back to the lake. He would have to hitch a lift into the nearest town and report the incident to the police. It wasn't going to be easy because he didn't speak the language. He didn't know what the Italian for "car" was, for instance. He didn't even know the word for "man".

"Impossible," he said out loud.

His voice sounded weak in the harsh landscape.

As he trudged along, his mind began to fill with all kinds of scenarios. Raymond had been kidnapped — but what for? The men would rob him at the very least. He might be beaten up as well, or even killed.

Billy imagined Raymond's gangster hat lying upside-down on a deserted road.

Though it was starting to get dark by the time he reached the end of the track, it didn't seem any cooler. He stood still for a moment, trying to remember which way they had come. To his right, on a bend in the road, he saw a cluster of lights. It looked like a restaurant. Perhaps he would find help there.

When he pushed the door open, he saw Raymond sitting at a table by the wall, eating a pizza. Billy was so astonished that he couldn't speak.

Raymond glanced up. "You took your time." He was chewing with such relish that knots of muscle showed beside his ears. "Aren't you hungry?"

"Yes, but what happened?"

"I got a lift." Raymond laughed. "You didn't think I was going to *walk*, did you?" He drank from a tall glass, then reached for another slice of pizza.

"But the men — those men —"

"What men?"

"The ones on the beach."

It turned out that they hadn't been involved at all. The cars belonged to a group of young Romans who had been taking drugs in the woods. Raymond had flagged them down and then smoked a joint with them. They had stopped at the restaurant because they were starving.

190

"They only left about five minutes ago," Raymond said. "Jesus, this pizza's good."

Billy shook his head. "I'm such an idiot."

Raymond ordered another beer. The waitress had straight black hair and sallow skin, and her lips were a curious deep-purple colour, almost aubergine. There were dark rings under her eyes. Raymond watched her walk back across the restaurant, then he turned to Billy. "She looks like a vampire," he said, "don't you think?"

Still standing outside the hospital mortuary, Billy noticed a movement at the far end of the corridor. Not a drowned boy or a fish, but a figure in dark clothes. This would be one of his colleagues, he thought, coming to relieve him. He checked his watch. Yes, it was nearly four. Another break, and then just a couple of hours to go. He watched as the policeman passed through alternating areas of light and shadow, almost vanishing one moment, only to emerge seconds later, bathed in a glow that was subterranean, oceanic. There was something hypnotic about the man's calm progress, something almost eternal, and yet Billy felt separate from it, excluded. Like death looking at life.

Finally the constable stopped in front of him. "Not late, am I?"

"No, no," Billy said. "Right on time."

CHAPTER
TWENTY-NINE

On his way to the snack bar, images from that day by the lake in Italy still lingered. He couldn't remember what had happened after he walked into the roadside pizzeria. Had Raymond spent the night with that waitress? Billy had a vague memory of sleeping in a stuffy back room with all the cleaning equipment, and Raymond not being there, Raymond being somewhere else . . .

As Billy passed a toilet, the door opened and Phil Shaw appeared. His face looked chapped and blotchy. Probably he had been dowsing it in cold water, trying to keep himself awake.

"On your break, Billy?"

"I'm going to get a cup of soup," Billy said. "I think I saw some in one of the machines."

"Mind if I come with you?"

"Course not."

At that moment, a nurse darted round them and into a nearby ward. On reaching the doorway, which was open, they both paused, curious as to the reason for her haste. Illuminated by a single lamp, an old man was sitting up in bed and vomiting stringy yellow fluid down the front of his pyjamas. "Oh God," he gasped between oddly effortless bouts of retching. "God, bugger. Fuck." One of the nurses attending to him held a grey cardboard container below his chin. He vomited again. "Disgusting," he said. "This is bloody disgusting." Another nurse arrived with a fresh pair of pyjamas. Phil touched Billy on the shoulder, and the two men moved on.

They covered fifty yards without speaking, then Phil gave Billy a sideways look. "Still want that soup?"

CHAPTER
THIRTY

Phil was shaking his head. "You know, I never really understood it . . ."

Billy smiled. "There's nothing to understand."

"But you seem like such a natural for a sergeant."

"I just didn't want to be one. I still don't."

"What's wrong with being a sergeant?"

"I didn't say there was anything wrong with it." Billy blew on his black coffee to cool it down. He could feel Phil watching him. "Not everyone's ambitious," he said. "I like being on the streets, I suppose. Close to the ground. Where things happen."

"Even at your age?"

Phil was mocking him, but he was also making a serious point, which Billy took on board. "Well, we all burn out sooner or later," he said, "whichever route we take." He was thinking of Neil, of course. Neil who now lived above a launderette. Neil who claimed that there was nothing quite as soothing as drifting off to sleep to the sound of half a dozen giant tumble dryers.

"I still don't understand it," Phil said.

"This may disappoint you," Billy said, "but I'm just keeping my head down, to be honest. It's only a few years till I get my pension." He paused. "I've put a lot into the job — maybe too much. I need to start thinking about my family."

Phil held Billy's gaze for a moment longer, then nodded slowly and looked down into his coffee.

It was different for Phil, Billy thought. He'd only done ten years. He still had a taste for the work, and someone in that position would find it hard to imagine what it felt like to be coming out the other side.

"Do you remember the barbecue we had at your place?" Phil said after a brief silence. "We were out in the garden, and suddenly that old bloke who was riding down the track fell off his bike."

"Harry Parsons," Billy said. "He hit a stone or something."

"He went flying. Cut his head quite badly."

"We had to call the ambulance."

"The sausages all burned, remember?"

"And the chicken drumsticks. Sue had to get a meat pie out of the freezer."

"We drank a lot that night, didn't we?"

The episode had upset Billy. He would have gone to the hospital with Harry if the paramedics hadn't told him it wasn't necessary. Though Harry had never actually set foot in their house — modesty stopped him venturing beyond the back door — he was like a member of the family. If Billy ever had good news, Harry would be one of the first to know — and Harry had seen him at his lowest too . . . One night, not long after Emma was born, Billy was standing on the track behind his house when something seemed to reach down into him and wrench the tears out by force. He kept glancing at the bedroom window, afraid that Sue might hear. Then a piece of the darkness near him shifted and came loose, and a voice said, "Is that you, Billy?"

"Yes," he managed. "Yes, it's me."

In good weather, Harry often sat up late in the allotments. He had his own shed and a couple of folding chairs. As he'd admitted to Billy once, he didn't have much to go home to.

"Are you all right?" Harry said.

"I think so," Billy said. "More or less."

"I was just sitting here, having a beer." The dark air flooded in around Harry's voice, seeming to cushion it. "Would you like a beer, Billy?"

"Yes," Billy said. "Thanks. That'd be great."

"I think there's one here somewhere . . ."

As Harry rummaged for a beer, Billy stepped closer. The apex of the shed's roof showed black and sharp against the sky. Harry pushed a cool can into Billy's hand and set up the other chair for him.

"That's clever of you, Harry, keeping a drink out here."

"Well," Harry said, "you've got to, haven't you?"

They sat side by side in the darkness. The beer tasted metallic, almost rusty, as if it had been made not from hops but from bits of old machinery.

"Sue asleep, is she?"

"I hope so."

To keep the birds away, Harry had hung CDs from horizontal canes. When the air stirred, they would fidget, knocking and clicking against each other.

Sometimes one of them glinted silver as it twisted on its string. After a while, a train clattered past.

"They go all the way to Liverpool Street, those electric trains," Harry said. And then, sometime later, "When my wife died, I couldn't stop crying for a month."

Pinching his eyes against the glare of the snack-bar lights, Billy sighed, then took a sip of his black coffee.

"Is he still alive?" Phil asked.

"Harry?" Billy said. "Yes, he's doing well. He still comes up to the allotments, even when it's raining. He's growing delphiniums again this year. He loves delphiniums."

"Good for him."

"When me and Sue got married, we invited Harry to our wedding. He came instead of my father. I'd never seen Harry in a suit before. Usually, in the summer, he just wears trousers and braces and a flat cap, and he'll have chalky stains all over him from the talcum powder he puts on after he has a bath. The suit, though. It was brown tweed, stiff as cardboard — and he'd stuck one of his own nasturtiums in his buttonhole. You know what my best man, Neil, said? 'Who's the scarecrow?' " Billy smiled at the memory.

"Instead of your father?" Phil said.

"What?" Billy said. "Oh right — well, I couldn't have invited him. I didn't know where he was."

Phil watched him across the rim of his paper cup.

"I never knew my father," Billy went on. "He left before I was born."

Shaking his head, Phil looked down at the table.

"He was a musician," Billy said, "you know?"

"That's no excuse."

Billy was tempted to ask Phil why his wife had walked out on him, and whether he was happier since she had gone — at four-fifteen in the morning, in these extraordinary circumstances, he might have got away with it — but in the end he thought Phil probably had enough on his mind without him adding to it.

"When all this is over," Billy said, "you should come round. I know Sue would like to see you."

Phil nodded, fine wrinkles multiplying at the edges of his eyes. "I'd like that."

Shortly afterwards, he was called to the control room in reception, leaving Billy in the snack bar by himself. Billy drained his coffee, wincing at the bitterness, then he threw the cup in the bin and started back to the mortuary.

CHAPTER
THIRTY-ONE

Billy was Glenn Tyler's second child. Charlie was the first, born five years earlier, in 1951. According to their mother, Glenn had been away at the time, touring America, and didn't set eyes on Charlie until he was eight months old, his sole contribution being the name — Charlie for Charlie Parker, of course. With Billy, it was different. Glenn had no record to cut, no live dates booked. There was no reason not to be there, which must have put the fear of God into him. He left two months before the birth, and this time he didn't even bother to suggest a name. Maureen had her new baby boy christened "William Douglas", after her maternal grandfather, whom she adored.

Glenn came back to Weston once, when Billy was seven. Billy had no memory of anything his father said or did that day, or even of what he looked like. It had been sunny, and his father had parked across the street, the powder-blue Cortina standing out against the curved white wall of the pub. He wore boots with pointed toes and pieces of elastic in the sides. A car, a pair of shoes — and that was it. His father who had returned, but without any warning, and just for the afternoon. "He only ever thinks of himself," Maureen said afterwards, on more than one occasion. "Does as he pleases. Always has."

Gathering his reports together, Billy slid them back into the folder. He didn't think he would be doing any more paperwork before he went home. He held his Thermos over his cup and shook it. Three drops — not even enough to cover the bottom. He swallowed it anyway, then put the flask and cup into his bag, along with the folder. Back in his chair, he leaned forwards, elbows on his knees, and stared down into the drain. He had only seen his father one other time, but that was ten years later, and his father never even knew.

Some weeks short of his eighteenth birthday, Billy saw a fly-poster on a wall in Liverpool, advertising live jazz at the Iron Door on Seal Street. THE GLENN TYLER SEXTET, it said in bold black capitals. Then, in smaller letters, ONE NIGHT ONLY! He stood quite still and waited for his heart to slow down. The wind, briny and cold, pulled at his coat, his hair. Glenn Tyler . . . That had to be his father, didn't it? Surely there couldn't be two Glenn Tylers who played jazz. Not yet knowing what he was going to do, he wrote the details down on a scrap of paper, which he folded and pushed to the bottom of his trouser pocket. He didn't say a word about it to his mother. As for Charlie, he was in London, at medical school, and wouldn't be home till Christmas.

When the night arrived, Billy told his mother he was having a drink with an old schoolfriend who had heard about a job. It was only a month or two since he had returned from his holiday in Europe with Raymond, and he was still living at home. He hadn't yet decided what course his life should take. He knew he needed to earn money, though. His mother had to work hard to make ends meet — she was employed as a pharmacist, in Boots — and he wanted to be able to give her something for his keep.

The band appeared on stage at nine o'clock. There were five men, all middle-aged, all white, but Billy couldn't see anyone who looked like his father, and his stomach felt hot, as if he might be about to vomit. The music had already been going on for several minutes when a man holding a saxophone emerged from the wings. Of course, Billy thought. *Sextet.* The man didn't so much as glance at the people who had come to see him: he simply lifted a hand in their direction. He was wearing a suit made of shiny silver material, with a black shirt underneath, and his dark hair was slicked back. Billy recognised him from a photo his grandma had shown him once, and also because if he narrowed his eyes he seemed to be looking at a taller, rangier version of Charlie. He felt sick again, but in a different way.

Standing against the wall, Billy fixed his gaze on the man in the silver suit. He didn't listen to the music, though he was aware of it as the hectic backdrop to his thoughts, which were halting and stilted. He noticed how the man launched into solos with his eyes closed, as if frightened of whatever was in front of him, and then, when the solo finished and he took the instrument from his mouth, his eyes opened again, and even though he was being applauded, the expression on his face was glowering, almost hostile, as if people couldn't possibly appreciate what he'd just played — or perhaps his resentment was aimed at the music itself, at his attempt to master it and his inevitable failure. Billy tried to see himself in the man — a feature, a gesture — but there was nothing obvious. At the same time, he knew he was looking at his father. He felt it somewhere deep down, a sharp tug in his guts.

At the end of the first set, the musicians put aside their instruments and occupied two tables near the stage. Cigarettes were handed round. A bottle of Johnny Walker appeared, and drinks were poured. There were two women sitting with his father. One wore a red cardigan that was cut low at the front, and her arm rested carelessly on his left shoulder. Even from across the room Billy could see her breasts lift when she breathed in. The other woman was dressed entirely in black.

Swallowing hard, he walked over to their table. He didn't say anything at first. He couldn't. His mouth felt numb, clumsy. The woman in black glanced up at him, but her face didn't change. She had arching eyebrows and dark wavy hair, and her teeth were as small and fragile as rice crispies. He cleared his throat.

"Mr Tyler?"

The name had never sounded so foreign to him — sour somehow, and thin, like lemon juice — and yet, in his everyday life, he used it all the time.

His father's face came up slowly, lazily, and he was slanting his eyes against the smoke from his own cigarette.

"What can I do for you, kid?"

"Nothing," Billy said. "I enjoyed the music, that's all."

"Thanks."

Billy held his hand out over the table. His father laid his cigarette on the edge of the ashtray, in a smooth groove, and they shook hands.

Father and son, Billy thought. Flesh and blood.

As he was turning away, he imagined he saw a glimmer of recognition in the look Glenn Tyler gave him. Up to that moment, Tyler had been playing the big man, casual, amused, not paying too much attention, but now his eyes seemed to tighten. No, it wasn't recognition exactly. More like uncertainty or wariness. Or even, maybe, curiosity.

"Hey, kid," his father said.

Was it the handshake that had affected him? Had he felt a vibration, a charge — a kind of resonance? Or was it Billy's face? Something visual he couldn't quite put his finger on. An echo of Maureen, the woman he had married and then abandoned . . .

Billy acted as if he hadn't heard. He was making for the door that led out to the street. He had seen all he wanted to.

"Hey!"

Billy kept on walking.

Outside, the rain was coming down in great blown sheets. A filthy night. Lowering his head, he began to run, like someone guilty of wrongdoing.

After half a mile he slowed to a walk and turned into a cobbled alleyway. He was soaking wet, and panting;

his throat burned. Cardboard boxes had been stacked against a wall of blackened brick. The back of a warehouse, by the look of it. Near by were several tall metal bins. The rain whitened as it dropped through the glare of a security light. Replaying the past couple of hours, he saw himself staring gormlessly at his father up on stage. He saw himself approach the table with the bland, blurred look of an idiot.

Hey, kid.

He went over to the closest bin and kicked it as viciously as he could. It toppled, then rolled into the middle of the alley. Rubbish spilled on to the cobble-stones. A bottle smashed. Not satisfied yet, not even remotely satisfied, he kicked another bin, but this one must have weighed more because it didn't move at all. Pain flared in his right foot, and he bent down, clutching the toe of his shoe. "Fuck," he said. "Shit." Rain dripped down into his eyes. He picked up a piece of glass, pushed his coat-sleeve back and drew the makeshift blade across the outside of his forearm. It was like a magic trick, blood conjured out of nothing.

He caught the last train out of Lime Street. From Runcorn station, it was a twenty-minute walk, most of it uphill. The rain had stopped, but the pain in his foot was worse, and by the time he neared his house he was limping badly.

His mother was still awake when he got in. She looked up from the book that she was reading, and the soft, delighted look she usually greeted him with was quickly replaced by one of alarm as she noticed the blood on his sleeve.

"What happened to you?" she said.

"I got in a fight," he said. "Someone came for me with a bottle."

"Oh, Billy . . ."

He pushed his shirtsleeve back and showed her.

"That's a nasty cut," she said.

"It was my fault. I said something I shouldn't have."

"Why on earth —"

"It won't happen again, Mum. I promise."

She sat at the kitchen table, and he stood beside her, at her shoulder, as she swabbed the wound with iodine. It stung so much that it brought tears to his eyes. Different tears from the ones he'd imagined.

"You really ought to have stitches," his mother said.

Billy told her it would be fine. "You've done a grand job," he said, and leaning down, he gave her a kiss on the top of her head.

"What about your friend?" she said. "Did you see him?"

"Yes. There wasn't any work, though." He winced as he shifted his weight from one leg to the other. "I think I've hurt my foot."

Their GP told him that he had broken three toes. He would tape them together, he said. Time would do the rest. "Just don't kick any more cars," he added, peering at Billy over the rims of his spectacles.

Billy grinned. "It was a dustbin, actually."

He showed his damaged foot to Charlie when he came home for Christmas the following week. Charlie explained that the only important toe on your foot was the big one. If you lost your big toe, you wouldn't be able to walk, he said. You might not even be able to stand up.

"So I broke something that doesn't matter?" Billy said.

Charlie just looked at him and smiled.

CHAPTER
THIRTY-TWO

This time she didn't startle him. He sensed that he could rouse her simply by letting his thoughts drift in a particular direction. When he turned to face her, he saw that she was wearing the lilac suit again. Her eyebrows were plucked, and brown lines had been drawn on in their place. On the table in front of her were two packets of cigarettes. She must be thinking of staying for longer than usual. She'd come prepared.

No, he wasn't startled, nor did he feel nervous. He had never appeared on TV, or on the front page of a national newspaper. The media were not in the habit of discussing his fate. He was an ordinary person, and yet her fame — her notoriety — had no impact on him.

"I'm ordinary too," she said, little puffs of cigarette smoke emerging with the words. "If I hadn't met him, I would have gone on being ordinary."

That was debatable, of course. But it was the first time she had referred directly to the man who had been her lover, her mentor, the man who was now serving a life sentence in Ashworth, a high-security prison for the criminally insane. He had outlived her, even though he had been on a hunger strike for the past three years, and was being force-fed through a tube. He had outlived her, even though he was the one who wanted to die. He wouldn't have been too happy when he heard the news.

"I've got a question for you," Billy said. "Another question."

Half an inch of ash teetered on the end of her cigarette. "Still no ashtray?" she said, looking round the room. "Oh well." She held her cigarette over the drain and flicked the filter with her thumb. The ash tumbled softly through the air and disappeared. she turned back to him again, her pencilled eyebrows raised, which gave her a raffish, faintly sarcastic air.

"Who did you love most?" he said.

"My mother." She hadn't given herself time to think. She hadn't needed to, perhaps. Either she had seen the question coming, or she had simply told the truth. She was still watching him, waiting to see how he would react to her answer, daring him to make something of it.

"What about your father?" Billy said.

"I don't want to talk about him."

Her father had been away fighting in the war until she was three. When he returned, she was sent to live with her grandmother. Later, crippled by an accident at work, he became a drinker, moody and violent.

"Your mother . . ." Billy nodded slowly. "I thought you might say that."

"You don't believe me?"

He looked away. It wasn't that he didn't believe her. It was just that the answer seemed predictable. He had somehow known that she wouldn't be able to admit to loving the man with whom she'd committed those atrocities, the man whose name was now linked eternally, inextricably, with hers. From a distance of thirty years, she would have found that love hard to credit, let alone acknowledge. She would have had to call it something else — something less idealistic or more extreme. An obsession. A madness. She might even have blotted it out altogether. The knee-high boots and miniskirts. The nickname he had given her. The sado-masochistic sex. What's more, she'd probably been in love with people since. That fellow inmate, for instance, the one who was a singer — and there were rumours of affairs with prison guards as well. The love she remembered, though, was the one that came first. A daughter's love. He tried to imagine the woman as a little girl, but it made him feel uncomfortable. It was as if he were placing her on the same footing as her victims; it seemed insensitive at best, at worst a kind of violation. Yet there must have been a time, mustn't there, when she was innocent? People didn't want to think about that, of course. There was one image of her in the popular mind — the dyed-blonde hair, the brooding gaze — and that was it. There was no before, no after. No childhood, and no old age. Those photos taken in various prisons over the years — who were they supposed to fool? All those different hairstyles. That wasn't her . . . And as he sat there at the table it suddenly occurred to him that he had never seen a picture of her as a child, not even one. Didn't her mother have any? If not, what had happened to them? Had they been suppressed? Destroyed? It was a strange absence, unsettling, almost unjust, though he thought he understood the need for it.

"What about you?" the woman said.

He brought his eyes back to her again. She was always turning the tables on him — or trying to. The result, perhaps, of half a lifetime of being questioned by parole boards, psychologists, criminologists and priests . . . If she temporarily deflected attention away from herself, she would have time to marshal her thoughts, to dissemble, to conceal. Or perhaps she was simply brighter than he was. After all, she did have a degree from the Open University, which was more than he would ever have.

"Who did you love most?" she said, her face seeming to tighten around her cigarette as she inhaled.

"I'm not dead," he said.

"So far, in your life" — and she drew the words out, mocking him for being so pedantic — "who did you love most?"

He could have said his mother too, but that didn't seem to be the point of the question. At the same time, he felt he ought to be quick, like her. The answer wouldn't come, though, and the longer he hesitated, the more difficult it became. He ought to know, surely. He shouldn't have to think.

"Oh dear," the woman said. She had a triumphant smile on her face, a smile that was almost lascivious, as if it excited her to identify weakness and uncertainty in others. "Maybe I should help you," she said, "by mentioning a few names."

"Like who?"

"Venetia."

"No." He shook his head. "No, you're wrong."

"You were mad about her. Anyone could see that."

"It wasn't love. It was —"

"You worshipped her. You would have done anything —"

"Shut up a minute, will you?"

Her look of triumph returned. He had shouted. Lost control.

"You're not giving me a chance to think," he said. "All this talking, all these questions."

"Oh?" she said. "And whose idea was this?" She leaned over and dropped her cigarette into the drain. "I don't know why I'm asking, really," she said, straightening up again, her face a little flushed. "I already know the answer."

"What is it, then?" If Billy sounded defiant, it was only because he was without resources; it was pure bluster.

"Raymond," she said, looking off to one side, as though it was so obvious, so plain for all to see, that she didn't even have to meet his gaze. "Raymond Percival."

Billy let out a brief, explosive laugh, but even as he was ridiculing the idea, he saw Raymond walking ahead of him towards the reservoir, his bare back in shadow, his skin as cool and pale as peeled fruit.

"You followed Raymond everywhere," the woman went on. "You did everything he said." She lit another cigarette. She took her time. "You were so *obedient*. Even dogs aren't that obedient."

He shook his head, but knew that it was true.

"The way you looked at him sometimes. The thoughts you had. You never actually put them into words, but they were there, weren't they?" She broke off to inhale. "You behaved just like a bloody girl," she said, then laughed bitterly. "I should know."

He stood up quickly, the legs of his chair screeching on the tiled floor. His face was burning. He could feel her watching him to see what he would do next. She was feasting on his embarrassment, his shame.

"The way you looked at him," she said.

Turning to face the mortuary doors, he noticed a wedge-shaped gash at about waist-height. The door-frame was varnished wood, but the dent was sufficiently deep to reveal the wood's true colour, palest yellow, not unlike unsalted butter. He touched it with his fingertips, feeling the sharp edge, the cleft. A porter had misjudged the width of the trolley he was wheeling, or a funeral director had been too cavalier with a coffin. You'd think someone could have repaired the damage, though; it wouldn't have taken much.

Now he knew why it seemed familiar, this rough-and-ready space, so stark and practical, and so neglected: it was like all the places he had rented when he first left home, places he had shared with strangers, or else lived in by himself.

"I love my wife and daughter most," he said.

He was silent for a moment, his fingers still touching the damaged door-frame.

"My daughter," he said.

"Well," she said, and her voice was rasping and dismissive, "I suppose you got there in the end."

212

CHAPTER
THIRTY-THREE

Three months ago, in August, there had been a night when he had woken suddenly. Not sure what had disturbed him — a noise? a dream? — he went to the bedroom window and looked out. Darkness filled the garden. To his right was the cornfield, its contours barely visible. He could see how it sloped upwards from right to left, though, and how it curved down again as it approached the woods. How, like a wave, it gathered itself and then appeared to break. But why had he woken? As he peered out into the field, something glinted, and he knew at once that Emma was there. She must have turned her head, the lenses of her glasses catching what little light there was. She had wandered out of her bedroom before, many times, but she'd never left the house. They were always careful to lock up at night. This time they must have forgotten, or else she had managed to open one of the doors herself — and yet she wasn't usually capable of such initiative. Should he call out? No, that might startle her. He should go down, though — and quickly. If she went beyond the confines of the field, it could be dangerous. In the woods, he would never find her — and then there was the road. It was very straight, and people always drove too fast. He turned from the window.

"Who's that?" Sue called out from the bed.

"It's only me, love," he said. "Go back to sleep."

He hurried out of the room and down the stairs, stopping by the back door to pull on a pair of wellingtons. At the side of the house, he paused again. The night smelt musty, thrilling. Cow parsley, fox fur. The breath of owls.

Pushing through the long grass at the far edge of the track, he stumbled into the remnants of a wire fence. His T-shirt snagged on a post as he climbed over. He freed it and then stood still. There she was, about fifty yards away, the dark shape of her head and shoulders showing above the corn.

He began to walk through the field. "Emma?"

She swung round, her head at an angle. She seemed curious, or even sceptical, as if he were a second-rate magician and she was intent on seeing through his tricks.

"Daddy," she said, "what are you doing?" She sounded surprised, but also disapproving.

He came to a halt a few feet from her. At times she appeared so sure of herself that she completely wrong-footed him. He had imagined that she might feel disorientated, even scared, and that he would lead her back to the safe haven of her bedroom. As often happened, though, she saw things differently. In her eyes, he was the hopeless one, the one who was out of place. He was the one who needed help.

"I came to look for you." He didn't sound very convincing, even to himself. He had already taken on the character she'd given him.

She extended an arm in front of her and drew it in a slow, majestic semicircle through the air. "Night," she said, as if she owned it. As if, without her to tell him, he might not have known what it was called.

"It's very late," he said. "You should be asleep."

She muttered a few rebellious words, which he didn't quite make out, then steered a look towards the woods, her jaw jutting and determined, like an explorer preparing to strike out into uncharted territory. Billy glanced back at the house, but there was no sign of Sue. He would have to do this alone.

"Where's Parsons?" Emma said.

"He's at home in bed," Billy said, "like everybody else."

He looked away in case she noticed he was grinning. He was just thankful that she was there, that she was all right, that she was herself — so indisputably, uniquely, herself. What if he hadn't woken? Who knows where she might have ended up. She didn't realise that bad things could happen. She had no fear. He had to feel it for her. In the last days of 1999, when he climbed up on to that deserted moor, he had imagined a man leading a boy along a shallow gully. He had been able to see it all, almost as if it were happening in front of him — two figures walking away, hand in hand, one in a dark coat, the other in shorts — and in that moment he had thought of Emma and how vulnerable she was. She was even more trusting. She knew even less. She wouldn't have had the first idea. That was what he had thought, and then he'd felt awful, because Emma was still alive . . .

After several failed attempts, he finally managed to lure her back into the house with the promise of a midnight feast. Once she had devoured her biscuits and chocolate milk, he tucked her in and kissed her on the forehead. She had to go to sleep, he told her. He would see her in the morning.

"Sing," she said.

Though tired, his grin returned. Not for nothing did he call her "Captain" — or even, sometimes, "Chief Inspector".

He sang a few numbers from musicals to start with — *Mary Poppins* and *West Side Story* — he followed those with a medley of his all-time favourites, including "You've Lost That Lovin' Feeling", "Waterloo Sunset", "Massachusetts", and "Help Me Make It Through the Night". He even sang songs he didn't know he knew, songs they used to play in tacky Greek and Spanish discos when he was young: "Una Paloma Blanca", "Sweet Caroline", and "Lady in Red". He went on singing long after Emma had fallen asleep. He was singing because he was worried. He was singing because he was relieved. He sang until his voice hurt, then he kissed Emma one last time and crept back across the landing. As he pulled off his wellingtons, he noticed that Sue was awake. He could see a glint on the pillow where her eyes were.

"You're a dark horse," she said.

His heart beat high in his throat. Had he let something slip? What had she found out?

"All these years we've been together," she said, "and you never told me you liked Neil Diamond."

She could still make him laugh, even at half-three in the morning.

"I don't like Neil Diamond actually," he said as he slid beneath the duvet.

"Liar," she said.

He held on to that fragment of conversation. He would go back over it when he was parked down by the river, setting it against all their anxieties and disagreements, wanting it to weigh more.

You're a dark horse, he would say to himself as he turned the car around and started for home.

Or, *Liar*.

CHAPTER
THIRTY-FOUR

Venetia, though. Nothing had prepared him for the effect that she would have on him. Even her name. It was unlikely, expensive — the sort of name one of Raymond's girlfriends might have. Born to a Scottish father and an Indian mother, she had spent most of her childhood in Glasgow, only moving to Liverpool when she was fourteen, and her voice had something of both cities in it, with the lilt or rhythm of Bombay underneath. Three ports, one voice. Was it the sound of her that he fell in love with? Perhaps. But the sight of her, on Lacey Street, was enough to bring him to a standstill. For a few seconds, he forgot to breathe. Her hair so black and shiny that he could almost see himself in it. Her eyes as well. Her skin was dark too, but also lemony, somehow, as if yellow had been overlaid with a patina of translucent black.

Venetia McGarry.

The first time he saw her, she was driving a white Ford Fiesta. She had pulled up at the junction with Victoria Road and was signalling right. She looked him in the eyes, but only for a moment, then she leaned forwards in her seat to see whether anything was coming. She had a bald tyre, he noticed. Front left. For some reason, he didn't book her, though; he simply stepped back from the kerb so she could look beyond him. Once she had established that the road was clear, she smiled at him, and he waved an arm out sideways, meaning not just that he was letting her go first, but that she should go with his blessing. The whole incident lasted fifteen seconds at the most, and though he thought about her on and off for the rest of the day, he certainly never expected to run into her again.

When he saw her the second time, in a pub in Liverpool, more than six months had passed, and she had no memory of ever setting eyes on him before, not even when he told her exactly what had taken place and where. She was surprised that he remembered it all in such detail. Flattered too. Later, she said that although she found his story extremely convincing she didn't believe it, not for a moment. She assumed he was making the whole thing up. Though that, in itself, was quite charming, she thought. Romantic even. That he should go to the trouble of inventing a previous encounter. Not at all the kind of chat-up line she was used to. Spooky that he'd guessed the colour of her car, though. What was he? A mind-reader? Giving her an ambiguous smile, he looked away. Had he not remembered seeing her and been able to describe it, had he not been equipped with that memory, it was quite possible that nothing would ever have happened between them. As it was, he could turn back to her and tell her something else: her front left tyre had hardly any tread on it.

"It was illegal," he said, "but I decided to let you go."

"Wasn't that dangerous?" she said.

And with those words something began.

Three months on, when it was all over, he couldn't rid himself of the suspicion that she had remembered more than she had led him to believe. That morning in Widnes, as she looked through her car window, she would have noticed the uniform he was wearing. The idea could have occurred to her there and then. Not that she necessarily thought she would run into him again. Someone *like* him, though. A *policeman*. But if that was true, it undermined every moment they had spent together, and no matter how sceptical he felt, or how bitter, he couldn't bring himself to admit that the entire relationship might have been a sham. It was just too much to lose.

Billy had gone to Paradise Street with Neil Batty, and when Neil left the pub at around nine, he started talking to Venetia, who was sitting at the next table. She had friends with her — Simon, her flatmate, and Beryl, who was on the dole — and after a while the four of them went upstairs. On the first floor was a bar that had a pool table. Something by the Specials was playing as they walked in, Terry Hall's voice floating high above a typically nervy but hypnotic beat. Venetia was drinking Southern Comfort on the rocks. He was captivated by her, but paralysed; as in a dream he felt that if he reached for her she'd always be an inch beyond his fingertips. All he could do was gaze at her when she wasn't looking. He couldn't understand why everyone wasn't gazing at her. She was that gorgeous. Then, without any warning, she moved towards him through the smoke-filled air, and suddenly she was up against him, sideways-on, like a conspirator, and he felt a heavy object drop into his jacket pocket.

"That's for you," she said.

Off she went again, with her long hair pouring down her back and her double Southern Comfort on the rocks. Halfway across the bar, she turned and smiled at him over her shoulder.

Christ.

He fell in love with her right then — or was it moments later, in the privacy of the Gents, when he reached a hand slowly, tentatively, into his pocket and watched it emerge with the black ball from the pool table?

The most important ball in the game. The one that's worth more than all the others. The difference between winning and losing.

"Where the fuck's the black?" a man yelled.

Nobody knew. The ball had disappeared.

It was a mystery.

The second he took that ball out of his pocket he knew what it meant: she had decided she was going to sleep with him. His heart jerked, as if his body had been speeding and he had just stamped on the brakes, and he stayed in the Gents for longer than he needed to. He was putting off returning to the bar, delaying the look that would surely pass between them, and the understanding they would have.

But nothing happened that night. In fact, nothing happened until the following Tuesday, and even as she left his flat on Wednesday morning she told him not to get used to anything because it might not happen again. Her life, she said, was complicated enough already. Though disappointed, wounded too, somehow he had seen this coming. He knew he was lucky to have been with her at all, and he was already grateful for the little he'd received. At the outset, then, she learned a couple of things about him: one, he didn't feel that he deserved her, and two, he was entirely at her disposal.

She would visit his flat. He was never allowed to visit hers, though. She didn't want her friends to see them together. She wouldn't meet his friends either. She gave him her phone number, but didn't tell him where she lived. She didn't let him take any pictures of her and wouldn't even go into a photo booth with him; she didn't want their relationship recorded. What went on between the two of them was to remain private, secret. Hidden. If the world found out, pressure would be brought to bear on them, and that, she said, would be the end of it. He did his best to abide by her rules, but as the weeks went by it began to seem unnatural, stifling, even cruel. When he tried to tell her how he felt, she interrupted.

"Look, this isn't *serious*," she said. "We're just having fun."

He nodded gloomily. Fun.

Once, in early March, she let him take her away for the weekend. To spend two consecutive nights and days with her was unheard of, but even as he counted his blessings he knew the weekend would never be repeated, so his mood as they drove up the motorway that Friday evening was one of thinly disguised despair.

It was late when they arrived at the hotel, and the bar was already closed. Luckily, Venetia had brought some champagne with her. After the long drive north, he needed a drink, but the simple act of following her into an unfamiliar room excited him so much that he had to make love to her immediately, before they could even open the bottle. In the past, she had always insisted on having the lights off and the curtains closed, as if she belonged to a different generation, another time. That night, though, they did it with the TV on, and he could see her as she lay beneath him on the quilted counterpane, her narrow, boyish hips, her thin legs, almost stick-like, and her surprising breasts, which were out of proportion to the rest of her. Her body seemed more voluptuous than usual, in fact, and he wondered if she was having a period, but when he was inside her, it didn't feel like it. Afterwards, she smeared his sperm over her nipples with the tip of her forefinger. "I like the feeling when it dries," she said. "It goes all tight." And he was so tired and dreamy that he barely noticed this veiled reference to previous experience, other men.

Rousing himself at last, he popped the cork on the champagne and poured her a glass. Later, he sat on the floor beside her while she had a bath. From the bedroom came the lurid, almost delirious soundtrack of a Hammer horror film. When she stretched out in the water, with her head resting against the side of the bath nearest to him, her black hair hung over the edge, and he touched the ends of it without her knowing. Violins played a high, thin note. A woman screamed, then screamed again. Venetia's hair balanced on the palm of his hand like something standing upright. He still thought she was holding back — even in that moment, when he seemingly had everything he could possibly have hoped for. Was she just too lavish for him? Or was she only giving a part of herself, the least she could get away with? Even before that weekend, he had started hoarding items that belonged to her — lip salve, nail varnish, a pair of laddered tights. She didn't notice: she was always losing things. He even kept some split ends that she had cut off in his bathroom when she was drunk one night. If she had known that he had some of her hair in a plastic film canister, and that he opened it from time to time and smelt it, she would probably have called him a weirdo and left him on the spot. But he was only trying to fill the gaps, get closer. *We're just having fun*. He didn't want it to be fun. He wanted it to be for ever.

Waking early the next morning, he turned in the bed and ran his right hand over the curve of her hip and down between her legs. She leaned sideways and took something from her bag on the bedside table. At first he thought she was going to pass him a condom, but then he saw her fit a mask over her eyes. The mask was beige, with the words AIR INDIA on it.

"You're not going to wear that, are you?" he said.

"Yes," she said coolly. "Do you mind?"

Though startled, he could already envisage the erotic possibilities — how her blindness might give him licence. "Well," he said, "if that's what you want . . ."

After they had finished making love, she told him that he had gripped her so tightly when he came that

224

she felt as if he had somehow reached through her skin, all seven layers of it, right into her muscles, even her bones, as if he had penetrated her body all over, and not just in the one place.

"I didn't hurt you?" he said.

"No," she said. "I liked it."

Later that morning, they walked along a short stretch of the Pennine Way. As he stared off into the distance, the shadows of clouds blue-black on the smooth sides of the fells, he asked her about the eye-mask. What was it exactly, he said, that she didn't want to see?

"I'm shy," she said.

He laughed. "You? Shy?"

She was standing knee-deep in rough grass, a piece of saxifrage in the palm of her hand.

"What are you afraid of?" he asked.

"I'm not afraid."

"Is it me?"

Her hand closed over the small white flower, and she gave him a look that came at him straight and level. "It's nothing to do with you."

This was both succinct and ambiguous — was she telling him not to overestimate his own importance, or was she trying to reassure him? — but he also sensed a kind of shakiness or trepidation, and he knew he'd stumbled on something that might help him to explain her. She wouldn't elaborate, however, and he decided not to press her. Instead, he took her hand, which he would never have dared to do if they hadn't been the only people for miles around. She affected not to notice, but he thought her fingers tightened around his.

Rare though they were, such moments gave him hope: in time, perhaps, she might go a little easier on him . . .

That evening they drank pints of Guinness in the hotel bar, served by a man from the Midlands. In his early forties, with a gold tooth and a wicked tongue, he was soon making Venetia laugh with tales of local scandal, and Billy saw that for all the intimacies of the past twenty-four hours he had no hold over her, no claim whatsoever.

At dinner Venetia took charge of the wine list, ordering a white to go with their starters, then switching to red for the main course.

Billy shook his head. "It's amazing, the amount you drink."

"It must be the Scottish side of me," she said. "My father —" She checked herself. "I'm not sure I should tell you."

What he learned that night would alter him for ever. Certain stories lodge like rusty hooks in the soft flesh of the mind. You cannot free yourself.

Sitting in the mortuary with his eyes shut, Billy heard the rasp of a lighter.

"You'd know all about that, of course," he said.

CHAPTER
THIRTY-FIVE

His eyes still closed, he saw the woman not in lilac or maroon, not in a suit at all, in fact, but in a kind of gown. Shapeless it was, and hooded. Brown or black.

"They'll never forgive me, will they," she said, "not even now I'm dead?"

"No," he said. "I don't think they will." He paused, and then decided that he might as well tell the truth. "It's strange, but I think people hate you even more now. It's like what you did has got worse with the passing of time — or maybe it's taken this long for the full horror of it all to sink in."

She fell silent, as if the idea hadn't occurred to her before. At times, he wasn't sure whether she was still there, but then he would hear a swift, sharp intake of breath as she inhaled, or the faint scrape of a shoe against the floor as she altered the position of her legs. Though he was in danger of falling asleep, he resisted the temptation to open his eyes. He didn't want to see her again. He had already seen enough of her, he felt, to last a lifetime.

"Sometimes I dream I'm standing in a crowd," she said at last, "or else I'm walking along, surrounded by hundreds of people. I don't know any of them. They're

227

all strangers. But it feels like — like luxury." There was another silence. He imagined a cigarette butt falling in slow-motion through the air and vanishing between two bars of the drain's dark metal grille.

"To be part of a crowd," she said. "You don't know how I long for that."

"They'd probably tear you to pieces," he said.

"In my dream, no one recognises me. They've never heard of me. They don't notice me at all."

"You did something people couldn't bring themselves to think about. You forced them to imagine it. You rubbed their noses in it."

That was what they meant, he realised, when they called her a monster. She had shown them what a human being was capable of. She had given them a glimpse of the horrific and terrifying acts that lay within their grasp. She had reminded them of a truth that they had overlooked, or hidden from, or lied to themselves about.

"That's why they can't forgive you," he said. "I mean, maybe if you'd broken down in court —"

She let out a short, sardonic laugh. "I'm not a bloody actress."

"They needed *something*."

"They wouldn't have believed me."

He thought about that. Over the years, there had been a number of people who had taken her side. They saw her continuing imprisonment as political, driven not by the rule of law but by popular opinion. Other murderers were freed when they had served their sentences — why not her? Clearly, she was no danger to society. In fact, the opposite was true: were she to be released, society would be a danger to her. And here was the savage irony: taxpayers' money would have to be used to protect the woman from what the taxpayers themselves would try and do to her. No government would willingly put itself in the position of having to defend such a policy. Instead, the responsibility for her fate was handed swiftly from one Home Secretary to another, like a particularly hazardous game of pass-the-parcel.

"You're probably right," he said. "I don't think there was any way back from what you did. They'd never have let you out, not in a million years."

"It already feels like a million years." He heard her light another cigarette. "I smoked myself to death," she said. "What else was I going to do?"

"You did make it worse for yourself, though," he said. "You made mistakes."

"Mistakes? What mistakes?"

"Afterwards, I mean. You said things you shouldn't have. To journalists."

He thought she might bridle at that, but she kept quiet.

"And that picture they took of you when you got your degree," he said, "the one that appeared in the papers."

"What about it?"

"You shouldn't have smiled."

"So now I'm not allowed to smile . . ." She sounded crestfallen, even defeated, but when she spoke again, a few moments later, her voice had all its old bluntness. "And you," she said, "are you so innocent?"

CHAPTER
THIRTY-SIX

Billy went over to the stainless-steel sink in the corner and brought handfuls of cold water up to his face. He had been honest with her, brutally so, and she had put up very little resistance, though she had hit back towards the end, when he was least expecting it, but now that she had gone, he was left with an uneasy feeling. He'd talked too much. He hadn't listened. He hadn't paid attention and, as a result, he felt there was something he had failed to understand. He turned off the tap, then tore off a couple of paper towels and dried his face and hands. Failure, he thought. Firstly, she had failed to realise what she was getting into. Then she had failed to object, to disassociate herself. Something was lacking in her, and it had made her lethal. *But what about me?* he thought as he dropped the sodden paper towels in the bin. *Am I so innocent?*

Almost twenty years had passed, but he could still see Venetia sitting across from him in that prim, drab hotel dining-room in the North Pennines.

"If I tell you —" Venetia said, then stopped.

"What?" he said.

"It might change everything . . ."

"You decide."

She took a breath and then began. When she was a little girl, she said, she hardly saw her father. He was always off somewhere — at work, or out with clients, or travelling. She would long to spend time with him, fantasising endlessly about all the things they might do together. Grimacing, she tipped more wine into her glass. George McGarry was his name, she went on, and he was the chief executive of a shipping company — a man of great energy and charm, by all accounts. In his forties he married a lively but delicate woman from Bombay. They had two daughters. Margaret was four years older than Venetia, taller, and more reserved.

"I always felt she should have said something," and now Venetia looked away, into the room. "But I suppose it was asking too much. Besides, I probably wouldn't have believed her. I wouldn't have wanted to believe her."

Billy felt as if the contents of his stomach were beginning to go sour, and he reached for some water.

"I didn't really see my father until I was eight or nine," Venetia went on, "and then suddenly, from one day to the next, he seemed to realise that I existed. I couldn't have been more thrilled. This was my dream, and I'd almost given up on it. He started calling me V. V, darling. V, my sweet. He would pick me up after school and we would go to the cinema, or if it was summer we would drive out into the country. He had a beautiful car. A Daimler, I think it was — all soft leather and polished wood. It was like his work, the secret, glamorous side of him — the part of him I'd never been allowed to see."

She looked across the table at Billy, and the expression on her face was one he didn't recognise. She seemed to be pleading with him, but he wasn't sure what she wanted. To change the past, perhaps. Impossible, then. The look had a nearness about it too, a confidentiality, and for the first time, possibly the only time, he felt properly included in her life, and it hurt him in a way that was almost physical, both because of the unexpected beauty of the moment, and because he was certain that it wouldn't last.

"It keeps coming out wrong," she said. "Do you want me to go on?"

Staring down at the tablecloth, he nodded.

"Promise me something," she said.

"What?"

"Promise you won't feel sorry for me."

"If I feel anything," he said, "it won't be that."

Her face was drawn to the dark window. "The first time it happened, we were in his car. We had been to a museum, I think, but he took a different route home, and we ended up on a quiet road that ran through woods . . ."

One of her hands lay on its side on the table, the fingers curled. Her head, angled away from him, was absolutely still, as if the story she was telling was an animal that could be frightened off by even the slightest of movements.

"He parked the car, then turned and looked at me," she said, "and I thought he was going to talk about school, how I hadn't been doing very well, and I had all my excuses ready, but then I noticed that there was something in his eyes that I couldn't remember seeing before, something strange and glittery, and his breathing was noisier than usual. I could hear each breath, and when he spoke, his voice was husky."

She gazed down into her drink. Billy wanted to reach out, put his hand against her cheek or stroke her hair, but he knew it would be wrong to touch her.

"It was husky, almost as if he had a cold, or he was going to cry. 'You know I love you, don't you, V?' he said, and suddenly I didn't want him to call me V any more. 'Venetia,' I said. 'That's right,' he said. 'You're too grown-up for nicknames, aren't you?' He looked through the windscreen for a while, then he turned to me again. 'I love you so much,' he said. Then he said, 'Do you love me?' 'Of course I do,' I said. I wanted to come out with a joke and make him laugh, but his eyes still had that weird glitter, and the air in the car had gone all thick. 'Will you do something for me?' he said. 'Of course,' I said. And that was when he reached down and undid his flies . . ."

Her face was still lowered.

"It went on for six years," she said.

"Venetia," Billy said.

He couldn't say anything else. He felt, oddly, as if he was implicated in her father's behaviour, as if he was also guilty. Because he was a man, perhaps.

Fathers, though, he would think a few years later: they were like the poppies that appeared in the summer, so vivid against the new ripe yellow of the corn, so handsome, but if you pressed their petals between finger and thumb the red went black and wet.

Back upstairs, he lay next to Venetia on the bed and watched TV. He fell asleep without meaning to. When he woke, it was two-thirty in the morning and Venetia had gone, but there was a strip of light under the bathroom door, and he could hear a tap running.

"Are you all right?" he called out.

She didn't answer.

Leave her, he thought. *Let her be.* Throwing off his clothes, he climbed beneath the covers and was asleep again before she reappeared.

On Sunday, as they drove back to Liverpool, he asked her whether she ever saw her father. Sometimes, she said. On special occasions. Though he was quite ill now, with angina. He'd been put on a strict diet and wasn't allowed any excitement. Two months ago, on his seventy-first birthday, she had bought him the richest cake she could find. She thought that if he ate enough of it he might die. She cut him slice after slice, and because he loved her so much he kept on eating.

"It didn't work, though," she said. "He's still around."

Billy took his eyes off the road and looked at her. She wasn't joking.

After that weekend, things were different between them. He no longer felt sidelined or short-changed. He didn't see her for ten days, but he wasn't jealous of the time she spent away from him. He now had a sense of what he might be worth to her.

On the Wednesday evening, she rang his bell at half-past six. She was wearing a white blouse and a dark-grey pencil skirt, which told him she'd come

234

straight from work; she was temping at a firm of stockbrokers that month, and they insisted that she dressed conservatively.

"Whisky," she said, handing him a bottle of Famous Grouse. Then she held up a bag of ice. "Rocks."

As the drink took hold, they returned to the subject of her father. He had called recently, she said. Accused her of neglecting him. How could she be so inconsiderate, so heartless? Did she have no feelings for him whatsoever? In the end, she had to unplug the phone. If she'd let him go on any longer, he would have lost his temper — or else he would have started crying.

Towards midnight, they began to try and think of ways of killing him. Obviously they couldn't afford to be caught, nor did they want to incriminate themselves; it had to look natural, or like an accident — or, at the very least, like a crime that had no motive. What they were saying was so terrible that they got completely carried away, each attempting to outdo the other, their ideas becoming ever more lurid and unrealistic. At some point, though, Venetia's face went still, and she covered her mouth with one hand. She was looking at Billy's uniform, which hung on the back of the door.

"What is it?" he said.

"My father," she said. "He's always been afraid of the police." She paused. "You could do something."

"Like what?"

"You could frighten him, somehow," she said, her eyes on him now. "Frighten him to death."

To frighten someone to death. That was just a figure of speech, wasn't it? He wanted to laugh, but he could tell that she was serious.

Two days later, on a foot-beat in the centre of Widnes, he saw Raymond Percival. At first, he thought he must be imagining it. The man standing outside the Landmark had bleached hair, and he was wearing a long black coat, but when his head moved and the club's security light slanted across his face, there was no mistaking that superior, contemptuous expression. How long had it been? Eleven years? Twelve? And here he was, in Widnes of all places. He had some people with him, older, the women in high heels. As Billy approached, still not certain what to do, Raymond flicked his cigarette into the gutter. He didn't notice Billy — or if he did, he chose not to register the fact — and Billy kept on walking, his right hand almost brushing the back of Raymond's coat. He only stopped when he had turned the corner, and then, in the quiet of a dead-end street, he leaned against a wall. He thought of the slogan Raymond had quoted once, and said the words out loud: "Sexton's have solved the mystery of elegant living." Then, laughing, he looked up into the murky, grey-orange sky. He hadn't spoken to Raymond. They hadn't even exchanged a glance. Simply to have set eyes on him, though, after all these years! For Raymond to appear out of the blue like that at such a crucial time . . .

The following week, Billy called Venetia at work and asked where her father lived. She gave him the address.

"What are you going to do?" she said.

"I don't know yet," he said. "Maybe nothing."

He had to set her free, but wasn't sure how far he could go. There were so many factors to take into account. Sometimes he wondered what Raymond would have done in his position — Raymond who was always so confident, even when he was in the wrong . . . One thought, above all others, was ever present in the back of Billy's mind: no matter what he did, he would be unlikely to profit from it. In the long run, favours win you nothing but resentment. Gratitude's a double-edged sword.

One Saturday night, at about eleven, he let himself out of his flat. He was wearing a bomber jacket and a pair of jeans; the roll-bag in his right hand contained his uniform. It had rained earlier, but the sky was clearing. Clouds moving fast. He walked over to the next street, the bluish-white glow of TVs filling almost every front room. *Match of the Day* was on. In the gutter near his car was an umbrella blown inside-out, which made him think of the girl he and Neil had found in a club a few weeks back. She'd drunk too much and ended up on the toilet floor with her dress over her face. As he unlocked his car, he could hear people shouting in the distance. Some pub kicking out.

He drove over the Runcorn — Widnes bridge, its struts criss-crossing above his head. Once on the south side, there was almost no traffic. Sometimes a taxi would cruise past in the fast lane, men full of beer being ferried back to their four-bedroom houses after a day at the football or the races. He slowed for a roundabout, then followed the signs to North Wales.

The road was even emptier now. To the west, over the marshy fields, he could see flames burning in the tops of chimneys at the oil refinery. Twenty-five to twelve, and most of the clouds had blown away, though the weather-man was forecasting rain before morning.

He took a right turn, on to the A540. The smell of silage stole into the car. He was entering the Wirral, where Venetia's father lived, and a knot formed in his stomach. He switched the radio off; the voices were too warm, too reassuring. What he was about to do lay to one side of all that.

Beyond Heswall, Billy parked on an unlit lane and walked off into a copse with his bag. When he was hidden from the road, he quickly changed into his uniform. At home, he had removed his silver epaulette numbers and replaced them in a jumbled order, on the off-chance that McGarry made a note of his number and reported him. He doubted that anyone would think of checking officers as far afield as Widnes. Still, it was best to take precautions.

As he continued towards West Kirby, the houses fell away. At first, the land opened out into a kind of heath or common — a golf course wouldn't have looked out of place — but then high walls of gorse-studded rock closed in around the car. He turned left at a junction marked by an obelisk, the road doubling back on itself and looping down towards the river. The cul-de-sac where McGarry lived appeared on his right — he had memorised the address — but he drove beyond it, parking in a pub car-park at the bottom of the hill. Since he was in uniform, every action had to be carried out with absolute conviction and authority. He was on duty now. He was the law.

From the car-park a footpath led back up the hill. Trees dripping and creaking, uneven walls of ivy-covered brick. There were some steps, then the path narrowed. Billy emerged halfway along the cul-de-sac, with McGarry's house directly in front of him. His footsteps echoed as he crossed the street. To his left, a thin moon tilted above a steep slate roof.

McGarry's front door was on the right side of the house and set well back from the pavement. Billy didn't hesitate. As he started up the path, a high leylandii hedge screened him from the next-door neighbours, but he could still be spotted by the people living opposite. Not that they would be able to describe him. It was dark, and he was more than fifty yards away. Once people noticed a uniform, it tended to blind them to all sorts of other details. *A policeman*, they would say, and they might have some vague notion of his size or height, but that would be all. In any case, Billy's aim was not so much to come and go unseen as to conceal his actual identity. If a neighbour saw a policeman arrive, so much the better. It would put McGarry under still more pressure. After all, the police don't appear in the middle of the night unless it's serious. Were a neighbour to bring up the subject, casually, in conversation, McGarry would be unlikely to tell the truth. Given what Billy was about to say, he also doubted that McGarry would go to the authorities. If he did, he would only draw attention to the secret he had hidden successfully for so many years. In the end, then, having thought the whole thing through, Billy wasn't convinced that he would need an alibi at all.

He rang the bell twice, firmly, and stood back. He glanced at his watch. Twelve twenty-three. Somewhere in the depths of the house he imagined that he heard a click. He was about to ring again when a voice spoke from the other side of the door.

"Who is it? Who's there?"

The Scottish accent was unmistakable. Billy had come to the right house.

"Open the door," he said. "This is the police."

Not a sound from inside. Had McGarry's heart lurched at the mention of the word "police"? Was Billy's strategy already beginning to take effect?

At last a key turned in the lock, and the door opened, revealing an old man in a dark-red dressing-gown and leather slippers.

Billy took out his pocketbook and consulted a blank page. "Mr McGarry?" he said. "Mr George McGarry?"

"Yes?"

"I'm a police officer. I need to talk to you — in private."

"I was asleep."

"I'm afraid this can't wait." Billy stepped past him into the hall.

Once the old man had locked the front door again, he opened a door to his immediate left and switched on the light. Billy followed him into a library. Its many shelves were filled with non-fiction, mostly, and works of reference, but there was also evidence of McGarry's interests and accomplishments: paintings of racehorses

240

and battleships hung on the walls, and the mantelpiece was crowded with sporting trophies — rowing, tennis, golf — all of which McGarry seemed to have won himself. On the sideboard, flanking a glass case that contained a scale model of an ocean liner, were two photographs in silver frames, one of Venetia, the other of a girl who was fuller in the face, and lighter in colouring. This would be Margaret, the sister. Significantly, both pictures had been taken when the girls were much younger.

The old man was surveying Billy from a position just inside the door, the whites of his eyes visible below his pupils so that he appeared to be looking into the air above Billy's head, or at some judgement that might, at that very minute, be hanging over him. Of the energy and charm that Venetia had alluded to, there was no sign, illness and old age having taken their toll. His face was flushed, and the skin around his mouth and eyes was pouchy, loose, discoloured; he looked like what he was, a man in his early seventies with a bad heart. None of this was entirely unexpected. What Billy hadn't reckoned on — or even considered — was the family resemblance. When Venetia told him how her father had abused her, he had imagined a deviant, a pervert, someone who stood out from the rest of society, but this old man not only resembled any other old man you might see on the street or in a shop, he also resembled his daughter. *He looked like Venetia.* This bizarre similarity wrongfooted Billy for a moment, and he found himself wondering why Venetia hardly ever mentioned her mother. In that hotel in the North

Pennines, she had described her mother as "delicate", he remembered, and it occurred to him that Mrs McGarry must already be dead.

"Well?" the old man said. "What is it?"

The curt tone, a relic of McGarry's arrogance, gave Billy his ground back.

"Some allegations have been made against you," he said. "Some very serious allegations."

"Allegations? What allegations? What are you talking about?"

The old man turned and lowered himself into a nearby chair. He was avoiding eye contact and using too many words, which Billy interpreted as signs of unease, if not of guilt.

"Sexual abuse," Billy said, "of minors."

"*What?* How dare you!"

"We have it on good authority, Mr McGarry, that you've had sex with underage girls. You've been interfering with young girls —"

"Don't use those words in my house." Rising out of his chair, the old man seemed about to launch himself at Billy; white froth had gathered at the corners of his mouth. "This is my house. You're not using language like that in here."

"You never spared a thought for them, did you? You never *cared* about them. You only ever thought about yourself."

As always.

"Get out of here," the old man said.

Billy lowered his voice. "You're a child-molester, McGarry. You're a paedophile, a kiddy-fiddler. You're a nonce." He could feel all the words lining up now, ready to spill; he was almost smiling at how straightforward it was. "Do you know what happens to people like you in prison? Your life's a misery from the second you wake up to the second you go to sleep — if you dare to go to sleep, that is. You'll be praying for sleep, but you won't want to risk it. Because of what might happen while you're not looking. Sooner or later, everybody in there will find out what you are. The screws will see to that. Do you know what they do to people like you?"

"There aren't any people like me," the old man shouted hoarsely.

My God, Billy thought. He must have run through this scene a hundred times, but he had never imagined such defiance. For a moment, the room whirled, a surreal merry-go-round of horses, books, and silver cups. He walked over to the window and parted the curtains. The street was quiet. Hardly any lights on in the houses opposite. Nobody about.

"This is a nice area," he said, still looking through the window, "but I'm not sure how much longer you're going to be able to live here."

He had the eerie feeling that the old man might be about to attack him with a blunt object, and he quickly faced back into the room. Though McGarry's mouth was twitching and the skin under his eyes had turned a mottled whitish-grey, he was motionless, seeming to hang in the middle of the room, as if suspended, and Billy was reminded briefly of the incident in Weston

243

Point, the wild arcs of the walking stick, the bits of glass showering through the air.

"Everyone's going to find out what you did," Billy said, his voice still even, calm, "and when that happens, the past will count for nothing. All this" — and he glanced round at the paintings, the trophies — "all this will turn to shit. You'll be the scum of the earth from that point on — for ever. Your good name, if you've got one, will be dragged through the mud. The newspapers will take care of that.

"Even if you're proved innocent — which is a verdict I can't see myself — they'll never believe it," and he angled his head towards the bay window behind him, "not out there. The people out there will make your life hell because, for them, there's nothing worse than somebody like you." He paused. "No, not hell," he said. "Much worse than that."

"You can fuck right off." McGarry spat the words in his direction. "Fuck off out of here."

Billy felt an irresistible force propel him across the room until he was so close to the old man that he could smell the wet-hay smell of his breath.

"I don't think you've been listening to me, McGarry," Billy said through gritted teeth. "I'm going to have you. You're going to fucking pay." And he gave the old man a shove in the chest.

McGarry toppled backwards into his armchair. "That's assault," he said, but his voice had lost all its power.

"Well," Billy said, "you should know."

He was still standing over the old man, but the old man stared right through him. The dark-red dressing-gown had fallen open, revealing a triangle of thin, translucent skin, the white of the breastbone almost visible beneath.

"I don't feel very well," the old man said.

Billy left the room. Unlocking the front door, he let himself out. McGarry would never admit his own guilt. He was incapable of that. Still, at least someone had told him the truth . . . Billy stood under a streetlamp and checked his watch. He had been in the house for just eleven minutes.

He set off down the hill. The night smelled of the river. Above a cluster of black trees, the moon looked thinner, sharper. Climbing into his car, he fitted the key in the ignition. His actions felt heightened but claustrophobic; if he moved his hand, it seemed to leave staggered versions of itself in the air behind it.

After Heswall, he saw a farm off to the left. Dark windows, nobody awake. Parking his car, he walked until he found some bags of silage piled in the corner of a field. He began to hit the nearest bag, his fists slamming into the shiny plastic. He carried on punching until his arms felt slow and heavy, then he stood back, panting. There was a breeze now, and it had brought clouds with it. He waited for his breathing to calm down, then returned to his car and drove away.

When he had left the Wirral, he switched the radio on. News and sport. The weather. He kept thinking he could smell rotten vegetables. At some point, maybe, the bag containing the silage had split. He took his right hand off the wheel and brought it up to his nose. Oh God, that was awful. But he'd had to release some of his frustration. McGarry, though ... He still couldn't believe the fury — the *self-righteous* fury — of that old man. *How dare you. Fuck off out of here.* Perhaps the fact that he had woken from a deep sleep had insulated him from the shock he might otherwise have felt at Billy's appearance on his doorstep — or perhaps the defiance was a symptom of his fear.

Billy had been shocked by his own behaviour too. The words that had streamed out of him, the quiet, vicious threats. The air of menace. He'd been better at it than he'd imagined he would be, which wasn't an entirely comfortable thought. In going over certain aspects of the encounter, he had to keep reminding himself that he was the one who was in the right.

He didn't speak to Venetia for more than a week. He couldn't decide how much to tell her, what to say. When he finally called, her voice sounded smaller than usual, and flatter, and he knew right away that something had happened. She had some strange news, she said. Her father had died.

"What?" he said. "When?"

"I just heard."

She didn't say when exactly the death had occurred, and he didn't ask.

Still holding the phone, he looked out of the window. A woman was wheeling a pushchair down the middle of Frederick Street. Her child was clutching a brightly coloured plastic windmill, and Billy heard the spokes revolving in slow-motion, the sound as weighty and

246

liquid as a helicopter's rotor blades. He felt as if his head might float backwards into the room, leaving his body where it was.

"Well," he said at last, "I suppose it's what you wanted . . ."

Venetia didn't answer.

"Isn't it?" he said.

"I don't know."

"You don't know? Listen, I'm at home. Could you come over?"

"No. There's too much going on. The funeral . . ."

Frederick Street was deserted now. Turning away from the window, Billy stared out across his living-room. "Do you need anything?"

"Don't call me again," she said.

They didn't see each other for several weeks. At work, he seemed to be waiting for something without necessarily knowing what that something was. People kept asking him if he was ill. Once, he went to the pub on Paradise Street with Neil, but Venetia wasn't there.

"Remember the last time we came here?" he said.

Neil nodded. "I only had two pints. I had to leave early."

"There was an Indian girl sitting behind you."

"Indian girl?" Neil looked blank.

On the pretence of visiting the Gents, Billy checked the bar on the first floor. It was empty, but he saw that they had bought a new black ball for the pool table. He cupped it for a moment in his hand, then sent it rolling slowly down the table. He watched as it rebounded off the far cushion with a noise that was like a soft full stop.

Then, one evening, his bell rang, and when he opened the door she was standing on the pavement. He knew that a long time had gone by because he didn't recognise anything she was wearing. The lemony gleam she used to have had faded: her skin looked dry, and slightly dusty. He asked her in. Upstairs, he offered her a beer — it was all he had — but she shook her head. She'd stopped drinking, she told him.

"I'm sorry about your father," he said. It seemed to be what she expected to hear.

She nodded, but said nothing.

Later, when they were sitting on the sofa, he leaned over and put his head on her lap. He tried to work out how many times he had made love to her. It wasn't much more than ten. Less than twenty, certainly. It startled him when he realised quite how little he'd been happy with. He was facing out into the room, his cheek resting against her thigh. The taut yet supple curve of muscle. The flutter of a heart somewhere above.

He felt her hand on his head, pushing it away.

"You're too heavy," she said.

"I miss you," he said.

None of their sentences fitted together.

They met up one last time. A beautiful evening in Liverpool. Above St George's Hall the clouds were edged in gold like invitation cards or pages from the Bible. Outside the station he thought he smelled tar and ropes, as though a tall ship had sailed past just minutes earlier; the air still had ripples in it, all that remained of the wake. He had travelled into the city with a desolate lightness in his heart. The fact that she was prepared to meet him in a public place could mean only one thing.

"It's over," she said.

She had to repeat the words because it was so noisy in the pub. Half-five, and people had just left work. Everyone excited. Summer here at last.

"I don't love you," she said.

"You never did," he said.

She sighed and looked away.

"Well, did you?" He leaned forwards, moving his face into her eye-line.

"If you're going to make a scene," she said.

He leaned back again.

He picked up his drink, but found he couldn't swallow it and pushed it to one side. He had never been able to look at her without wanting her. He had never had enough of her, nowhere near. Was it any wonder that he was upset? In giving him so little, she had bound him to her all the more closely. Didn't she realise that?

"What were you doing with me, anyway?" he said.

Once again, she had no answer.

He consoled himself with this one thought, which was unworthy, if not downright cruel: she would never know the truth about her father's death. She may have talked to Billy about revenge and furnished him with the name and address, but she had no way of proving that he had actually done anything. She didn't know that he had driven out to the Wirral. She knew nothing of the eleven minutes he had spent in George McGarry's house. Had his unexpected visit brought about her father's death, or would it have happened anyway? No one could possibly say, not even Billy, and he found a certain comfort in that element of doubt.

As he reviewed their brief history, a smile spread across his face. Ironically, the very aspect of their relationship that he had most resented was now providing him with a measure of protection. No one was aware that they had slept with each other. No one had ever seen them together. No one even suspected that they might be friends. In the eyes of the world there was no connection between them whatsoever, and never had been.

"What's so funny?" Venetia asked.

On that warm night, in that loud pub just down the road from Lime Street station, he looked across at her and saw her father. That mouth, those eyes. *You can fuck right off.* He shook his head.

How he had loved her, though.

CHAPTER
THIRTY-SEVEN

With the end of his shift less than an hour away, Eileen Evans looked in on him, and he was grateful to her for making the effort. She didn't know what it meant to him to have some company. For the past twenty minutes, he had been fighting an overwhelming desire to go to sleep. He had no coffee left, not even a drop. All he could do was stay on his feet. Pace up and down. If he rested his head on his arm for so much as a second he'd be gone. Out cold.

Taking a seat, he bent over the scene log and noted Eileen's arrival in the mortuary. While he was writing, he asked whether she'd seen Phil.

"He went home a couple of hours ago," she said. "He'll be back at eleven."

Billy put his pen down, then sat back in the chair. Eileen was leaning against the radiator with her arms folded across her chest.

"What about you?" he said. "Have you had any sleep?"

"Not really." She gave him a look that he remembered from when he met her, in reception; it was searching and yet resigned, as if she believed that the quality she hoped to find in him was unlikely to be there, as if she'd grown used to such disappointments. "It's been a long night." She lifted a hand to smother a yawn. "Another long night, I should say." She yawned again. "Still — excuse me — it's nearly over now."

"I'll be glad, actually," he said. "I meant to have a nap yesterday afternoon, but somehow I never got round to it. It's been pretty hard to stay awake."

"Have you got far to go?" she said. "When you leave, I mean?"

He told her where he lived. "It's a village. Near Ipswich."

"I don't think I know it."

He began to describe the place for her. It was only small, he said, and most of it was arranged along a single road. He told her about the allotments at the back of the house, and about Harry Parsons and his secret hoard of beer, and he told her about the field where, only a few months ago, his daughter had gone wandering at night. He wouldn't have seen her if she hadn't had her glasses on. He laughed softly when he realised how that sounded, and Eileen laughed with him.

"Was she sleepwalking?" Eileen said.

"She's got Down's," he said. "She just hasn't got it up here." He tapped one side of his head with his index finger. "She hasn't got a clue, really."

He found himself talking about the time Emma went missing in a shopping centre. When Sue rang him, he thought at first that she was calling from the swimming-pool. The background acoustics were the same: voices, laughter, shouting, everything echoing and merging in the huge, hollow space behind her voice.

"I've lost Emma," she said.

She sounded so calm that he thought he must have heard it wrong.

"I came out shopping with her," Sue said, "and now she's disappeared."

He asked Sue where she was. In Tower Ramparts, she said. By the lift. He told her to stay put. It was only half a mile from the police station to the shopping centre, and he ran the whole way. When he pushed through the gilt-and-glass doors, his shirt was sticking to his back. He saw Sue immediately. She was the only person in the place who wasn't moving. In the context of a shopping centre, her stillness looked unnatural, suspicious.

He took her by the arm. "You didn't do something, did you?"

"Do something?" she said. "What?"

After all their years together, you'd think they would be on the same wavelength, but they often had difficulty understanding one another; there were none of the short cuts that a long relationship ought to have brought with it.

"Sue," he said quietly, "did you do something?"

She shook her arm free. "Would I look like this if I'd done something?"

Well, yes, he wanted to say. Maybe. Because her face was drained of colour except for beneath her eyes, where the skin had darkened, and her irises were lighter than usual, as they often were if she was frightened.

"When did you last see her?"

"I don't know. About twenty minutes ago."

"She was here? Beside you?"

"Oh God." Sue turned in a slow circle, as if she were in a trance; she didn't seem to be able to make any sense of her surroundings.

He told her to start looking on the first floor, and in the various restaurants, while he searched the ground floor and the exits. They agreed to meet by the lift again in ten minutes.

"What's she wearing?" he asked.

Sue told him.

Unable to find any security guards, Billy ran upstairs to the Centre Management Suite and asked the man in charge to broadcast the following announcement at regular intervals:

Would anyone who sees an eight-year-old girl with Down's syndrome please accompany her to Centre Management immediately? She has shoulder-length blonde hair, and she is wearing a pink T-shirt and jeans. Her name is Emma Tyler.

Having checked all the exists, he began to cover the shops systematically, one by one, ridding his mind of everything but Emma's hair, her spectacles, and the distinctive, slightly tilted angle at which she often held her head. He talked to himself constantly under his breath so as to stop thoughts forming. *Come on, Emma. Please. Where are you?* In particular, he was trying not to think about the parents of children who had gone missing. He didn't want to become one of them. He wouldn't be able to bear it. "Come *on*," he murmured to himself. "Where *are* you?"

What hellish places these shopping centres were, with their piped pop music, and their groups of sullen teenagers, and their endless bloody discounts and bargains. Every vertical surface had been fitted with mirror-glass, which made the public spaces look twice as busy as they really were, and he kept catching glimpses of himself, a big man, hot and anxious. The glass shop-fronts gleamed. So did the gold rails. Everything reflecting, distorting, confusing.

Once, as he passed a record store, he thought he heard her. That unmistakable tuneless booming sound she made whenever she joined in with *West Side Story* or *Beauty and the Beast*. He rushed into the shop, calling her name, but stopped before he reached the end of the first aisle. A girl with Down's was standing at a listening post with a pair of headphones on, singing along to what was obviously one of her favourite CDs. She was older than Emma. Her hair was brown. He saw how oblivious she was to the world around her. Emma would be no different. It was unlikely she'd be feeling abandoned or lost. She probably wouldn't even have realised she was on her own.

When he met Sue by the lift, as arranged, she was shaking her head.

"I can't do this any more," she said.

He told her to wait where she was.

On his third circuit of the ground floor, he noticed a door marked FIRE EXIT. It opened on to a windowless space that had the dimensions of a warehouse, a vast interior of poured concrete and metal stacking-systems, and there under the stark lights, there among the cleaning equipment and the fire extinguishers, was a girl in a pink T-shirt and jeans. Arms in the air, she was swaying to the piped music, but her eyes were on her feet, checking that they were doing what they were supposed to. He wondered whether she had noticed the announcements. If she had, she would probably have imagined that there was a direct connection between the repetition of her name and the songs that were being played. She would probably have assumed that the music was for her. She would have felt special, and that would have encouraged her to go on dancing. In her mind, she was at a party, or in a show. Certainly, she seemed quite unaware of how inhospitable, how inappropriate, her surroundings were. For a few moments, the sight of her held Billy where he was, fifty yards away.

Sue was waiting by the lift when Billy appeared with Emma. At first, she didn't react — she hadn't believed that he would be successful, perhaps — but then she dropped to her knees.

"Emma, Emma," she said. "Are you all right?"

"I was dancing," Emma said.

Sue had her arms around her daughter now, and she was holding her tight. "I thought you were lost. I didn't know where you were."

"Naughty." Emma had adopted a strict expression, which she had copied from a teacher at school.

A brief, involuntary laugh came out of Sue, then she began to cry.

Billy could see Emma's face over Sue's right shoulder. The strictness faded, and a look of sympathy, almost of pity, took its place. One of Emma's hands lifted into the air, then faltered. Peering at the side of Sue's head from close up, she started, rather clumsily, to stroke Sue's hair.

"There," she said.

Once again, Billy couldn't bring himself to move. Mother and daughter in each other's arms, and strangers passing on either side, their heads turning, sensing a drama, perhaps, but knowing nothing of the real story — and him just standing near by, watching . . .

Things like that were always happening, it seemed, or on the point of happening. He turned to Eileen as if seeking confirmation, but carried on before she could open her mouth. Sometimes it got too much for him, he told her, and he would drive to the Orwell estuary after work. The thought of going home frightened him. Or exhausted him. He didn't know which. Maybe both. He had a hard time working out whether he was lucky or unlucky. He had no clear view of the value of his life. Usually, he was down by the river for an hour or more, trying to cobble something together, some new version of himself. Not that it would last. Well, not for more than a couple of days, anyway — or sometimes it fell apart the moment he walked through the front door. Some days he'd sit in the car, not think at all. He would just switch off. Or he would read about the birds that passed through the area, and it would occur to him that he wasn't so very different, the way he stopped by the water, gathering his strength, and then moved on. He felt Eileen's silence near him in the room. He couldn't decide what he should tell and what he shouldn't tell. There didn't appear to be any barriers or boundaries. When he touched his cheek, he found that it was wet.

Eileen walked over and put a hand on his shoulder.

"I'm all right," he said. "I'll be fine." He smiled at her through his tears. "It's just that it's difficult sometimes, and no one's very strong, really, are they?"

"No," she said quietly.

"Thank you, Eileen. Christ." He used both hands to wipe his face. "I didn't sleep yesterday, that's all it is. Normally, I have a nap in the afternoon."

"You must get some rest when you go home," Eileen said. "We all must." She took her hand off his shoulder and stepped over to the wall again.

"I suppose I've been thinking too much," he said, "imagining things . . ." His eyes moved to the locked fridge. "Phil said you had the key."

She nodded, then patted her jacket pocket. "It's in here."

"But you're not allowed to open the fridge, are you?"

"Not unless I'm authorised."

"So you couldn't open it for me?"

"No."

"That's what I thought. It makes you curious, though, sitting here all night . . ."

A silence fell between them, and Eileen made no attempt to fill it.

"Did you ever see her?" Billy said at last.

"Once or twice." Eileen gave him a look that he had already noticed on the faces of other people who were closely involved in the operation. There was wariness in it, and a fear of being indiscreet, both perfectly understandable in the circumstances, but there was also a hunted quality, a coating of guilt, as if merely to have been associated with that murderer of children, no matter how innocently, was to have laid oneself open to suspicion or recrimination, or even to have committed a kind of crime oneself.

"What was she like?" he asked.

"Well," and now Eileen's eyes drifted away, towards the far end of the room, "I was never with her for more than a couple of minutes at a time, and never on my own." She paused, as though trying to summon one clear image. "She seemed, I don't know, very frail . . ." Another long pause, and then she looked directly at Billy. "If I hadn't known what she'd done —"

"You would've thought she was normal," he said.

"Normal. Yes." Eileen seemed surprised that he had been able to assist her. Grateful too. But then she took a step backwards, and one of her hands shot out in front of her, the fingers spread, as though she were trying to keep something at bay. Her other hand had risen towards her face.

"Eileen?" Billy said. "Are you OK?"

She waved at him with the hand that was sticking out, but didn't look at him, the rest of her body rigid, braced, quite motionless. Then she sneezed four times, in rapid succession.

259

"Bless you," Billy said.

She took out a tissue and blew her nose. "I don't know what came over me," she said.

"Maybe it's cold in here — colder than the rest of the hospital, anyhow."

"Yes," she said, turning towards the door, "that's probably it."

Though his observation might well have been true, he had the odd feeling that he was covering for her — or even, perhaps, for both of them. Equally oddly, she appeared to be colluding with him. There was the sense, for a few short moments, that they had found themselves in a dangerous predicament, and that, if they had survived, it was only because they had, at some level, joined forces and because they had stood firm.

He stooped over the scene log.

"You won't tell anyone, will you?" he said. "About me getting — you know . . ."

She was sideways-on to him, by the door. "I don't think there's any need, do you?"

In sounding offhand, and choosing not to look at him when she spoke, she had allowed him to save face, and he liked her immensely for that.

He saw her out, then glanced at his watch. Thirteen minutes to go.

CHAPTER
THIRTY-EIGHT

"So what's it like?"

Virus Malone stood just inside the mortuary with his hands in his pockets, rocking slightly on his heels.

"There's a ghost," Billy said.

Virus looked at Billy placidly, as if it was only a matter of time before he retracted his statement.

"When she appears," Billy said, "keep calm. She'll try and talk to you. Don't answer. Oh, and tell her she's not allowed to smoke. No smoking in the mortuary. It's against regulations."

"Same old Billy." Virus shook his head.

Though the two men had worked together in the mid-nineties, Virus had been transferred to the other side of the county just before the millennium, and they hadn't seen each other in quite a while.

"So how's Newmarket?"

"The racing's good — and, you know, it's a bit quieter. You're not there, for a start . . ." Looking at the floor, Virus grinned and rubbed the back of his neck — for some reason, making jokes had always embarrassed him — then his eyes travelled round the room again. "So what's it been like," he said, "really?"

"All you do is sit here," Billy said. "Time goes pretty slowly."

Virus nodded. Now, finally, he had a framework within which he could function.

Billy signed himself out, then handed the pen to Virus and watched as he began to record the fact that he had taken over as scene loggist. *I am Police Constable James Malone . . .* His writing was unexpectedly small and tidy, and the letters all leaned forwards, like people walking into the teeth of a gale. Billy hoisted his bag on to his shoulder. At the door, he turned and said, "Careful you don't catch anything."

Virus gave Billy the finger, but he was grinning.

Out in the corridor, the mood had altered. A new day had started, and nurses were hurrying this way and that. Some pushed trolleys or wheelchairs; others were carrying charts. The air smelt of breakfast — hospital breakfast: damp toast, stewed tea, watery scrambled eggs. Walking back to the main entrance, Billy felt ambivalent about having been relieved. On the one hand, he badly needed rest. Putting in a twelve-hour shift on very little sleep had left him veering between moments of great clarity and sudden bursts of panic and despair. He still couldn't believe that he had broken down in front of Eileen Evans; he hoped to God it didn't go any further. On the other hand, the operation wasn't over yet, and he would be missing out by not being there. Though he knew his place — he was just a bobby, a cog in the machine — it would have been satisfying to be able to see it through. But perhaps that satisfaction wasn't something he had worked for. In the end, perhaps, it wasn't something he had earned.

From his various conversations with Phil Shaw, and with other personnel, in both the police and the hospital, he had learned a good deal about what would be happening that day. He knew that undertakers were being brought in from somewhere at least two hundred miles away — Sue had been spot on about the difficulty of finding a firm willing to handle the body — and that they were scheduled to arrive at five o'clock that afternoon. While the body was being transferred from the fridge to the coffin, with Phil looking on, police vehicles would be moving into position outside. The crematorium being used was situated to the northwest of Cambridge, near the junction of the A14 and the M11. It was a good twenty miles from the hospital, in other words, and traffic would have to be controlled for the entire length of the route. The journey would take about forty minutes. At no point would the hearse be stationary.

The funeral was due to take place at seven-thirty, after the crematorium had closed. About a dozen people were expected to attend the short service. Owing to illness, the woman's mother would not be among them. The body would be cremated, and when the ashes had cooled they would be placed in an urn. Once again, the sergeant would be on hand to oversee every stage of the process.

Towards eleven, he would leave the crematorium in an unmarked car, the urn in his possession. Hopefully, any journalists or members of the general public would have dispersed by then; a raw, cold night was forecast, with the possibility of rain, and it was unlikely anyone would want to hang around in that kind of weather. The sergeant would be driven to a secret location where he would surrender the ashes to an unidentified third party. The moment the ashes left his hands, his job — and the job of the police — would be over.

On reaching the cafeteria, Billy stopped and looked in, hoping to say goodbye to Mr Prabhu and wish him well, but he wasn't there. He would be having a word with the medical staff, or maybe he, too, had gone home to get some sleep. Moving on again, Billy nodded at the two volunteers who were manning the reception desk, then he left the hospital.

He stood on the steps that led down to the car-park and breathed the damp, leafy air. It was still dark. To the north, white smoke was rising from the sugar factory. He knew much of what the day would hold for the police, but there were still questions, weren't there? Who was the unidentified third party, for instance? And who would decide where the woman's remains were scattered? Which piece of land would be considered neutral enough, or resilient enough, to become her symbolic resting place? Or would she be scattered over water? And would that be the end of it? Would people finally forget? Forgive? Billy didn't know the answers to any of these questions. All he could do was speculate. He remembered how the ash from the woman's cigarette had fallen soundlessly into the drain, and how, later, he had examined the metal grille and been unable to find any trace of it, not so much as a single

264

grey-white flake. Perhaps that was how it would be. Not rest exactly, but disappearance. Not peace, but silence.

Once back in his car, Billy checked his mobile — no new messages — then put it on the passenger seat and turned the key in the ignition. Though it was cold, he decided not to use the heater; it would only make him drowsy. If he drove fast and the traffic was light, he could be parked by the estuary in time to see the river change colour — though there wasn't much colour involved, not in November. The water just gradually made its presence felt: from black to charcoal-grey, or steel-grey, or even, sometimes, silver — like looking at a glass-topped table in a darkened room. But he hadn't forgotten his promise to have breakfast with Sue. He wouldn't stay for more than a few minutes.

He turned out of the hospital. Wednesday morning. Curtains still drawn in many of the houses. Soon children would be sitting up in bed, knuckles in their eyes and tangled hair. Soon they would have to start preparing for school. He remembered the butterflies he'd had when he was young — that strange, sick feeling . . . The short days were the hardest: you got up in the dark and came home in the dark. The road curved gently downhill. He passed a pub, an empty car-park, a playground. Over one round-about, and then another. It was on the faces of other drivers too. A rumpled quality, a puffiness. Not just the last vestiges of sleep, but a certain vulnerability; you could almost see them swallow, dry-throated, at the thought of what being awake involved.

He accelerated on to the A14, the town behind him now. Behind him, too, was the sugar factory, its thick, creamy smoke pouring upwards in his rear-view mirror. His eyes felt heavy. He wound the window down an inch or two, and cool air streamed into the car. Westbound, there was a tailback. Eastbound, though, the road was clear except for a lorry with a Dutch numberplate.

Maybe we could go away . . .

Sue would have been thinking about the holiday they'd had shortly before she got pregnant with Emma. In Amsterdam, they had found themselves outside a coffee shop, and she had startled him by suggesting they should buy some dope. "But I'm a police officer," he said. She laughed at him. "Billy," she said, "it's *legal* here." Though full of misgivings, he handed her the money and watched as she disappeared through a black glass door. *I'm buying drugs*, he thought. Then he remembered what she had told him. *It's legal here.* The words just didn't ring true, somehow. But he had done worse things . . .

That afternoon they drove out to the coast and parked on a road that overlooked the sea. Susie produced a packet of cigarette papers, and Billy was surprised again, this time by her dexterity. Shutting the windows, they lit the joint. The car soon filled with smoke. It was a Sunday, and families kept walking past. People with small dogs and children.

"It doesn't *feel* legal," he said, sinking lower in his seat.

When they had finished the joint, they went for a walk along the beach. A cold wind tore in off the North Sea. Waves crashed against the sand like walls collapsing.

"It's not working," Billy shouted, and he could hear the relief in his voice.

As soon as they turned inland, though, he began to talk nonsense. Then he had a fit of the giggles, something that hadn't happened for years. In a souvenir shop, he took eight bars of chocolate up to the cash-till, but just before paying he had a moment of doubt. Nudging Susie, he showed her what he was buying. "Do you think this'll be enough?" he said.

Back in Amsterdam again, they decided to go to the cinema. They would be safer in the dark, they thought, where nobody could see them. They bought tickets to *In the Name of the Father* and sat in the front row.

After a while, Billy leaned over and whispered in her ear. "I don't understand this film at all."

"It hasn't started yet," she whispered back. "This is the adverts."

When the pub blew up, Billy laughed. He couldn't help it. The whole thing seemed so artificial, so exaggerated. Ludicrous, really.

"People died," Susie told him earnestly. "In real life."

Billy's laughter became uncontrollable, and they were asked to leave.

They returned to their hotel and had showers, then Susie painted her toenails, which seemed to take hours. Later, they lay on the bed, watching TV. Once, as Susie leaned forwards, her bathrobe loosened and Billy saw the curve of a breast, the underside, heavy and soft.

Then, inexplicably, he fell asleep.

In the middle of the night he woke up with an erection. Susie was sleeping deeply, one arm abandoned on the outside of the covers. His penis felt harder than it had ever felt before, and it wouldn't go down, no matter how long he waited. In the end, he decided to put it inside her. He didn't know what else to do. She was facing away from him, which made it easy, and she was already wet, which made it easier still. It was almost as though she had been expecting him. He pushed into her gently, stealthily, and then stayed there, without moving. He could feel the muscles inside her contract around him, gripping him. Was she awake after all? If she was, she gave no other sign of it. He came without touching her, except in that one place. Just by thinking about her, imagining her — even though she was right next to him. He could feel the pulsing in his penis as the sperm pumped out, but his penis didn't move at all. Still inside her, he fell asleep again.

The next morning she sat up in bed and looked at him. "Did you do it to me in the night?"

He nodded.

"Did I wake up?"

"I don't know," he said. "I don't think so."

She lay back, her head resting on the pillow. "I don't mind, you know. I don't mind it if you do that." She was staring at the ceiling. "What was it like?"

"It was amazing," he said. "It was like our bodies weren't there at all, only the parts of us that were touching. They were there all by themselves, and they were much bigger than normal, and it was dark all around them, as if they were in a cave . . ."

Susie's head turned on the pillow, and she looked at him again. "I think you're still stoned," she said.

A brittle rattling began, and Billy glanced over his shoulder. On the back seat of the car were all the newspapers that he had bought at the weekend, their pages vibrating in the draught. He wound the window up a fraction, enough to stop the noise.

Amsterdam, though.

That was the first and last time he ever smoked dope, and he didn't regret it either, not for a moment, but if they were to go back to Amsterdam in the near future, with Emma, it wouldn't be like that. It would just be an extension of the life they were already living. What Sue had really been trying to say, he thought, wasn't so much that she needed a holiday, or that she would like to return to a place where they had once been happy, but that she wanted to recover some spirit or quality that they appeared to have lost. Well, he wanted the same thing. It wouldn't be easy, though. In fact, he wondered whether it could actually be done.

On a footbridge up ahead someone had written RURAL REVOLT in giant capitals. Labour had been in power for five years now, and all the excitement and the optimism had gone. All the shine too. They were always interfering, trying to tell people how to live their lives. Why couldn't they deal with the things a government was supposed to deal with — health, education, transport — and leave the rest of it alone? Whoever was

269

responsible for the graffiti had damaged public property, but Billy found himself approving.

He checked his rear-view mirror, then concentrated on the road in front of him. It was empty.

Then a lorry piled high with timber, which he overtook.

Then nothing.

CHAPTER
THIRTY-NINE

As he came over a rise, not far from Stowmarket, Billy saw the lights of a petrol station below him and veered off the dual carriageway, braking hard. The cold air wasn't enough: he needed a soft drink, something sugary to help him stay awake.

Parking outside the shop, he went in and picked up a bottle of Lucozade and a newspaper. He'd been hoping Keith would be behind the till — when Billy worked the late shift, he often dropped in and Keith would let him have a sandwich and a cup of coffee for nothing — but it was a man he'd never seen before, young and overweight, with floppy brown hair and a twist of gold wire dangling from his right ear.

"Traffic's bad," Billy said. "Going west, I mean."

Not bothering to look up, the young man nodded. "There was an accident, apparently. Lorry shed its load . . ."

"When was this?"

"About an hour ago." He rang up the soft drink and the paper, then glanced through the window, towards the pumps. "Any petrol?"

Billy shook his head. "No."

Behind him, a slot machine gave off a series of muffled and incongruous sounds. The whinnying of horses, pistol shots — an Irish jig.

He reached into his pocket, bringing out a five-pound note and Mr Prabhu's business card at the same time. He placed the money on the counter. "I've been working all night," he said. "I'm hoping the Lucozade will give me a bit of energy."

The man handed Billy his change and turned away.

It was usually tiredness that caused accidents, Billy thought as he left the shop — that, or a momentary lapse of concentration. Some time after Sue's crash, when she was no longer having the nightmares, he had asked her whether she had an explanation for what had happened, imagining she would blame treacherous road conditions, or the car's light steering, but she had told him it was all her fault. She'd simply lost control. "But *outside Emma's school?*" he said. Even months later, he still found this aspect of the crash astonishing. "That's the whole point," Sue said. "I was thinking about the time I took her to Whitby, and how I nearly —" She broke off, unwilling — or unable — to complete the sentence.

As he walked to his car, Billy saw that it was getting light. Mist cloaked the wispy trees that divided one side of the A14 from the other. On a whim, he took out his mobile and dialled the number on the hi-fi dealer's card.

He answered almost immediately.

"Mr Prabhu?" Billy said. "This is Billy Tyler. We met in the hospital cafeteria."

"PC Tyler," Mr Prabhu said. "Of course. So you've decided to take me up on my offer?"

Billy laughed. "No. Actually, I was just wondering about your wife. Is she all right?"

"She's out of danger, I'm happy to say. It seems the operation was a success."

"That's wonderful. You know, I looked for you earlier, at about four, and then again when I left the hospital at seven, but there was no sign of you. I thought you must have gone home."

"No, they let me sleep in the ward — on a chair. My neck's killing me."

"Well, anyway," Billy said with a smile, "I'm glad your wife has come through it all OK."

"It was very thoughtful of you to ring, PC Tyler. Thank you so much."

"Well, goodbye, Mr Prabhu."

"Goodbye — and have a safe journey home."

Ending the call, Billy felt something slacken inside him, something that had been stretched to breaking-point. He had wanted to talk to someone who would be glad to hear his voice. He had needed good news.

He slid the phone into his pocket and put the Lucozade on the roof of the car, then flicked through the paper. There, on page 26, was a photo of the crematorium where the woman's body would be burnt that evening. The caption said FURNACE HEADING FOR HELL. Tucking the paper under his arm, he reached for the Lucozade and drank it standing beside the car. After two or three long gulps, he tipped his head back and stared at the sky. Another cloudy day. Thick cloud too. He thought of people in planes, and how they would be above it all, and he wished he could be catapulted straight upwards, into miraculous sunlight. He finished his drink, then dropped the bottle in a rubbish bin and climbed back into his car.

Ten minutes later, he passed the turning that led to his village, the trademark brick façade of a Travel Inn visible off to the right, but he only left the dual carriageway a few miles further on, at the last exit before the Orwell bridge. Ahead of him as he drove down the hill was Ipswich harbour with its marina full of yachts and its static, dark-blue cranes. He rounded the roundabout. A fire had been lit behind a wooden fence next to the boatyard, and smoke was drifting across the road. The acridity of the fumes told him that what was being burnt was probably illegal. Rubber, it smelt like — or plastic. Two Christmases ago, his brother had flown back from San Francisco, where he was now a successful paediatrician, and Billy had driven to Runcorn with Sue and Emma to see him. On Boxing Day night, sitting up late over a whisky, Billy had asked him what he remembered about their father.

"Not much," Charlie said. "He gave me a toy saxophone once. It was gold." He swirled the whisky in his glass. "I burned it."

"Really?"

"In the garden," Charlie said. "I threw it on the bonfire. For a few moments nothing happened, then it sort of went all floppy. It made a real stink." He sipped

274

his whisky. "I used to think that was the real him, that stink. I still do, actually."

"Remember when I broke my toes?" Billy said, then told him the story of how he had gone to the Iron Door in Liverpool.

"What?" Charlie said. "You saw him play?"

Billy nodded.

"Was he any good?"

"I don't know," Billy said. "I couldn't tell."

Now they were both laughing, two brothers who rarely saw each other, and it was the kind of quiet laughter that never quite dies away. Just when you think it's stopped it starts again.

Billy followed the narrow road that led out along the river. He should go and stay with Charlie one of these days. In fact, maybe that was the trip they should be planning. Not Amsterdam, but San Francisco. He would have to save, of course — or borrow — but imagine it! San Francisco, with its madly plummeting streets. Alcatraz, the Golden Gate — the fog . . . Pleased with himself for having such a good idea, he felt less guilty about visiting the estuary, and he put his foot down, speeding between the soaring concrete stanchions of the Orwell bridge. Looking to his left, he saw flat, slick expanses of mud. Low tide.

Somebody had parked a beaten-up silver Volvo in his lay-by, but there was just enough room beyond it, and he was able to reverse into the gap. He turned the engine off, but left the keys in the ignition. He seemed to remember that the woman who fed the swans drove a Volvo. She usually showed up later in the day, though: he would see her at around three in the afternoon, when he came off an early shift. Yawning, he leaned his head against the headrest for a moment.

CHAPTER
FORTY

Trevor was high above him in a half-built house, busily hammering a nail into a rafter. *Trevor?* he called out. *What are you doing?* Trevor looked down, his body foreshortened, as if he were bearing the full weight of the bright-blue sky and it was crushing him. Billy wanted Trevor to join him on the ground, but he couldn't seem to make Trevor understand. Trevor didn't even glance at him again, let alone speak. The hammering went on and on — endless nails being driven into endless wooden beams.

Billy's eyes opened. In a panic, he looked around. He'd forgotten something — or he was late for something. No, wait. He was in his car. Though all the windows had steamed up, he could see somebody peering at him through the glass. His body stiff with cold, he reached across and wound down the window on the passenger's side. A wide face, corkscrew curls. It was the woman who fed the swans.

"Are you all right?" she said.

"I'm fine," he said. "I must have nodded off, that's all."

"Your lights are on."

"So they are." He switched them off. "Thank you." He yawned, then sat up straighter in his seat. "What time is it?"

"About nine."

"Is it? God." He rubbed his face with both hands. It felt rubbery and slack, and he needed a shave. "What are you doing here, anyway?" he said. "I thought you only came down in the afternoons."

"Normally I do. Today my son's in a concert, though. At school." She looked past him, into the back of the car. "Is she dead?"

He glanced over his shoulder. On top of the pile of papers from the weekend was Saturday's *Telegraph*, the famous picture of the murderer occupying half the front page.

"She died on Friday," he said.

"I had no idea." She shook her head. "So terrible, what she did."

He nodded absently.

"People like that," she said, "I think they do deals."

He stared at her with her frizzy hair and her face all spread out like a house with its windows flung wide open. "What do you mean?"

"They go further than anyone else, and they have to pay a price for that." Her eyes moved to the picture behind him. "That's why she's got that look." Turning to Billy again, she smiled almost sadly. "You don't know what I'm talking about, do you?"

"Maybe I'm still half asleep."

She gave him a steady, slightly patronising look that told him tiredness had nothing to do with it.

278

When she had driven away, he reached over into the back seat and got hold of the paper. Propping it up against the steering-wheel, he scanned the article on the front page. There was nothing in it that he didn't already know. The facts of her death, a description of the tape. A brief account of how the murderers behaved in court. *Sullen, defiant. Passive.* In his memory, it was this apparent passivity that had upset people most of all, since it had been seen as a form of arrogance, a clear indication that the couple in the dock were not only unrepentant but contemptuous, both of those who sat in judgement over them and — far more shocking, this, if true — of those who had suffered at their hands. *Do what you like,* their silence seemed to say. *It makes no difference to us.*

His eyes lifted to the woman's face. That gaze, always described as empty. The black mouth curling a fraction, as if suspecting the photographer of weakness or inferiority. And now, suddenly, he had an inkling of what the swan lady might have been getting at. The woman and her lover had gone where no one else could follow. They probably thought of themselves as mavericks, dare-devils — pioneers. They were special, in other words. Unique. But then to be arrested, charged, held under lock and key . . . It would all have seemed so humdrum. Pathetic, really. No wonder they had joked about it when they wrote to each other from their separate cells. What did it mean to be put on trial? What did that have to do with anything?

He ought to be heading home, he knew that, but there was something he had to do first. Folding the

Telegraph, he stepped out of the car. A still grey morning, sky the colour of an unlit light-bulb. The mud-flats glistening. Down by the river's edge gulls glided through the air, their wing-tips seeming to clear the land by no more than a few inches. He opened the back door and gathered up the rest of the newspapers, then he locked the car and set off along the grass verge. This wouldn't take long, he thought. Apart from anything else, it would warm him up. Get his circulation going.

The road snaked right, then left, then right again before it slid beneath the bridge. On one of the bends was a red house that stood alone, with fir trees in the garden, and just beyond it, if he remembered correctly, was a bus stop. He walked fast, facing the oncoming traffic, the papers wedged under one arm. He kept his eyes on the ground. Though the grass verge was raised, it hugged the road, and sometimes the slipstream from a passing vehicle would push him sideways. He saw a powder-blue Cortina parked in front of a white wall. He saw a boy's head sinking below the smooth, dark water of a reservoir. He saw a woman in a black wig, smoking. All these images were linked.

Once, he glanced over his shoulder. His car had shrunk to the size of a toy.

Before he even reached the house, he came across a tall grey wheelie bin. Positioned at one end of a lay-by, it had been fastened to a metal post with a padlock and chain. The words printed on the lid — NO GARDEN WASTE — were partially obscured by bird droppings. This wasn't the bin he remembered, nor was it where he had expected it to be. Given its location, he could have driven. Oh well. Lifting the lid, he peered inside. Big Mac cartons, a Kit-Kat wrapper, the remnants of a Happy Meal. A crushed Coke can. The nation's diet in a nutshell.

When he heaved his stack of newspapers into the bin, Saturday's *Telegraph* stayed on top. The woman's face stared up at him, stubborn, provocative, daring him to act. Flipping the paper over, he pushed it as deep as it would go, then closed the lid firmly and stood back.

He looked around.

The day was grey and glassy, as before. Traffic roared over the great arc of the bridge. In front of him, perhaps a hundred yards away, a yacht swung slowly anti-clockwise on the water. The man who dug for ragworms and razorfish had told him what that meant.

The tide was on the turn.

CHAPTER
FORTY-ONE

A Mercedes flashed past, one glimpse of the young blonde woman behind the wheel enough to convey her style, her wealth, her sense of purpose. Billy glanced at his watch. It was nine-thirty. Five minutes back to the car, then a fifteen-minute drive. He could be home before ten.

As he hurried away from the lay-by, his left foot caught in a dip in the grass verge, and he fell sideways, then tumbled down the bank, landing awkwardly at the edge of the river. He hadn't hurt himself, but his trousers were covered with mud, and water had seeped into one of his shoes. He was still sitting there, unable to believe what had happened, when his mobile rang. Even without looking, he knew it was Sue. She would have taken Emma to school, and then returned to an empty house. She'd be wondering where he'd got to.

He took the phone out of his pocket with his left hand, which wasn't quite so muddy. "Is that you, Sue?"

"Billy," she said, "where are you?"

Climbing to his feet, he shook his head. "I'm on my way back." And then, before she could speak again, "Listen, did you get my message?"

"No."

"I sent you a text — last night . . ."

"I haven't checked my mobile yet. What did it say?"

"I was hoping we could have breakfast together," he said.

"You're not too tired?"

He smiled. "No."

"How long are you going to be?"

"Twenty minutes. Maybe less."

Once Sue had hung up, he wiped the mud off his phone and pushed it back into his pocket, then he looked down at his trousers. What a mess. He would have to take his uniform to the dry-cleaner's later on. Still, at least he didn't have to go to work till Sunday. Four days off — and he needed it as well. Maybe at the weekend he could drive Sue and Emma to the village that perched right on the tip of the peninsula. There was a pub out there — the something Arms. They could have lunch. He could already imagine it: the smell of the wooden furniture, waxy, slightly sweaty, almost human, the pints of beer and plates of battered cod, the cloudy, grey-green water just beyond the door. Afterwards, they would walk along the beach, perhaps, and if he looked hard enough, if he was lucky, he might see a redshank or a godwit, and it would surprise them that he knew the name of a bird. Well, it would surprise Sue, anyway. Emma's reactions were less easy to predict. He wondered what she would say if she could see him now. *Mucky.* The word would be delivered at top volume. Her head would be tilted at an aggressive angle, and her hands would probably be on her hips. *Mucky pup.* He found that he was laughing.

On Sunday evening, he had left Emma in the bath while he went downstairs to check that their supper wasn't burning. When he was in the kitchen, though, he panicked, imagining that she might be drowning, and he ran back up the stairs and burst into the bathroom.

"Quiet," Emma said in that toneless voice of hers. "Too noisy." Without her glasses, she was very short-sighted, and her eyes had a blankness to them that could seem cold, almost hostile.

Grinning, he apologised, and sat down on the floor beside the bath.

"That's better," she said.

Later, when he pulled out the plug, she turned round so that her head was near the taps. Lying on her stomach, she watched the water disappear down the plughole. She was leaning up on her elbows, with her face propped on her hands, and her air of concentration was intense, as if she were studying some rare phenomenon.

She would never study anything, of course.

He had wondered then what would become of her. What would he and Sue decide to do about her future? Would she always live at home, with them? Who would care for her when they were dead?

Or would she, with her damaged heart, die first?

He laid his forearms along the edge of the bath and rested his chin on top. He, too, watched as the bath slowly emptied itself. He noticed how her head revolved ever so slightly, echoing the miniature whirlpool that formed in the water as it was sucked down the hole. The strange noises that it made, all squawks and cackles . . .

At last Emma peered up at him.

"Gone," she said.

Looking at his daughter stretched out in the bath, he noticed how strong her body was, and how well made, her skin so sleek and rosy, so unblemished.

"You're beautiful," he said.

She climbed out of the bath and stood on the mat in front of him, arms held away from her sides.

"Dry me."

How she loved to issue commands! He reached for the towel that was warming on the radiator.

As he knelt in front of her, rubbing her legs, she placed one hand on the top of his head, then she leaned down and looked right into his face.

"Daddy," she said.

Also available in ISIS Large Print:

So He Takes the Dog

Jonathan Buckley

Buckley is expert at stringing together the tiny dramas of individual lives to make a narrative necklace
Daily Mail

On a beach in southern England, a dog returns to its owner with a human hand in its mouth. The hand belongs to Henry, the homeless eccentric who has been wandering the south-west of England for the last 30 years, most recently living rough in the town. The local policeman and his accomplice, in piecing together his movements prior to his death, talking to those who knew and watched him, uncover an extraordinary life. But their investigations tellingly shed light on the town itself, and the story of Henry and those who tell it begins to affect the narrator-policeman's own life in ways he never expected.

ISBN 978-0-7531-7816-4 (hb)
ISBN 978-0-7531-7817-1 (pb)

Alentejo Blue

Monica Ali

For some, the Portuguese village of Mamarrosa is a place from which to escape; for others it is a place to run from trouble. Vasco, a café owner who has never recovered from the death of his wife, clings to a notion that his years in the USA make him superior to the other villagers. One English tourist makes Mamarrosa the subject of her fantasy of a new life, while for her compatriots, a young engaged couple, Mamarrosa is where their dreams finally fall apart.

At the book's opening an old man reflects on his long and troubled life in this seemingly tranquil setting, and anticipates the return of Marco Afonso Rodrigues, the prodigal son of the village. When he does finally appear, villagers, tourists and expatriates are brought together, and their passions and disappointments must inevitably collide . . .

ISBN 978-0-7531-7798-3 (hb)
ISBN 978-0-7531-7799-0 (pb)

Ludmila's Broken English

DBC Pierre

From the Booker prize winning author of *Vernon God Little*

Ludmila's Broken English charts the unlikely meeting between East and West that follows Ludmila Derev's appearance on a Russian brides' website. Determined to save her family from starvation, Ludmila's journey into the world and womanhood is an odyssey of sour wit and even sourer vodka.

Thousands of miles to the west, the Heath twins, Blair and Bunny, are separated after 33 years conjoined at the abdomen. Released for the first time from an institution, they are suddenly plunged into a round-the-clock world churning with opportunity.

A wild and raucous picaresque dripping with the flavours of British bacon and nasty Russian vodka.

ISBN 978-0-7531-7672-6 (hb)
ISBN 978-0-7531-7673-3 (pb)

Unfeeling

Ian Holding

Holding's confident and measured prose rarely falters
Observer

Davey is in the attic when the militia comes. At 16, he's almost the man his father wants him to be, and almost the child he was. Locked in shock, he is barely aware that beneath him his parents have been murdered and his family's farm, Edenfields, "reclaimed".

The neighbouring farmers — his parents's closest friends — take him in and try to care for him, try to bring him back into their community of normality: the club, the church, after a few weeks, his boarding school. They look to cope. But Davey is on a different path. One night he escapes from his school and embarks on a harrowing, terrifying journey across Africa, home to Edenfields, looking for redemption.

ISBN 978-0-7531-7596-5 (hb)
ISBN 978-0-7531-7597-2 (pb)